THE WITCH HANDBOOK TO MAGIC AND MAYHEM

(Book 1 in the Stolen Spells series)

by

Tish Thawer

www.amberleafpublishing.com
www.tishthawer.com

The Witch Handbook to Magic and Mayhem Copyright© 2023 by Tish Thawer. All rights reserved.

No part of this book may be used or reproduced in any manner whatsoever, including Internet usage, without written permission from Amber Leaf Publishing, except in the case of brief quotations embodied in articles and reviews.

First Edition
First Paperback Printing, 2023
ISBN: 979-8387423444

Cover design by Molly Phipps of We Got You Covered Book Design
Edited by The Girl with the Red Pen
Character Illustration by Cameo.Draws

This book is a work of fiction. All characters, names, places, organizations, events and incidents portrayed in this novel are either products of the author's imagination or are used fictitiously. Any resemblance to actual persons, living or dead, events or establishments is solely coincidental or used herein under the Fair Use Act.

Amber Leaf Publishing, Missouri
www.amberleafpublishing.com
www.tishthawer.com

Praise for *Weaver*

"Visually stunning, Thawer's *Weaver* is a fresh YA Fantasy that will capture your heart and convince your mind dreams really do come true."
~ **Stacey Rourke, Award-winning Author**

"Atmospheric. Magical. And swoon worthy. Thawer's YA Fantasy is full of *Practical Magic* vibes and will have you rushing to bed in search of a Weaver of your own."
~ **Belinda Boring, International Bestselling Author**

"Lush and atmospheric, *Weaver* is a beautiful, carefully-crafted YA fantasy."
~ **Casey L. Bond, Author of House of Eclipses**

"An illustrious YA Fantasy that blurs the line between dreams and reality, obscuring together two worlds into one visionary romance."
~ **Cambria Hebert, Award-winning Author**

"A beautifully written YA fantasy, wrapped in darkness and love. *Weaver* is full of stunning imagery and unforgettable characters that will keep you turning the pages until morning."
~ **Rebecca L. Garcia, Author of Shadow Kissed**

"Spellbinding and packed with mystery and breathtaking landscapes, the world of the Weaver will assuredly enchant you."
~ **Cameo Renae, USA Today Bestselling Author**

Praise for *Guiding Gaia*

"The imagery Thawer developed is amazing. Her love of Gaia radiates from each page of this compelling story I eagerly lost myself in. If you liked *Lore*, this is your next must read!"
~ **Award-winning Author, Stacey Rourke**

"Guiding Gaia is the story you've been waiting for - beautifully written with twists and turns that keep you addicted, devouring each page until the epic end!
This is Tish Thawer at her very best.
A must read for 2021!"
~ **International Bestselling Author, Belinda Boring**

"Thawer brings a breath of fresh air to the genre with this beautifully told story.
I love this unique perspective of Gaia, her strengths and her vulnerabilities."
~ **Bestselling, Award-winning Author, Kristie Cook**

"Guiding Gaia is the book I needed most this year without even knowing it.
Tish Thawer has taken the history of this mythos and seamlessly turned it into something unexpected and extraordinary. This is one YA tale you don't want to miss."
~ **Paranormal Romance Author, Brynn Myers**

Praise for *The Witches of BlackBrook*

"Tish Thawer's intriguing story line is weaved and crafted into a magical and spellbinding web that kept me up until the wee hours of the morning biting my finger nails and cheering for the sisters. Strong story line and well-developed characters that will sweep you away. I was completely floored by this amazing book and I recommend it to everyone!"
~ Voluptuous Book Diva

"Tish Thawer is an amazing wordsmith. I have devoured several books by her and she never disappoints. The blend of history with contemporary is just genius and I can't wait to see what this author will come up with next. Add this to your list as a must-read recommendation from me! An EASY 5 out of 5 stars!"
~ NerdGirl Melanie

"Overall, The Witches of BlackBrook was a grand slam for me. I was so enchanted by this spellbinding tale of hope, love, and a bond that can't be broken. There was something special about it and I honestly think it had something for all different types of readers. Whether you're into romance, historical, paranormal, new adult, etc. the author effortlessly weaves so many elements together to create a flawless experience for whoever picks it up. If you're looking to be enchanted and escape your mind for a couple hours, I highly suggest picking up The Witches of BlackBrook and diving on in!!"
~ Candy of Prisoners of Print

"Don't go looking for fairies. They'll fly away if you do. You never can see the fairies, till they come looking for you."

~ Eleanor Farjeon

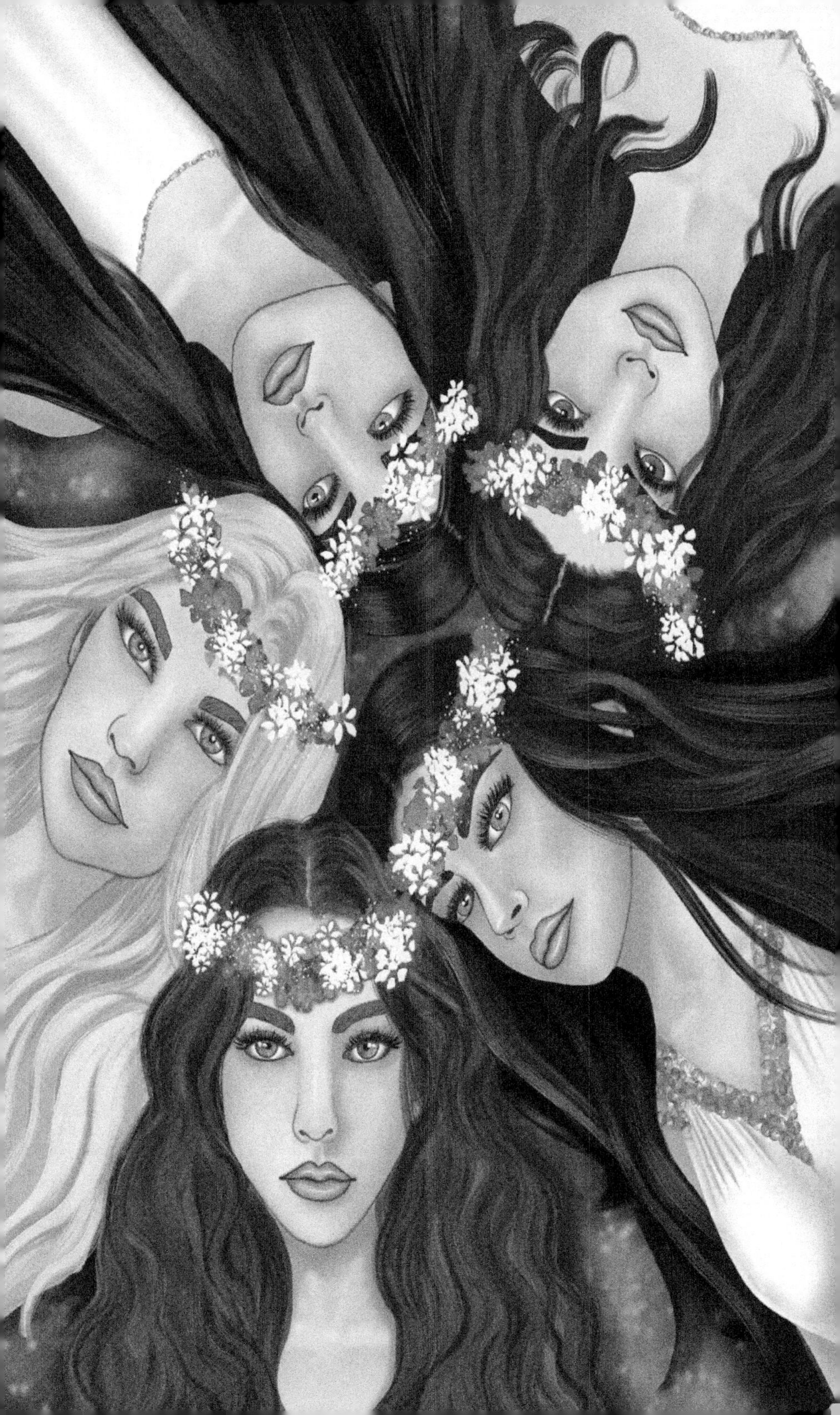

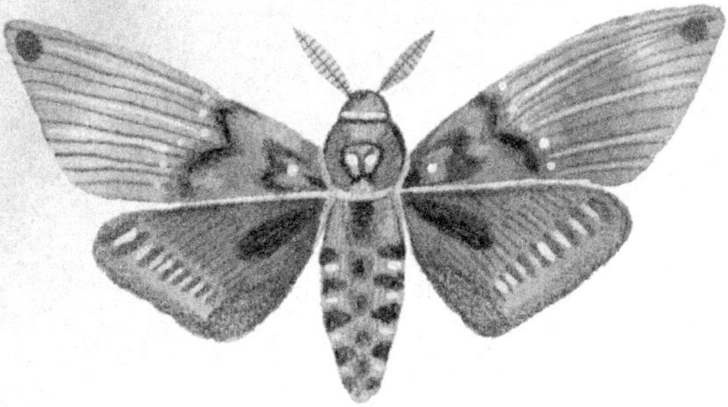

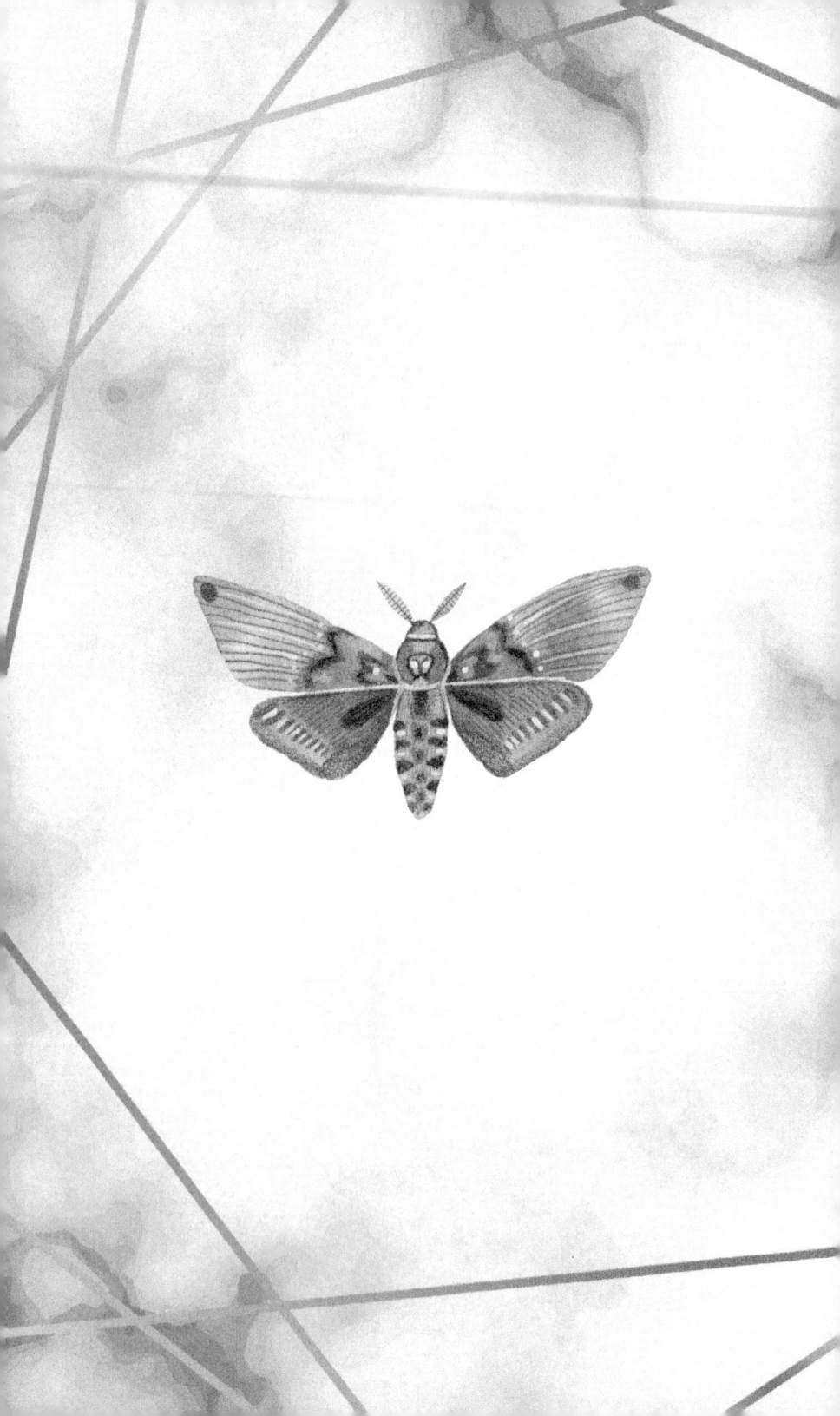

I
Magic

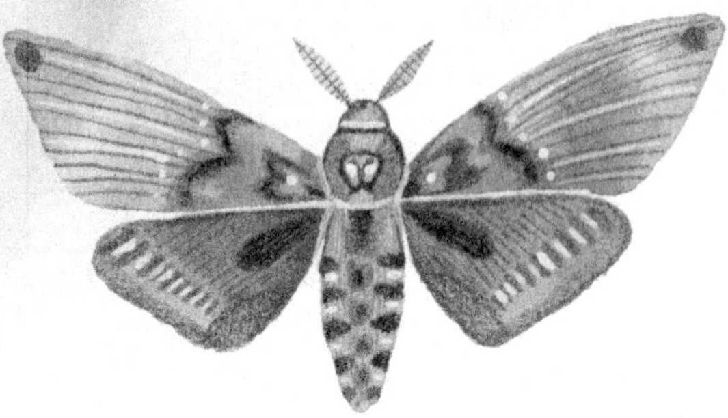

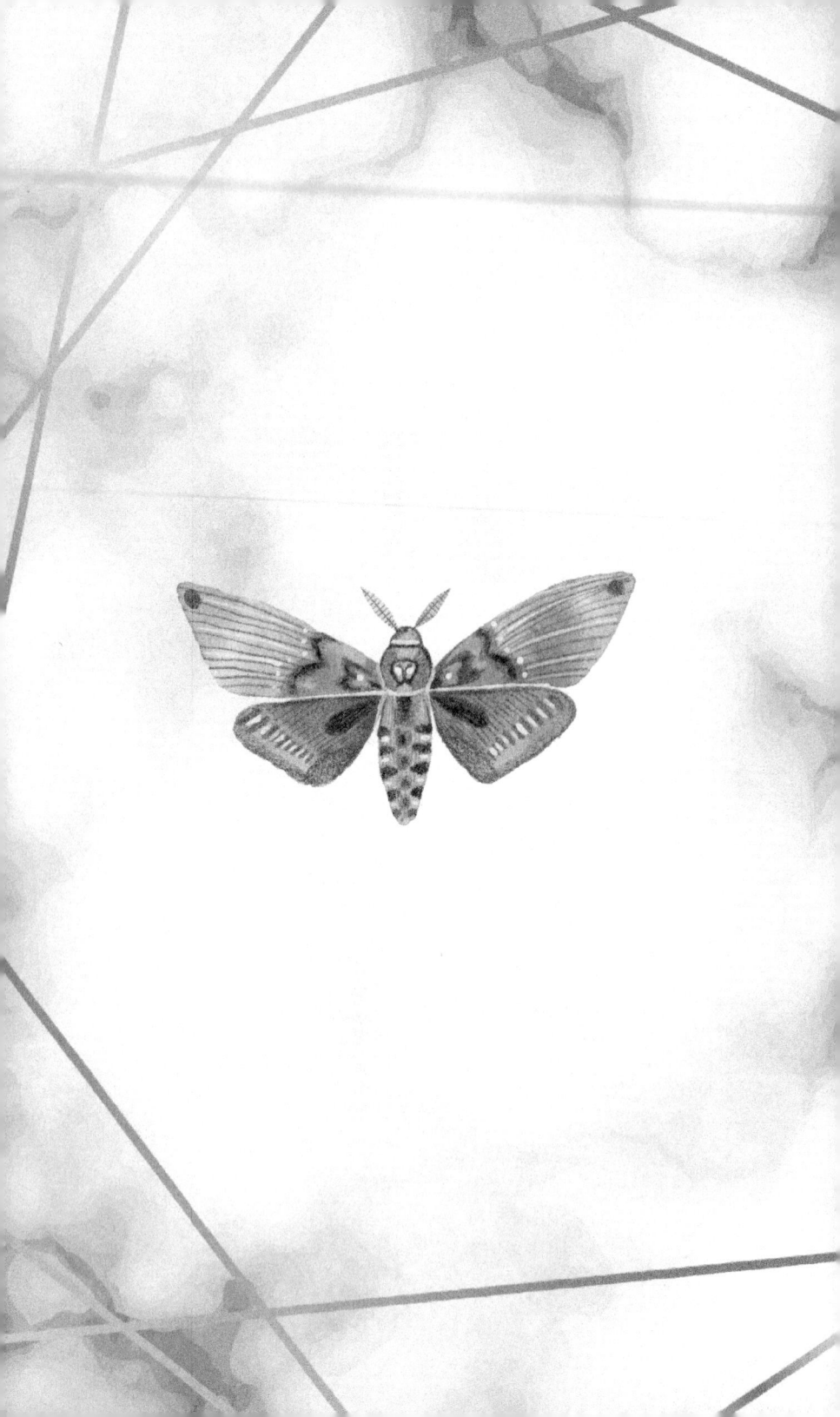

Prologue

FERINDALE - *Twenty years ago…*

"Brother, this is insane! You have to let the old ways die." There was deep-seated madness in his eyes—a look I'd never seen before tonight. I knew in that moment, I wasn't going to win this fight. The death of his wife only a few hours ago had changed him… had changed everything, and now his resolve was set.

"If they do not realize what is gone, they can never truly miss it. Isn't that right, crone?" The King's voice fell in sinister waves against my skin as he stared at the decrepit witch hiding in the shadows.

"*We* will know, Brother. And I, for one, cannot stomach the thought of you hurting an innocent child."

"Hurting?" he scoffed. "No one will be hurt. The child will be cared for, raised in safety… loved, even."

The weight of my black cape fell heavily against my legs as I bent to sit on the marble steps below my brother's throne. "The deception will ruin you, I guarantee it." I dropped my head when his hand landed roughly on my shoulder.

"Is that a threat?"

"No. Only the truth. You simply cannot do this!"

His grip tightened. "Actually, *Brother*, it's already done. You will not ruin my plans," Thadius seethed as he directed my attention to the witch's den. "This kingdom is now mine, and I refuse to lose it to a child due to some archaic fairy law."

Carefully rising to my feet, my stomach clenched at the sight of the swaddled babe in a woven basket at the base of the stone hearth. The crone's Book of Shadows lay open, splayed across her worn wooden table, smeared with bits and pieces of gnarled blood and bone.

Thadius continued to rant while the crone's lyrical words hung like fog in the air. Flipping to the last page in her book, she muttered beneath her breath and the child began to cry.

"What are you doing?" I jerked against my brother's grasp, not caring when he drew his blade in protest.

"She's binding its magic. We can't make the exchange until it's done."

I glanced at the waiting portal pulsing off to the side, its green center glowing brightly. It was the only gateway between *our* world and the *human* one... and the only chance of bringing this to an end.

Spinning wildly, I twisted away from my brother's clutches and shoved him to the floor. Grabbing the book from the table, I scooped the child into my arms and ran for the portal, disappearing a moment later.

I couldn't let him create a changeling and permanently seize the throne—even if it meant I had to escape to a world in which we were sworn never to go.

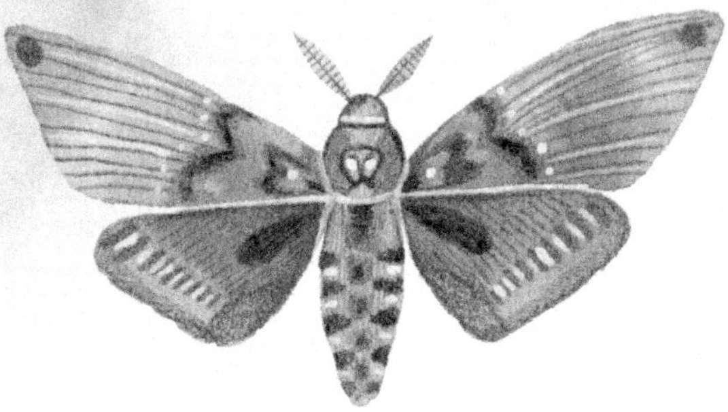

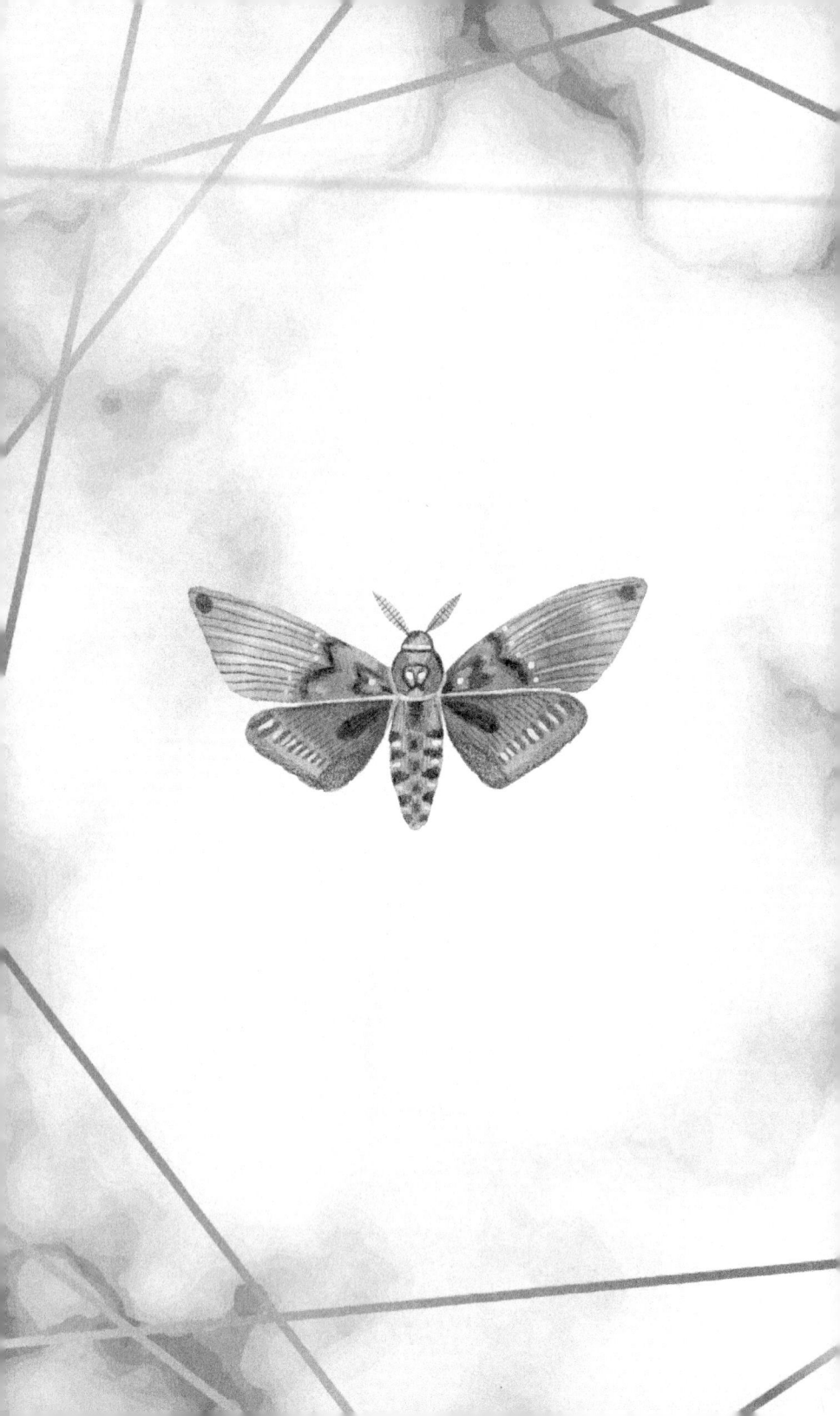

One

ESSEX, CT - *Present day...*

"Practice safe hex!"

I cringed at the familiar adage my oldest sister, Aster, called out to the young couple exiting the shop. They were so happy, beaming as they clutched their first Book of Shadows tightly in hand. "Why do you always say that?" I asked, brushing a sweep of fire-red bangs out of my face as the dark purple front door closed with a ding from the bell that dangled above.

Aster raised a brow, looking at me over her tortoiseshell reading glasses. "You know why, Lily."

"I mean, sure, I get it, but do you have to say it every time someone leaves? It almost sounds... *dirty*." I crinkled my nose.

Aster chuckled. "It's only dirty if your mind is in the gutter."

I huffed a laugh and rolled my eyes. Squinting past the foggy panes of the front windows, I watched the couple meander farther down the street. Gray clouds hinted at more rain on the horizon, and I, for one, absolutely loved it.

Aster tucked a loose strand of her cornsilk hair behind her ear as she lifted a feather duster to the next row of books. "Have you given any more thought to what we talked about?"

The brittle spines of the classic tales always seemed to be covered in a light layer of dust, regardless of how much she cleaned. I always wondered if books naturally attracted more dust, since our other shops didn't require that much care. Flames flickered in the fireplace and I stared into their depths, pointedly ignoring Aster's question as she continued to tend to her precious books.

"Lily?" she prompted, refusing to let me off the hook.

I sighed. "Not really. With our duties being what they are, I honestly don't see how I could leave for college, or what the point would be." I waved my hand in the air, dismissing the thought. "I already know what I'm meant to do… the same as you and the rest of our sisters."

"But that's exactly the point." Aster stopped cleaning and set her focus directly on me. "The rest of us are here, protecting the portal as our ancestors have done for centuries, which means… now's the time for you to live your life. You're eighteen, Lil—go to college, travel, and see the world while you still can. The rest of us will be here to guard the portal until you get back."

A familiar knot formed in my gut.

"We'll talk about this later," Aster continued. "Looks like you're up next." Joining me in the center of the room, Aster placed an arm over my shoulder as the store around us began to shift.

Books flew through the air in a flurry of magic, spinning and disappearing as my candles popped into existence and took their place upon the shelves. Brass light fixtures morphed into brushed silver ones, lending the shop a more modern feel. The square traditional rug beneath our feet rippled and turned into a thin round mandala print, just as the dark planks of the hardwood floor shifted to a light gray instead. Flames erupted in various corners, sending the fragrant scents of beeswax and lavender blossoming throughout the space.

With an almost palpable sigh, my candle shop settled into place.

"All set." I pulled from Aster's one-arm hug and made my way behind the transformed counter just in time. "Good afternoon, Ms. Buckman," I greeted one of my regulars as she walked through the front door.

"Hello, dear. Did my candles arrive?"

"Yes, ma'am." I reached beneath the dark wood desk to retrieve her special order. "Here you go. That'll be twenty-three dollars and eight cents."

"Goodness gracious. I remember when candles were only a few cents apiece."

"I know, Ms. Buckman. Inflation stinks." My genuine smile stopped the older woman's complaining—as it did each and every time. "See you next week?"

"Yes, and Lily, please order more of the lavender tapers and the vanilla votives, if you don't mind."

"Of course." I wrote down the order in an old-fashioned receipt book, then handed her a copy as I bid her goodbye. "Take care now." I waved as the bell chimed, marking her exit as she shuffled out the door.

"When is Daisy getting here?" Aster asked, noticing the shop beginning to shift again.

I joined her back on the rug as my candles disappeared, replaced by vials of oils and herbs now lining the shelves. An aroma of earthy scents filled the air as Daisy's apothecary rushed to settle into place. Snapping out a hand, Aster caught a glass bottle on its way to crashing to the floor.

"I'm here!" Daisy called out, running through the back entrance with her trademark witch's hat sitting askew atop her frizzy brown hair. As the second youngest sister—now twenty-four—she had recently taken over the apothecary all by herself, no longer relying on our mother's help. Tossing a handful of dried flowers onto the long worktable that had replaced my desk, she set a beaker filled with some sort of amber liquid next to the mortar and pestle that had appeared out of thin air.

"Cutting it kind of close, aren't you?" Aster frowned as she set the saved bottle on Daisy's workstation. "You know the shop responds to our emotions, so next time it summons you, perhaps you could arrive on time to avoid such chaotic shifts."

Daisy squinted and looked up from her work, noting things sitting slightly askew. But before she could respond, her customer arrived, pushing through the front door and tolling the bell again.

"Hi, Daisy. Thank you so much for the oil you gave me last week. I absolutely loved it." The middle-aged woman ran a hand up and down her arm. "My skin feels so soft and smells delicious." The woman leaned in close and lowered her voice to a conspiratorial whisper, even though we could all plainly hear what she had to say. "I think the hubby liked it, too." She grinned from ear to ear. "Can I get some more of that one and perhaps something for my daughter as well? She suffers from eczema, and this spring has been a doozy."

"You got it!" Daisy beamed as she set off to prepare the requested concoctions, ignoring Aster's lingering stare.

Aster rolled her eyes and turned away, nodding for me to follow her downstairs.

Entering the stone entrance hidden at the back of the shop, we wove our way down three flights of stairs, twisting underground until we reached the thick wooden door. Lifting a heavy key from around her neck, Aster slid it into the old metal lock.

I took a deep breath and followed her through the secret passage, blinking as the blue light from the fairy portal wavered brightly in the center of the room.

Pulsing from behind the scrolling metal gate, the glowing portal to the fae realm stood ten feet tall with a bed of lush green grass and blooming flowers spilling into our world from its base. Aster and I walked toward the small pond off to the left and sat down atop a large rock near the room's back wall.

I lifted the frayed hem of my patchwork skirt and kicked off my sandals, dipping my toes into the cool water below. "None of you left to go to college or travel the world, so why should I? What if something happens when we're not all here together?" I stared at the pool, its reflective surface shimmering off the vine-covered walls. The portal hadn't opened during any of our lifetimes, but it remained our ancestral duty to protect its existence and guard the entrance to the fairy realm. A duty I didn't take lightly.

"That may be true, but we're all older, wiser, and far more experienced in our individual magic now. You leaving won't be a big deal." Aster sat down on the boulder next to me. "And you said it yourself... none of us ever got to leave, and we don't want you feeling the same bitterness we did growing up." She reached for my hand. "You deserve better than that, Lil."

I leaned over and rested my head on my big sister's shoulder. "Thanks, Aster. I'll think about it." Closing my eyes, I let the pulse of the room settle my racing heart. This space had a rhythm of its own and was one of the only places I'd ever felt at peace.

I should have known better.

Two

By the time Aster and I climbed the stairs and emerged from the basement, the shop had morphed and shifted again.

Energy vibrated against my skin as Iris laid out her newest stock of amethyst clusters and fluorite crystals. Their blue and purple rays lit up the shop, the fractal light shimmering in the afternoon sun. "There you two are!" Iris called out, smiling wide as she tossed her jet-black hair over her shoulder.

"Are you recovered from last night?" I teased.

Iris and Fern—the twins—turned twenty-nine the day before. With five siblings under such a busy roof, we rarely kept up with all the birthdays and graduations, but we'd taken special care for the twins' latest, closing up shop early to celebrate and dance the night away. They, however, refused to give up on their party when the rest of us turned in for the night.

"I'm fine. Thanks for asking." Iris winked. "But Fern, on the other hand…" Iris nodded to the back of the shop where her twin sat in a forest-green winged-back chair, her head drooped to rest in her hands. "I'd say she had a little *too* much fun."

"I can hear you, ya know?" Fern kept her head down, her long raven hair almost reaching the floor.

"Yes, I know," Iris teased.

Aster and I burst out laughing, but before Fern could defend herself, Iris's customer walked through the door.

Our shop's magic only allowed in one customer at a time, and depending on their needs, shifted and summoned the required witch for the task.

"Hello," Iris greeted the young woman. "How can I help you?"

The new customer roamed Iris's crystal store with a blank look on her face—one we were all familiar with. Sometimes people had no idea why they were drawn to our store, or what it was they actually needed. But that was the beauty of the magic… we always knew.

"I just received a new batch of snowflake obsidian." Iris gestured to the bins now lining the far wall. "It's the perfect stone to carry with you if you're planning a trip," she intuited.

The customer's eyes lit up as she gravitated toward the stones.

Turning away, I knelt beside Fern and rested my hand upon her knee. "Fern, in all seriousness, are you okay?"

"Yes. I'm fine. I just drank too much of that damn wine and ended up with a massive headache."

"Oh!" I jerked my hand back, as if the pressure on her leg would somehow make it worse.

"We told you that you should've gone to bed earlier." Aster's reprimand came with a teasing smile.

"Yes, well, it's not too often we get to celebrate around here, so I wasn't going to pass up the opportunity… especially on my birthday." Fern shrugged, the corner of her mouth tipping up into a rare but welcome grin.

The bell above the door rang again as Iris bid her new customer goodbye, her perfect purchase in hand.

"With you both here now—and in the vein of missed celebrations—perhaps you can help me talk some sense into this one." Aster hitched her thumb in my direction. "The deadline for this year's enrollment is almost up, and she still isn't sure if she wants to go."

"Lil, are you kidding?" Iris started. "Why in the world would you miss the chance to go to college? And at Yale, no less?"

My shoulders sank.

Yes, I'd gotten into Yale—after Aster's constant pestering to submit my application—but that didn't mean I was ready to leave my home. "I'm sorry, but it's just not something I'm ready to do." I tossed my hands in the air. "I can't explain it, but leaving here… leaving our shop—it doesn't feel right."

I spun around and watched as Iris's crystals disappeared, sighing in contentment as a flush of lush flowers and greenery burst forth, filling the space. Fern stood, smiling and ready to greet her incoming customer as if the fragrant essence of her flower shop had instantly cured her hangover headache.

Taking Fern's place in the chair, I watched quietly as she helped a young bride pick out flowers for her upcoming wedding.

A wedding.

My chest tightened at the thought. How in the world would I ever get married if I truly decided to never leave? All my sisters had dated, but it was never anything serious since no strangers were allowed inside our home.

The old gray-washed brick building that housed our shop and home stood three stories high, not including the hidden basement. With the shop on the main floor, the second and third levels served as our living quarters. On the second was a modest kitchen, living room, and bathroom, while our bedrooms and two additional baths were located on the third. All of it was decorated in Mom's boho-chic style and protected by a magic put into place long before any of us were born, but only the shop shifted with the magic spell. Add the fact I was born here, learned how to control my magic here, and had been brought into my family's duty here, made it even more special, at least to me. This was my home. My heart. And while Yale may only be thirty minutes away, even that seemed too far whenever I thought about leaving Essex, Connecticut.

"I think lavender roses would be lovely for an early summer wedding." Fern's voice snapped me back to the moment, bringing with it another bout of stress.

From what Aster said, they'd all felt bitter at one point or another about being stuck here, but I never had. My soul was connected to this place. But seeing the excitement light this bride's face made me second-guess my decision… again. What if *I* wanted lavender roses at a summer wedding, or perhaps white lilies to match my name? Obviously, I wouldn't have either if I never roamed beyond the confines of my predestined life.

The bell above the door jingled as Fern waved goodbye to her customer and welcomed back a familiar face to us all.

"Hello, Ms. Buckman, you're right on time. Your flowers arrived this morning."

Her regular customer was, in fact, a customer of us all. The shop's magic prevented any cross-over confusion, as if each transaction culminated from just one visit. Ms. Buckman believed she received all her items at once, so we never had to worry when she kept walking back through our front door.

Staying out of sight in the back room, I watched the older woman move slowly through Fern's flower shop, bending and sniffing any flower that caught her fancy. She was tall and thin, almost hawkish, but had lines on her face that spoke of happiness and a life well-lived. My chest tightened with a strange feeling I'd never felt before. Envy.

Leaning back in the chair, I closed my eyes and thought about what a life outside our home might look like. I didn't have an idea what my "type" was when it came to men, but as a hazy image formed in my mind, I knew something was about to change.

As Ms. Buckman exited the shop with a bundle of fresh tulips in hand, the bell above the door tolled again, then all hell broke loose.

Flowers flew through the air, uprooted from their pots. Candles popped into existence and immediately back out again. Crystals spun wildly in the air or exploded from their bins, as herbs and oils crashed to the floor. Our shop was in chaos, wildly shifting from one façade to another.

Screaming, we rushed to the middle of the room.

Daisy joined us again as she raced back downstairs. "What's going on?" she yelled above the din.

"We don't know!" Aster yelled back, casting a protective bubble around us all.

Moments later, Mother rushed into the room, throwing her hands toward the front door and uttering a spell under her breath. She was the only witch who could truly close up the shop, halting its magic temporarily. It was something I'd never seen her do.

"Girls, are you alright?" Mom adjusted her loosely piled bun wavering slightly atop her head, a result of a flying candlestick whizzing by.

We all nodded, then froze as the bell rang again.

"Help me... please." A young man stumbled across the threshold, collapsing just inside the door with his hand outstretched and his eyes plastered directly on me.

Three

"Please," the young man begged, this time eliciting a flurry of reactions from my mother and sisters.

I stood still, frozen and waiting. I wasn't sure if he was the man from my vision, but for whatever reason, I couldn't peel my gaze away.

"What's your name, son?" Mother asked.

"Bennett."

Lily and Bennett. The thought popped into my head before I could stop it.

"Well, Bennett, can you tell me what's going on and why you so desperately seem to need our help?" Mother's voice was calm and collected, but I heard the distrust lying beneath her words.

"I don't know. One minute I was sitting in my dorm, and the next I was in the back of an Uber headed here. Only when I reached your shop did the pain subside." He wrapped his arms around his middle.

"Pain?" Aster inquired.

Bennett shook his head, as if hesitant to recall the memory. "It was like a swarm of killer butterflies fluttering in my gut, trying to rip me apart from the inside out. When the driver asked where I needed to go, the name of this shop popped out of my mouth." He looked up from beneath his shaggy brown bangs, his eyes pleading and still angled toward mine. "That's really all I know."

Mother looked over her shoulder with a raised brow. Once in a while, a customer would require the help of more than one sister, and today, it seemed like Bennett needed us all. "Well, it seems you're exactly where you need to be. Let's get you settled and we'll go from there." Mother extended her hand to help him up from the floor.

He was tall, muscular, and handsome, with strong shoulders and long legs that held him confidently, even as his eyes remained unsure. They reminded me of the color of the sky before a storm, mostly gray with flecks of blue beneath, and for some reason, they kept landing on me.

I shifted from foot to foot, glancing down at the floor while my mom and sisters did their thing. Aster pulled forward the high-back chair, setting it in the middle of the room, while Daisy ran upstairs and back down again, offering him a glass of water. Fern and Iris casually walked in a circle around him, muttering a spell under their breath, while I stood awkwardly in place.

My mom's and sisters' magic were more powerful than mine, and once combined, they'd lull Bennett into a sleep-like state where they could probe his mind to find out exactly what was going on. I'd only seen them do it once before—when the sheriff brought in a man charged with murder and asked if we could help find the body.

It was no secret what we sold here—our shop's name was *HEXX*, for goodness sake, but only a few select people knew the extent of what we could do. Our real secret, though, remained hidden from anyone who wasn't immediate family.

Visibly relaxing, Bennett's blinks became longer and longer until his eyes closed as he slipped under their spell.

Mother motioned us forward, signaling for all of us to join hands.

Reaching out to one another, we quieted our minds. Once the connection was made, we'd be able to see what Mother saw—which, so far, was nothing but a black empty space. I squinted my eyes tighter, trying to focus, when a buzzing sensation started at my feet. Climbing higher through my veins, it soon felt like I was being carried away by a swarm of angry bees. Daring to open my eyes, I let out a loud gasp.

At least ten abnormally large blue and green butterflies hummed through the air, their luminescent wings beating wildly above my head.

A surge of frantic energy filled the store as we all dropped our hands, freezing in place.

"What in the world?" I cried out.

"What are those things?" Daisy gasped.

"Where did they come from?" Fern and Iris practically screamed together.

Questions flew from my sisters' lips, but Mom and Aster just held each other's stare.

"They're called Morphineas, and they only come from the fairy realm," Aster supplied.

I sucked in a shocked breath and ducked out of the way as another dive-bombed me from across the room.

"Don't worry. They won't hurt you," she continued.

"And how do you know that?" I tried to stay calm as their large wings flapped around my head.

"How do you think?" Aster shrugged. "Books, of course."

"Well, do any of your *books* tell you why they're choosing to focus on me?" I covered my head with my arms as more Morphineas started to swarm.

Another look passed between Aster and Mom while the rest of my sisters stared in awe.

"Unfortunately not, but I think we better go check the portal right now." Mom's voice was tense but still controlled.

Aster, Mom, and I raced for the basement with the butterflies following closely behind. Fern, Iris, and Daisy stayed put, continually muttering the spell that would keep Bennett knocked out for the time being.

Descending into the cold stone tunnel, Aster pulled the key from around her neck and opened the door in a rush.

My mouth fell open.

The portal's deep pulse resonated in my chest as it started to glow brighter than I'd ever seen before. More Morphineas swarmed into the room through the tiniest of cracks, confirming without a doubt that the fairy gate was open.

"How is this happening?" I yelled above the clamor.

"I have no idea." Mom stepped up to the metal door and raised her hands, testing the magical locks on the gate.

Pulling me aside, Aster tucked us down behind the large rock at the pond's edge.

"Has anything like this ever happened before?" I asked.

"Absolutely not." Aster's eyes were locked on Mom.

Slowly, all the Morphineas drifted back through the portal, each one snapping and popping as it crossed the barrier of the wavering blue orb. "It's okay. Everything's okay," Mom breathed out on a ragged breath, slamming the gate shut as the last one disappeared.

A scream rent the air from upstairs and we all took off running.

Apparently, everything was *not* okay.

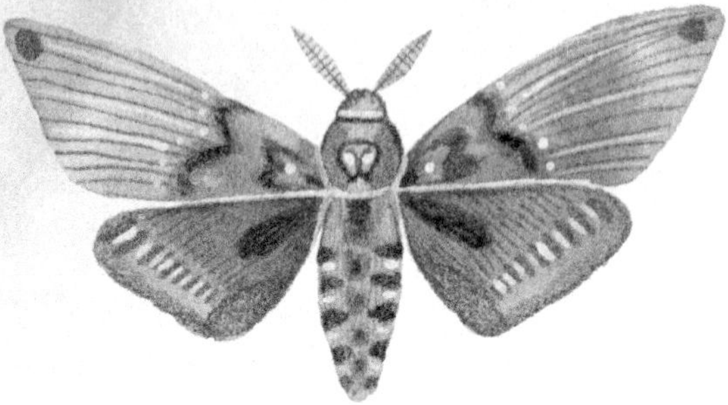

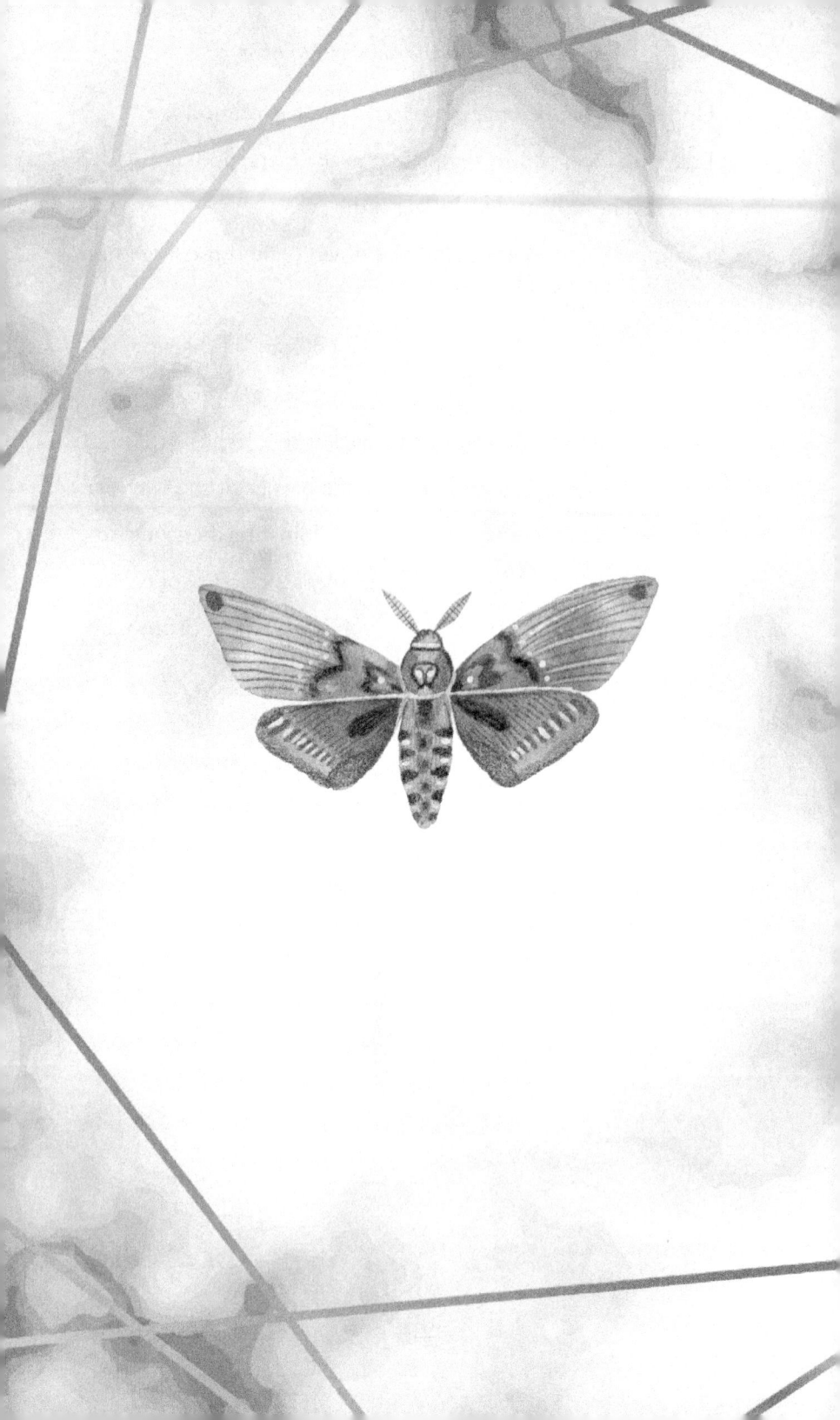

Four

Stunned into silence, Fern, Daisy, and Iris stood around the chair in the middle of the room, staring at Bennett as his eyes glowed with an unsettling violet hue.

"My Goddess, what happened now?" Mom bent down, bringing her eye-level with Bennett.

"We have no idea," Fern answered. "One minute he was sitting here under our spell, and the next, his eyes popped open and started glowing like a purple neon sign."

Mom leaned forward. "Despite his eyes being open and glowing, he still seems to be under the spell."

I circled the chair, leaning in to get a closer look. "Why would he have a reaction like this?"

His chestnut mop of hair, angled features and, of course, his strange gleaming eyes, individually made him seem odd or somehow *off*. But as a whole, some might think he was beautiful.

Aster cleared her throat and looked at Mom. "The more important question is how did the portal open in the first place?"

"What?" Iris gasped.

"It was actually open?" Fern shouted.

"Yes. There were a bunch more Morphineas downstairs until Mom cast them back and relocked the gate," I explained in a rush.

"I can't believe it." Daisy nervously wound the end of a frizzy curl around her finger.

"I can't either." Mom stood. "I need to test something. Girls, stand back and give me some room."

We all took a collective step back.

Muttering under her breath, Mom slowly released the hold on the shop's magic, and all hell broke loose again. Books crashed onto shelves, crushing the flowers that were already there. Candles sputtered to life next to vials of oils and herbs, causing them to bubble and burp while Iris's crystals started popping and exploding straight out of their bins.

Mom quickly shut it back down, a concerned look pulling her features tight. "Looks like we're going to be closed for a while."

"I can't believe this is happening." I walked to where my ruined candles were scattered across the floor, staring in disbelief at the unnatural mess. Bending down, I started to clean. Because honestly, what else could we do?

The rest of my sisters followed suit, each addressing their own wares.

The look on Fern's face as she picked up her broken blooms brought tears to my eyes. We each worked so hard in our respective stores, but loved and respected the others' items as well.

"Is there anything we can do to save them?" I asked, running a finger down the stem of a crushed pink tulip.

"I don't think so." Fern sank down onto the floor, crossing her legs and hanging her head as she pulled more of the ruined flowers into her lap.

"Hold on. Let's see what they can tell us first." Mother picked up a handful of flowers and scattered them around us in a circle. "Flowers grown with love and thrall, bear witness to what it is you saw. Shed light on things we cannot see. Bloom and bear witness, so mote it be."

The flowers twisted and coiled, bending in on themselves like snakes writhing in a fire. Bursting open, they released plumes of pollen that morphed into a strange grainy picture right before our eyes.

The outline of a man appeared, and we all sucked in a shocked breath. Though we couldn't see his face, one distinct feature was clear to us all… pointed ears.

"Are you saying what's happening is because of an actual *fairy*?" I covered my mouth, aghast.

Mother's sharp eyes snapped to mine. "I have no idea, Lily. I'm just as shocked as you. Though, obviously, from what Fern's blossoms showed us—and the fact that a portal which has remained closed for centuries has spontaneously cracked open—I'd say yes, that's a pretty good guess."

Tears welled in my eyes.

Mother had never spoken to me like that before.

Taking a deep breath, she looked around the room and sighed.

"I'm sorry, honey. I didn't mean to snap at you." Mom reached out and took my hand. "I'm just not sure what to do here."

In that moment, Bennett started to come around, sputtering and coughing as his eyes returned to normal. "What happened? I feel like I've been hit by a truck." He looked around the room, his brow creasing as he took in the mess. "Is something wrong here? It is safe for me to be here? Should I leave?"

All good questions, but none we had answers to. And the more pressing concern was whether or not Bennett himself was the threat. Besides his glowing eyes and the Morphineas showing up out of the blue, his ears weren't pointed, so we had no way to connect him to the fairy realm or the vision we'd all just seen.

"Bennett, you said you were in your dorm room when all this started. Can you tell me which college you attend?" Aster asked randomly.

"Sure. I'm a sophomore at Yale."

Everyone in the room turned to me.

"What?" I shrugged.

Aster stepped forward. "Ironic. Lily was accepted to Yale, too."

Five

Shaking off Aster's comment, Mother escorted Bennett upstairs with the help of Daisy, Fern, and Iris, wanting to *"keep an eye on him herself"*, but I couldn't let it go.

"Why are you looking at me like that?" I stared back at Aster as I took a seat behind the desk.

"You don't think it's a strange coincidence that the one time the fairy gate opens, the boy who triggered it came from the same college you are meant to attend?" Her eyebrows climbed into her hairline.

"You don't know he triggered it!" I snapped back.

"Be realistic, Lil. Something is going on here, and I think it concerns you." She pushed up the side of her reading glasses, straightening them on the bridge of her nose.

"Stop blaming me!" I shoved off my stool, cringing as it slammed to the ground.

Aster held up her hands. "I'm not blaming you. I'm worried about you." She nodded back to my computer. "Did you find out anything from your search?"

I shook my head, fighting back the surge of angry tears as I righted the stool. "No. At least nothing out of the ordinary. He's registered as Bennett Wilson and is a sophomore at Yale, just like he said."

A flash of his stormy eyes appeared in my mind and an odd feeling roiled in the pit of my stomach. I had no idea how any of this could be connected to me, but I couldn't deny the strange pull rising in my gut.

"What's his major?" Aster asked.

"Why does that matter?"

She shrugged. "I don't know that it does, but it may give us some insight into the type of person he is."

I clicked open another tab and typed in the request. "It doesn't say."

"Okay, then let's go ask."

The knot in my belly tightened and a nervous energy raised the hair on my arms. "No thank you. I'm good right here."

"Fine. You stay put and *I'll* go ask him." Aster smiled and started up the stairs, looking back over her shoulder one more time. "Lily, don't worry. We'll find out what's going on."

My head bobbed along with my heart. I honestly couldn't care less what Bennett was majoring in, or what his favorite color was, or why he kept staring at me… What *did* concern me, though, was how I could suddenly feel the pulse of the fairy portal pounding deep within my veins all the way up here.

I kept my eyes on Aster's back until she'd cleared the stairs before making a beeline for the hidden entrance at the back of the shop. We'd raced upstairs so fast when we heard my sisters' screams, I couldn't remember if Aster locked it or not.

Descending underground, my chest grew tight, its pounding growing louder and louder the closer I got to the wooden door. Blue light from the portal spilled out around the seams. With a twist of the handle, I walked back inside. We *had* left it unlocked.

The portal glowed brightly, but it remained secure behind the gate. Mom's spell had locked and resealed the metal door, but a deep thumping beat continued to rattle my bones and my fingers ached to touch the scrollwork. But I knew better. Staring deeper into the portal, the vibrant blue almost hurt my eyes. Then I heard it...

"It will never be yours," a voice whispered from beyond the gate... from inside the forbidden realm.

"MOM!!!"

"Are you sure that's what it said?" Mom asked for the fifth time as she stared at the portal, worry lines creasing her brow.

"Yes. That's what it said, in a low, sketchy-ass voice." I turned to face Aster, noting the tightness in her shoulders. "Okay, you two, what's really going on?" I was sick of them acting like they didn't have a clue. Between all the shared glances and the odd bits of information none of the rest of us had, it was obvious she and Mom knew far more than they were letting on.

After a long look at the floor, Mom replied, "Honey, I really don't know. We're just as confused as you are."

"Yeah, well, Aster thinks this has something to do with me, and since I'm the only one hearing voices, I think she might be right." I sank down onto my favorite rock, wrapping my arms around my middle and resting my head against my knees.

Growing up here, this had always been my safe place. A respite from my sisters whenever we fought or a peaceful place to meditate as I grew older. I'd spend hours staring into the sparkling pond, imagining what the fairy realm was like. My mind conjured unicorns, pixies, and all sorts of fantastical things. But this was home and safe and had always been enough. But now, everything was changing. Now, all I felt was fear.

"I just said I didn't think it was a coincidence all this started happening after Bennett arrived—a strange boy coming from the school Lily was meant to attend," Aster piped in, breaking my train of thought.

"How does that have anything to do with me?" I shouted, pushing to stand.

"Honey, calm down. We don't know if it has anything to do with you. Aster's just speculating." Mom raised a brow, piercing my sister with a pointed look.

Aster readjusted her glasses and crossed her arms over her chest. It wasn't like Mom to take sides, but in this case, I was glad she was on mine.

Mom pointed to the main door. "Let's all go back upstairs and see if Bennett can answer any of our questions." Leading us out of the portal room, she stopped to make sure Aster locked the door behind us this time.

I crept up the stairs behind my oldest sister, keeping my distance until we reached the living room two floors up. Bennett was asleep on the couch while the rest of my sisters stood huddled in the corner. Mom and Aster joined them, but their eyes frequently returned to me.

I shuffled past the couch and grabbed a chair from the dining room, returning to set it on the rug in front of Bennett's sleeping form. My eyes rose and fell in time with each deep breath he took. He had the build of an athlete, muscular but not bulky. With his plain white T-shirt, faded blue jeans, and Adidas sneakers, I thought he might be a baseball player, or a runner perhaps.

"Like what you see?" Bennett's voice drifted to my ears, quiet enough for only me to hear.

"What? Excuse me?" I shifted in my seat but kept my voice low.

"I'm just teasing," he whispered, flicking a look over my shoulder at the rest of my family. "Why aren't you over there with them?"

I peered back across the room, noting my mom and sisters still in deep conversation. "I don't know. It's not like any of us have a clue what's going on, but I figured if anyone had answers, it would be you."

[31]

"I already told you; I don't have a clue why I was pulled to come here. I just… was."

I stared into Bennett's eyes, wondering if he knew about the weird glowing that happened downstairs. "Can you tell me why your eyes were glowing purple?"

Bennett gasped, bringing everyone's attention straight to us.

Apparently, he did *not* know.

"Lily, what are you doing?" Aster raced forward, grabbing me by the arm and pulling me out of the chair.

"What?" I yanked out of her grasp. "I was just asking him some questions. Like you said we should."

She huffed, her eyes darting between the two of us. "Fine. But let's do it as a group."

Bennett sat up, adjusting himself and placing his feet flat on the floor. "Actually, all of you staring at me is a little overwhelming. If you don't mind, I think I'd be more comfortable talking to Lily alone." He smiled in my direction, eliciting deep frowns from everyone, including me.

Mom stepped forward. "Fine, but we'll be right over there." She ushered the rest of my sisters into the kitchen, all of them pretending as if they weren't straining to listen to every single word we said.

"Okay, now that we're *alone*…" I rolled my eyes, "what else can you tell me?"

He shifted on the couch again, slumping back into its deep emerald cushions. "I wish I had more to tell you, but I honestly don't know why I ended up here, or why my eyes glowed like you said they did."

I thought back to my online search and what Aster said. "Why don't you tell me a little bit about yourself? Maybe if we learn more about who you are, we can figure out what's really going on."

Bennett seemed to buy my logic and started peppering me with all sorts of personal details. Twenty minutes later, I'd learned he was an only child, had grown up in Nebraska, and that I was right... he *was* a baseball player. One who preferred Adidas over Chuck Taylors, since according to him, Chucks were *"only for show"*.

"Trust me," he continued to drive his point home, "if you really need to run from something, you'll be glad your shoes aren't just a stylish decoration."

I cocked my head. "You *do* know that Chuck Taylors are named after a basketball player, right? They're literally a sportsman's shoe."

Bennett sat there, stone-faced, staring at me like I'd grown a second head. "You're kidding."

"Nope. Look it up." I couldn't help but smirk at the bewildered look on his face.

"Wow, I guess it's true... You really can learn something new every day," he conceded.

"Yes, well, it would be nice if I could learn something new about you."

"Like how charming and funny I am?" he teased.

"No," I drawled, crossing my arms. "I'm looking for the truth, not a bunch of exaggerations."

He leaned in close, whispering conspiratorially, "Then here's a little truth for you… I'm single and ready to mingle."

"Oh my Goddess. You did *not* just say that."

"What? You wanted to know all about me, and I've told you everything important there is to know."

"I don't think your relationship status counts as an important detail."

He shrugged, crossing a leg over his knee. "It seems pretty important to mention when meeting someone as beautiful as you."

My eyes found the floor, hating that I couldn't stop my cheeks from flushing or my heart from racing, but I wasn't about to let him think he was getting to me. "Wow, that's the best line you've got?" I leaned in close, bringing us face to face. "You'll have to do better than that if you think you stand a chance with me."

Six

A loud cough broke us apart. I looked up to find everyone's eyes pinned on Bennett and me. Mom was standing in front of my sisters with her arms crossed, clearly unhappy with how close we appeared. I scooted my chair back, coldness spilling between us like a frozen rush of water, when Mom excused herself from the kitchen and headed upstairs, leaving the rest of us behind.

"Why is everyone staring at us like that?" Bennett whispered.

I looked into his wary eyes and forced myself to tell the truth. "They think you have something to do with a problem we're experiencing in the store."

"Yeah, I guess I can see how some random guy busting through your door with glowing eyes might put some people on edge." He shrugged, chuckling nervously under his breath.

I narrowed my eyes at him. "Seriously, though. You don't remember anything else about what happened?"

"Honestly, not a clue." He rubbed a hand through his mop of hair. "I was sitting there, talking to all of you, then suddenly I got super sleepy. The next thing I know, everyone is yelling and freaking out."

I took a moment to really study him, noting the sadness hiding in his eyes. I couldn't imagine what he was going through. Being forced to face a new reality—a supernatural one at that—and being blamed for such an unexplainable problem had to be difficult.

A creak of the stairs pulled my attention away. Mom had changed clothes and now donned a thick pair of canvas pants, a wool cardigan, and hiking boots, her hand-made bag slung across her chest. "I need to leave for a bit, but I'll be back as soon as I can. Everyone stay put." She nodded to Aster, indicating to us all that she'd be in charge.

I had no idea where she could be going at a time like this, but with the serious set to her shoulders, it was clear she had a specific destination in mind.

"Excuse me for a moment," I told Bennett, rising from my chair. "Hey." I grabbed Aster's arm. "Where is Mom going?"

She gently pulled out of my grasp, cocking her head. "I have no idea. You just saw her leave the same as me. Now, let's get dinner on the table." She headed to the kitchen, avoiding any further questions and creating a task for us all.

The five of us moved deftly around the kitchen, each completing our familiar jobs. Aster stood in front of the stove, doing most of the cooking, while Fern and Daisy chopped vegetables for the soup. Iris peeled potatoes while I gathered the drinks and set the table. The routine was familiar enough, but without Mom's uniting presence, it felt strange and strained.

Thirty-five minutes later, we each took a seat around the worn wooden table. Aster took Mom's usual spot, giving up her own for Bennett, which placed him right next to me.

"This is fantastic!" Bennett declared between spoonfuls of his vegetable soup.

Aster smiled. "Thank you. It's an old family recipe."

Silence descended as we dug into our humble meal. The only sound left in the room was the clink of our spoons against the ceramic bowls. I stared at the purple and blue swirls baked into the custom pottery. We owned the entire set of plates, bowls, serving dishes, and platters—all created by a local artist who was a close friend of Mom's.

Running a finger over the smooth rim, I wondered where Mom could be. Her hasty departure put me on edge. As I thought back to the grainy vision of the fairy displayed by the flower pollen, I wondered if that had anything to do with it. I wanted to blurt out all the questions running through my mind, but knew I couldn't with Bennett seated among us.

Fern, Iris, and Daisy kept sneaking looks in his direction, but every time I looked up, it was Aster who caught my eye.

I stared back defiantly.

I didn't think she *really* blamed me for what was going on, but I couldn't shake the feeling all her thoughts were centered on me. Then again, that was nothing new. Aster had always looked after me, acting like another mother instead of my big sis. The others had always deemed it normal since I was the youngest, but still, that didn't mean I had to like it. To me, it just seemed like one more person constantly riding me—one more person I constantly let down.

The downstairs bell chimed, pulling all our attention back to the stairs. Mom emerged slowly, her hair ruffled by the wind. With a deep breath, she eased off her cross-body bag and dropped it on a nearby bench. "Girls, I'd like you to meet an old friend of mine."

Moving aside, Mom revealed a tall, handsome man cresting the stairs behind her.

The whole room went silent.

His broad shoulders, dark hair, and pointed ears were the exact same as the figure we saw in our flower-induced vision.

"Hello. It's nice to meet you all." He lifted a hand, greeting the entire room, but his eyes landed on me. "My name is Gideon, and I'm originally from the land of the fae."

Seven

Shouts erupted as my sisters jumped from their chairs, spinning the room into utter chaos. Even Aster looked distraught, though she kept her questions and complaints to herself.

"Girls, stop!" Mom's reprimand took me back to when we were kids. "If you sit down and listen, we'll explain everything." She gestured to the table, pulling up an additional chair for our new and unexpected guest.

How in the world were they supposed to explain all this? And why on earth was Mom willing to reveal our secret to a complete stranger? I sank back into my chair, remembering Bennett seated beside me. Turning to face him, his eyes were practically bulging from his head as he stared at the male fairy. But even worse, they were beginning to glow again.

"What's really happening here?" Aster finally asked, her voice cooler than the rest.

Gideon sat down across from Bennett, pointing a finger directly at him. "I'm here to help figure out what is going on with this young man." He gestured to Mom. "Camellia seems to think it has something to do with the fairy realm."

Every head in the room snapped to Bennett, including mine. He remained completely still, entranced and bespelled again as Gideon whispered a spell of his own.

"What do you mean?" I scooted my chair back from the table.

"Your mother described his odd arrival and told me about the Morphineas. From the sound of things, I think she's right... this is definitely connected to my home."

"Connected how?" Iris asked.

"I don't know, but I'm here to find out." Gideon's vague reply didn't sit well with me. Or my sisters, apparently.

"And exactly how do you know our mother?" Daisy asked blatantly, her finger already red from the tight curl wound around her knuckle.

Fern and Iris pushed away from the table, escaping further into the kitchen as Gideon looked to Mom for direction. She gave him a slight nod.

"A long time ago, I was cast into your world and the portals were sealed behind me."

"Why were you cast out? Are you a criminal or something?" Fern snapped, interrupting what I thought would be a lush tale.

"No. Nothing like that—"

"Then what?" Iris demanded.

"Alright, that's enough!" Mom raised her voice. "Gideon has been a friend of mine for a very long time and is only here to help, so I suggest we get on with *that*." Mom crossed her arms and we all slowly returned to our seats. "Years ago, our portal flared late one night, sending a shock wave of energy through the entire house. Once I reached the basement, I found Gideon collapsed on the floor."

Gideon nodded, acknowledging her recollection of the story. "Yes. After crossing the barrier, I emerged from your portal."

"Barrier?" I raised a brow.

Gideon nodded. "It's the magical wall that keeps our two realms apart. The portal you guard is one of the few access points between the two worlds. As you know, crossing between them is strictly forbidden, but from the sound of things, I think someone from my former home is trying to get in and they're using Bennett to do it."

How is this happening? I thought to myself. I'd never heard of the barrier before. Though we'd grown up knowing the realms were closed to one another, it wasn't until this moment that I finally questioned why. "What happened before? Originally, I mean, that caused the realms to become forbidden to cross?"

Gideon stared at me, words stalling on his tongue until— "I believe it had to do with the rulers of that time. Wild magic flooded our lands, turning clans of magical beings into dark creatures of all sorts. Ogres, witches, poisonous plants… They spread like wildfire. It was then that the barrier and portals were put into place. The final task of the fae rulers were to appoint human witches to protect the access points and the lay lines around the world. It was all meant to keep both our people safe, for as you know, knowledge of the supernatural is not a commonly accepted thing."

I looked back at Bennett, wondering how he factored into all this. "What does this have to do with him?"

"Honestly, I'm not sure yet." Gideon reached across the table and lifted Bennett's chin, tilting his head from side to side as he inspected his glowing eyes. "A witch from the old realm must have found a way to reach across the planes and pull him to the portal. Once he was near enough, the magic in his veins must have activated it."

"I'm sorry… what? *The magic in his veins?*" I couldn't catch my breath. This was spinning out of control fast.

"Yes. It's obvious the boy has fairy magic somewhere in his DNA." Gideon released him and leaned back in his chair.

I stared at Bennett, my mouth agape, then looked to Aster. "I guess you were right. He *is* the reason the portal opened."

Aster shook her head, zeroing in on Gideon. "If the portal opened because of some latent fairy magic in *his* DNA, doesn't that mean *you* being here is putting it at risk of opening, too?"

We all shifted uncomfortably in our seats.

Gideon shook his head resolutely. "No. You don't have to worry about that. I perfected my wards a long time ago and haven't used much of my magic since landing in your realm. I won't be detected here."

Don't worry? Yeah, right! I *was* worried, and from the looks on my sisters' faces, they were, too. Mom had a secret fairy friend, some crazy old witch was using her magic to reach into our realm, and the boy I just met turned out to be part fae, so yeah… I was definitely worried.

"So, what now?" Aster asked.

Gideon looked to Mom. "There's something we need to start searching for."

"And what is that?" I snapped.

Turning to meet my gaze, he paused for a moment, taking me in. "We need to find the witch's handbook to magic and mayhem. It was stolen a long time ago and brought into this realm. It's the only way to keep this world protected and fix the magic of your shop." Gideon rose from his chair and started back towards the stairs, addressing Mom directly. "I need to take Bennett with me." He looked over his shoulder. "And Lily, too."

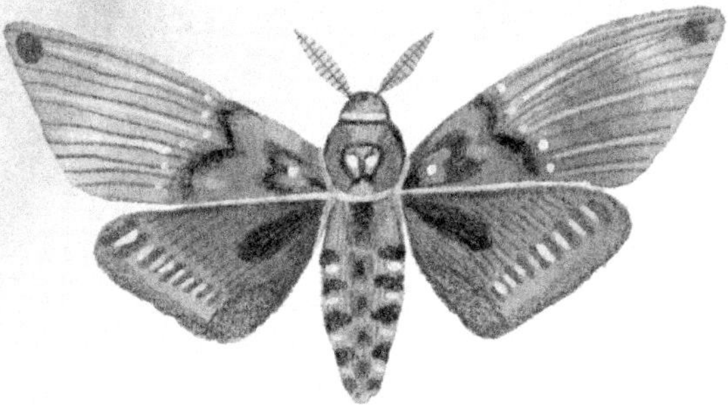

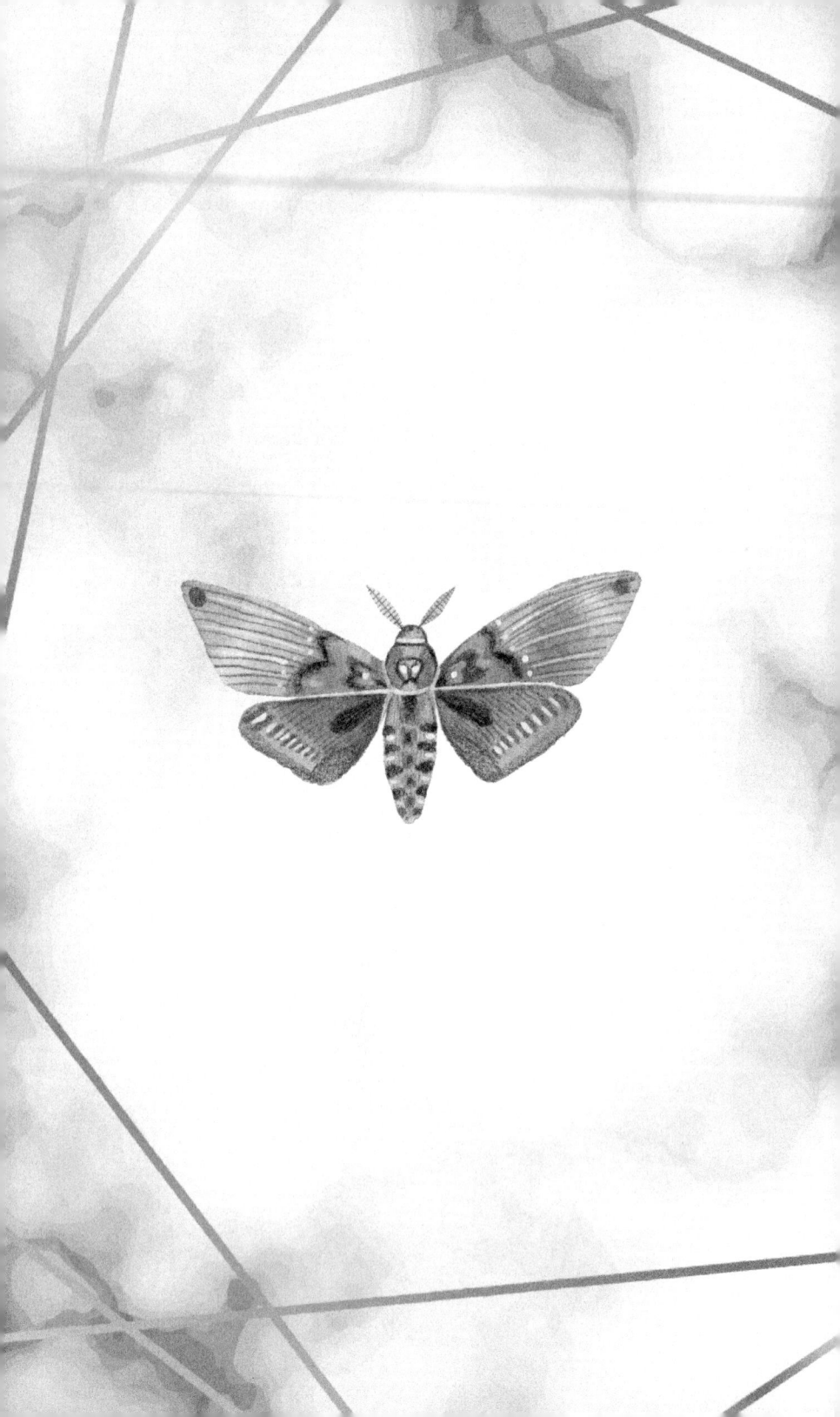

Eight

A fresh wave of shouts and protests burst from my sisters again, filling the room with a cacophony of worry, flailing arms, and violent shakes of their heads.

"No way! You are *not* taking Lily." Fern's hand clamped down on the back of my chair, while the others flitted around me like an angry swarm of bees.

"I promise to keep her safe, but I need to use Bennett to track the book's signature since the witch used him to activate the portal, and I need Lily's magic to break the spell."

Everyone fell silent. They were obviously confused as to why he'd pick me—the weakest witch of us all.

Finally, Fern asked, "Why Lily?"

"Because out of all your magic, Lily's is one of revelation. Rooted in light, it will help expose what's hidden. And that's the magic we need to find and open the witch's book."

"How do you know about our magic?" one of my sisters shouted. But as their heated conversation drifted into the background, I ran through our magical specialties in my head.

Aster and her books equaled unparalleled wisdom. Iris and her crystals worked mainly with grounding energy. Fern's flowers and Daisy's oils and herbs centered around healing the body and mind.

But mine… I didn't think my light magic would be strong enough to help anyone, even though what he said about it *did* make sense.

I looked up and met Mom's steady gaze, and everything around me faded away. *"It's up to you, sweet girl. You're the only one who can help Gideon bring things back into balance."* Her words drifted through my mind.

Tears formed in my eyes. I'd never felt like an important part of our family—having the least amount of practical magic between us—but if what they said was true, and helping Bennett and saving our store *was* up to me, I couldn't think of anything more important in the world.

"We'll go with you." I stood and placed a hand on Bennett's shoulder just as Gideon released him from his spell.

"Good. We'll need to gather a few things downstairs before we leave at nightfall," Gideon replied quickly.

Shocked expressions marred my sisters' faces as we weeded our way between them. "What?" I shrugged. "You all said I should get out of the house more." I grinned, aiming to lighten the mood.

Aster's eyes flicked between me and Bennett, then a sly smirk crept across her face. "I think it's a great idea. Now let's get you ready." Sliding her arm through mine, she pulled me away from the crowd, leading us upstairs and straight to my room.

As soon as the door closed, I collapsed onto my bed. "Oh my Goddess, what have I done?"

"I don't think you had a choice," Aster noted dryly. "That's a true fairy down there, and if he said he needs you to go… *you go.*"

Her words struck me like a slap to the face. I jerked upright, terrified of what she meant. "Do you mean he used magic to get me to say yes?"

"No, no. Nothing like that." She turned away and started rummaging through my closet. "The choice was yours alone. I'm just saying if a powerful fairy shows up and asks for your help, it's not like you can say no. Plus, why would you want to? This is sure to be the adventure of a lifetime."

Not sharing in her excitement, I fell back onto the mattress with a slew of questions pummeling my head.

Where are we going? What if there are more witches protecting the book? How in the world is Bennett part fae? And how did he even get here? Fear knotted my insides as tears pooled in my eyes. *What if I wasn't strong enough when it mattered most?*

A hard thump shook the bed as Aster dropped my leather duffel bag next to me. "Lil, get out of your head. I've got you all packed, so you just need to follow your instincts and let Gideon lead the way. You'll be fine."

I sat up again, questioning how in the world she could be so calm. "How is it that some strange male fairy—who has apparently been secret friends with our mother for years—shows up on our doorstep and you're completely fine with him leading your youngest sister away, just like that? What aren't you telling me, Aster?"

A flicker of concern crossed her face, but in the next moment it was gone. "Well, since Mom *is* the one who brought him here, I assume he must be pretty trustworthy." She pushed her glasses back into place.

I sighed. "I suppose you're right." Mom always made it a point to keep our secret quiet, so letting someone in, especially while things were going so wrong, was certainly a big deal.

Aster knelt in front of me, taking my hands in hers. "Look. I know you're scared. Especially to be venturing out on your own for the first time. But I have no doubt Gideon is beyond capable of keeping you safe, and from what I could tell, you and Bennett certainly have a connection. So, like I said, trust your instincts and try to have some fun."

I balked at her words. "There is no connection between me and Bennett."

Aster chuckled and stood. "Fine. Whatever you say. But you're going to be working side by side with him, so I think you better *find* a connection that you can make work." Aster grabbed my duffle and waited by the door. "Now come on. Let's head down to the store and get you stocked up."

"How long do you think I'll be gone?" I whispered as we descended the stairs.

"I have no idea, but I packed enough basic pieces to rotate outfits for a few weeks."

"A few weeks?" I squawked out loud.
Aster laughed as we reached the main floor. "Chill out, Lily. You'll be back home before you know it."

Joining Mom and the others downstairs, Aster started gathering supplies from our disheveled shop. I found Bennett leaning against the wall near the high-back chair, awake and seemingly back to his normal self.

"Hey." He lifted a hand.

I stopped short, keeping some distance between us.

He lowered his head. "So, I guess you know I'm part fae now?"

"Yeah. I know."

We stood in silence for a handful of heartbeats.

"I didn't even know myself, if that matters," he finally sputtered. Lifting his head, his tentative gaze met mine. "I've spent my whole life thinking I was a normal kid, and now—" He shoved his hands in his pockets. "I guess I've always been some kind of freak."

"Don't say that." I took a deep breath and continued forward. "I won't pretend to understand what it all means, but you are not a freak." I wasn't sure if I was saying this more for his sake or mine, but it felt right, nonetheless. "Besides, if you're a freak, then I guess you're saying I am too, and you're wrong." I lifted my chin. "I'm a witch, and proud of it."

Bennett laughed and took his hands out of his pockets. "Who knew when my day began, I'd wind up in a house full of witches who protect a fairy portal to a different realm that I'm apparently from?" He pointed to himself. "Definitely not me."

"Lily," Aster called from across the room. "Can you come here, please?"

Bennett followed me over to my eldest sister whose arms were full of dusty old books.

"You can't possibly expect me to take all those?" My eyes roamed the stack of titles cradled in her arms.

"No, no. Just help me lay them out on the table."

Bennett grabbed the first few from the top, and I took the rest.

Turning back to the shelf, Aster selected a couple more titles, then added them to the pile we'd already spread out in front of us.

Aster nodded in silent thanks. "I've looked up all I could on the witches of the old realm. While it may look like a lot, there's barely a mention between them. However, in each of these books, there *is* mention of a sacred tome, one coveted by the fae. Knowing what we do now, I'm wondering if the book they each refer to is this witch's handbook to magic and mayhem," she explained.

My eyes drifted over each cover, my nerves surging to the surface again. "Did you ask Gideon about it?"

"Not yet. But I figured I'd keep these here, ready and accessible, in case you need my help while you're gone."

Gideon slid between us in that moment. "Don't worry. I'll keep them safe."

Aster's eyes met mine, and for the first time in a long time, I wished my sister could remain by my side. "Are you familiar with any of these titles?" she asked Gideon.

He scanned the books with genuine interest. "No, I can't say that I am. But I heard what you said, and if they mention a tome important to fae, then you're probably right. There weren't many witches who lived in Ferindale or Dartmoor, but that doesn't mean there weren't more clans who resided outside the capital cities."

"Capital cities?" I asked, having no ideas beyond my own imaginations what the fae realm was really like.

"Yes. Ferindale is the capital of the Light Kingdom, and Dartmoor is the capital of the Dark." Gideon lowered his head, his eyes going distant and sad.

"And which are you?" I blurted out.

"Lily!" Mom reprimanded me from across the room.

"What? If I'm going to leave the only home I've ever known, I think I have a right to know!" I crossed my arms, not caring if she agreed. "I know you said we can trust him, but I think sharing a little more about himself is the *least* he can do."

With a forlorn look on his face, he met my eyes and shared only one word—"Dark."

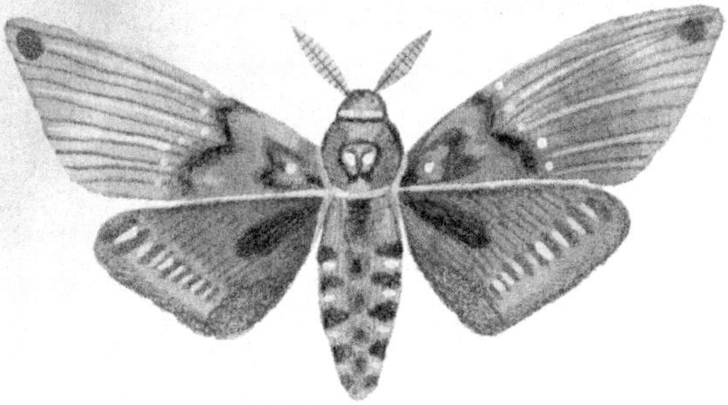

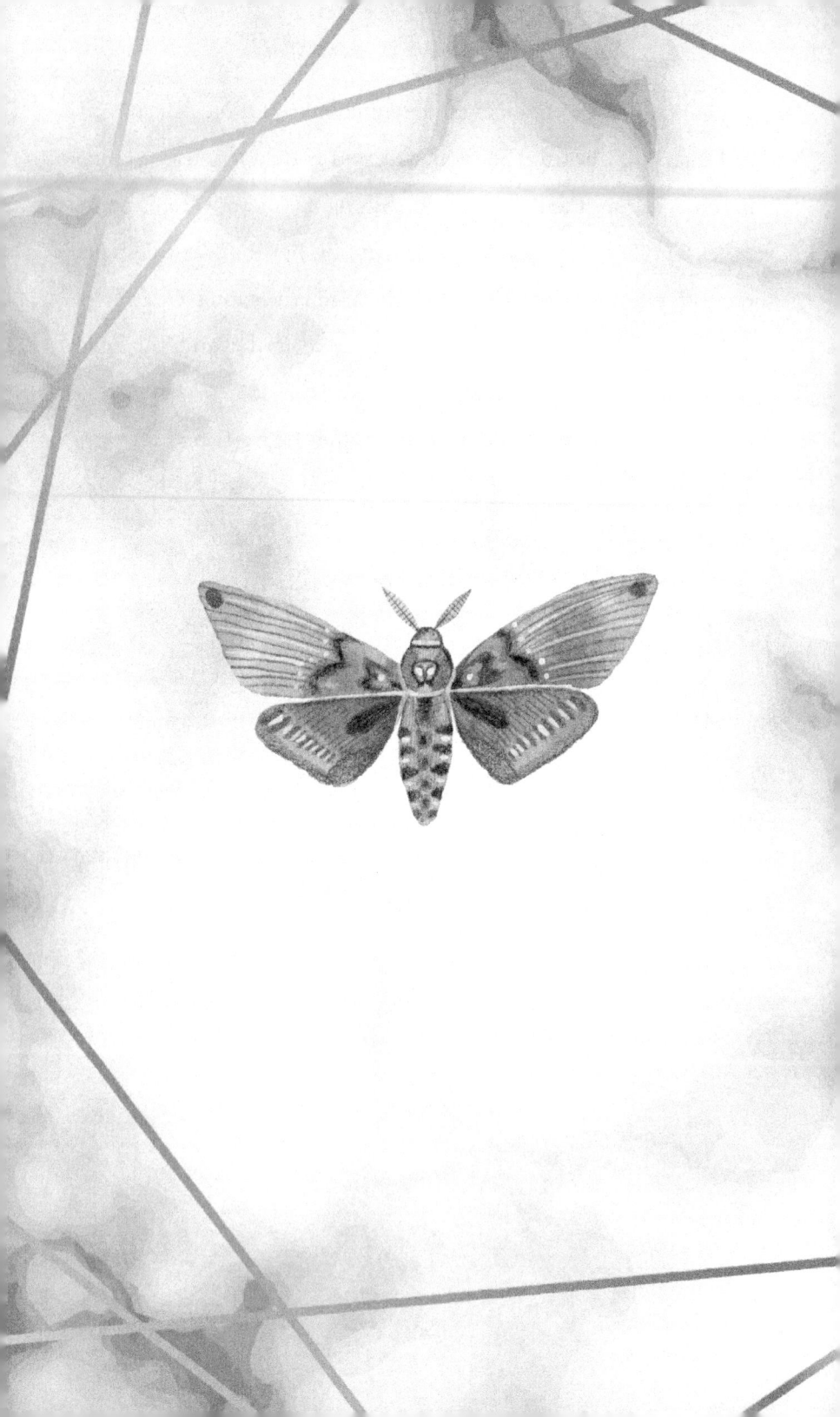

Nine

"Lily, that was out of line." Mom grabbed my arm and took me aside in the back room. "I told you Gideon is a friend. You should know I would *never* let you leave with him if I didn't trust him completely." Tears welled in my eyes and she lessened her grip. "Honey, I know you're scared, but Light or Dark doesn't mean good or bad."

"How do you know that? How do you know him at all?"

Mom recognized the fear in my words and pulled me in for a hug. "Baby, I told you what happened, and Gideon and I have been friends ever since. Trust me, you're going to be fine."

I held on tight, memorizing the feel of my mom's arms around me. I'd chosen to do this. Knew it was the right thing. But in this moment, I was a young girl scared to leave the safety of home and all those she loved.

"Come on now. Let's finish getting you ready." Mom kissed the top of my head and led me back into the shop.

With our supplies gathered—and after a slew of hugs and tears—I followed Gideon and Bennett out the front door, looking back one last time. With the shop on lockdown, the usually vibrant purple door somehow seemed muted and muddled. Leaving would break my heart, but this was something I had to do—to save our shop and home, to save Bennett, and from what Gideon explained, possibly save the world. Now, if I could just get past the terror setting in.

"Where are we going first?" I asked, hoping the information would help settle my nerves.

"Bennett's dorm."

I swallowed hard. *So much for that.* Not only were we headed to Yale, but into a boy's dormitory, no less. A chill ran up my spine, putting me even further on edge.

Bennett ordered an Uber to take us back to campus, leaving us to wait in silence on the corner for a few minutes until it arrived. But after looking up and down the street multiple times, something clicked.

I turned to Gideon. "Hey, wait. How did you get here with Mom?"

We had a truck that all of us shared for the shop, but I didn't remember her grabbing the keys when she left to get him.

"After your mother helped me when I arrived in your realm, I left her a way to contact me."

"And what way is that?" I pressed.

He lifted his chin, looking me up and down as if appraising whether I was worthy of the information. After a few uncomfortable moments, I heard a buzzing in my head. *"I will not speak the secret aloud, but I can tell you now if you're willing to accept the cost."*

"Cost?" I spewed, earning a deep frown from the stoic fae.

Bennett looked at me with creased brows, obviously confused at my outburst.

"Sorry," I sent back. "But I won't answer until I know the cost you speak of."

Gideon tipped his chin, silently agreeing. "The cost is the same as it was for your mother. You'll be sworn to secrecy, unable to share my existence with anyone."

"Except in emergencies, right?" I crossed my arms, thinking of how she'd just introduced us all.

A smirk pulled at his lips. "Yes, except in emergencies."

"Fine, I accept the cost."

Gideon nodded. "There is an old, gnarled tree deep in the forest outside of town. With the proper spell, you can summon me there."

"What's the spell?" I already knew which tree he was talking about. We'd all climbed it as kids. Mom would take us there often, laying out a blanket beneath its wide branches as we played and ate our picnic lunches.

Gideon took a deep breath, and I suddenly realized sharing this type of information cost him as well. "*King of Dark, King of Doom, hear my call as I claim a boon. Send my friend, in this time of need. Show me favor, for the secret I keep.*"

A surge of magic pulsed in my veins as I committed the spell to memory. "Thank you for trusting me."

He dipped his head. "Thank you for helping me."

"Uber's here." Bennett's voice pulled me back to reality, but I couldn't stop thinking about the spell.

King of Dark, King of Doom... Despite what Mom said about good or bad, Light or Dark, that certainly didn't bode well.

Thirty minutes later, we stepped out of the Uber and onto the Yale campus.

Bennett led us across a perfectly manicured lawn to a tall brick building. "My dorm's on the second floor."

With his glamor in place to hide his ears, Gideon and I followed in silence as I took it all in. I didn't want to miss one single detail.

The stone architecture was almost monolithic, with an air of the pseudo-Gothic style I loved. The lush landscape was clean and inviting—green and full of color even now in the middle of Fall. I was stunned by its beauty and could suddenly see myself walking the paths and ducking beneath the stone archways on my way to class.

"We'll have to take the stairs." Bennett held the door open, smiling down at me as I passed by.

"Are you on the second floor because you're a sophomore?" I asked.

"Yes. With four floors to the building, it's the easiest way to separate the classes for anyone who wants to live on campus."

"Is this fraternity housing, then?" I was almost embarrassed by how little I knew about college life.

"No, just campus housing. I never joined a fraternity." He shrugged flippantly, but I wondered if his decision was on purpose or if he simply didn't get in. The question seemed too personal to ask.

"Here we are." Bennett pushed open the door leading to the second floor and walked halfway down the hall. "You'll have to forgive the mess; I wasn't exactly expecting company."

The door swung open, and I thought I'd entered the fairy realm here and now. Green ferns hung from the ceiling while an array of potted plants decorated every flat surface available. I walked toward a hammock chair dangling in the corner and caught sight of his single bed pressed against the far wall. A modest desk, bookshelf, and dresser took up the rest of the space, but other than those minimal pieces of furniture, plants dominated the room.

"What did you say your major was?" I asked, completely shocked by the verdant state of his dorm.

"Molecular, Cellular, and Developmental Biology, with a minor in Botany."

"Wow!" Bennett Wilson was shaping up to be more than your average baseball player. "That's amazing."

"And useful," Gideon added. "Getting to the bottom of how your fae magic has stayed dormant until now will require this type of research. Since all fairy magic is rooted in the earth, your knowledge should prove quite helpful."

Bennett sank down onto his bed and shrugged. "Great. Glad to help."

I laughed under my breath as his sarcasm tinged the air.

"Good. Now, can you tell me if you came across anything new recently? A new plant, a gift from someone… anything that hadn't been near you before?" Gideon roamed the room, touching the leaves and blooms of all Bennett's plants, which for some reason didn't sit well with me.

"Hey, maybe you should stop touching all his things and let him think. I'm sure he'd notice if something was off with his plants," I quipped.

Gideon held his hands up in surrender. "My apologies. Please let me know if you think of anything." He settled himself against the door frame, waiting for Bennett to provide our next clue.

Rising from the bed, Bennett walked to his closet and pulled the accordion doors open. Multiple shelves filled the space, which carried a faint glow from the grow lights hanging above. "These are the most exotic plants I have, and this one arrived just yesterday." He grabbed a small terracotta pot filled with an exquisite purple plant and handed it to Gideon.

"This is it." Gideon's tone became serious. "It has fae magic pulsing within."

I walked closer and leaned in for a better look. "It's the same color your eyes were glowing. Do you remember where it came from?"

Bennett shook his head. "I order so many plants online, I just figured this was a backorder from one of the previous shipments."

"Did you keep the packing slip?" Gideon asked, impressing me with his modern knowledge of how things worked in our world. I knew he'd been here for a long time, but in my mind, all I saw was an ancient Dark fae.

"No. Sorry. Trash pickup was yesterday."

"Damn. Okay. Well, at least we found the trigger that awoke your magic." Gideon held up the plant. "We'll need this if we're going to use you to track the book."

I shook my head. "You know what? Until you acknowledge we're here to help you, you might want to stop using words like "use" and "trigger". Otherwise, neither of us are moving another inch." I dropped my bag on the floor and crossed my arms, shocking myself at how protective of Bennett I suddenly felt.

Gideon winced. "I'm sorry. I've lived alone for a long time, so my communication skills may be a bit rusty. But honestly, though my words may offend you, they do remain true. Bennett is the only one who can track the book since the witch directly triggered his magic to open your portal." He looked to Bennett. "You're our only link."

Bennett nodded, accepting his role, but I still didn't like it.

Gideon turned to me. "Lily, I am grateful to both of you for your help, despite my callous approach. Please accept my apology."

Taking a deep breath, I let my arms fall to my side and nodded back. What other choice did I have? "Fine. But remember, you just admitted it yourself. *You* need *us* if we're going to find this book, so maybe you could try not to treat us like pawns."

Gideon dipped at the waist. "You have my word."

I straightened at the sight of him bowing to me. "Well… thank you." I paused, shuffling awkwardly on my feet.

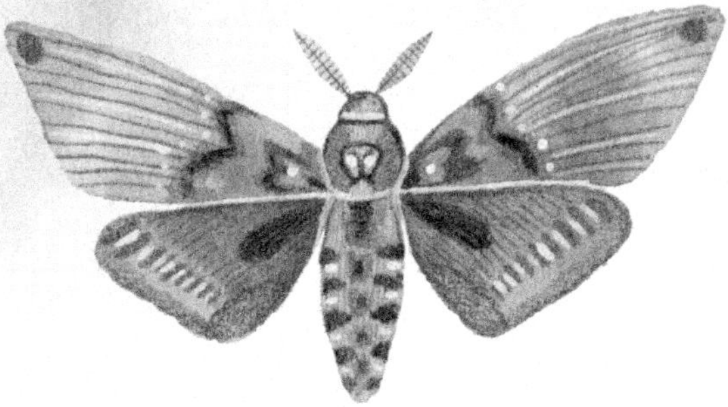

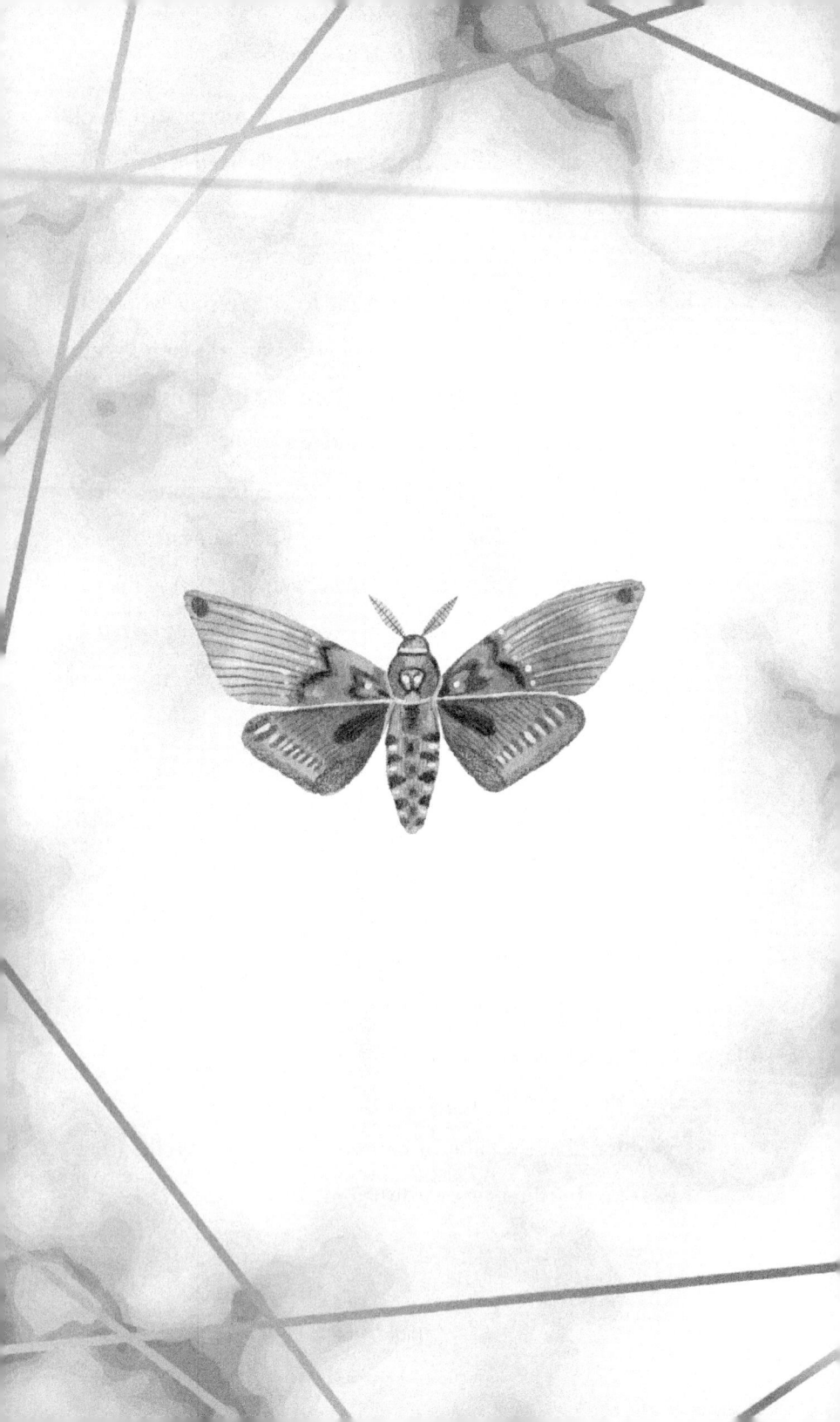

Ten

With the packing slip gone, Gideon informed me I'd need to use my "revelation magic" to figure out where the plant came from.

"Should we go somewhere else to do this?" I asked, worried of being discovered.

"No. We'll be fine here. Nobody bothers me." The sad inflection to Bennett's voice tugged at my heartstrings again. He may enjoy playing ball with his team, but in reality, he seemed to be quite a loner.

"Okay, I'll just need a little space." I sat on the rug in the middle of his room with the foreign plant placed in front of me. Bennett and Gideon moved away until their backs were pressed against the wall near the door.

Closing my eyes, I reached out with my magic and imagined a light encircling the pot. Focusing on the purple leaves, my mind asked the question of its origin and received the answer almost immediately.

I shot to my feet, lifting the pot with me. "It came from a florist right here in town. New Haven Blooms."

"Perfect. We can head over there now." Gideon gestured to the door, leaving me to shoulder my bag and carry the plant while Bennett locked up behind us, grabbing a duffle he'd hurriedly packed.

"How will knowing where the plant came from help us find the book?" I asked.

"Whoever sent that plant to Bennett knew it would trigger his magic. Once we pinpoint the person responsible, we can find out why they're helping the witch or if they have more information about her plans."

"Wait. You're saying there's someone *here*—in our realm—helping this witch on purpose?"

Gideon strode out the front door of the building, pausing to whisper a silencing spell before answering my question out loud. "Most likely. I think for the magic to reach through the barrier, she'd have to have someone's aid on this side."

"Why didn't you mention that before?" I slowed my pace to stay inside the spell's boundary, nervous our situation had just gotten a lot more dangerous.

"I thought it would be obvious," Gideon replied with a shrug.

"Maybe to *you*, but not to us! Remember, we don't know anything about the other realm or the barrier that keeps them apart."

"Again, my apologies for the assumption." Gideon stood on the curb, probably *assuming* Bennett was already calling for another car. Which he was.

After dropping the silencing spell, Gideon followed us into our second Uber of the day, providing the driver with our destination. None of us spoke on the ride to the florist, but I closed my eyes and tried to mentally prepare for what we might be facing. Unfortunately, since I had no idea what that might be, thinking about it only made me more anxious.

"Bennett, tell me about your time at Yale." I needed a distraction from my thoughts, and we hadn't really gotten into much detail beyond the basics.

"What do you want to know?" he asked.

Butterflies roamed in my stomach. "I'm not sure… just if you like it, I guess."

He nodded eagerly. "Absolutely! It's a great place, and all the professors are top-notch."

"What about the other students? Are you a member of any clubs or anything like that?"

He shook his head, pushing his shaggy hair out of his eyes. "Beyond my baseball team, no. I tend to spend most of my time studying my plants and reading."

I dropped my head, a little disappointed in his answer for some reason.

"But, if that's what you're into," Bennett continued, "there's tons of clubs and activities you can sign up for." I looked up and caught his smile. "Why? Are you thinking about enrolling?"

I shrugged. "Maybe."

"Your sister will be thrilled to hear it," he teased, obviously noting the tension between me and Aster when she brought it up before.

"Yes, well. We'll see."

"Here we are," the driver announced.

I looked out the window and found an unassuming flower shop tucked between two other buildings. Its whitewashed brick facade was clean and inviting, and the picture windows were bursting with riotous flower arrangements and floral displays. "This looks lovely."

"Indeed, it does. Now, let's find the owner." Gideon emerged from the car and strode toward the shop without an ounce of trepidation.

Meanwhile, shouldering my bag again, I clutched the purple plant to my chest and crept in slowly behind him, a complete ball of nerves. A bell dinged overhead as we entered, reminding me of home.

"Afternoon!" a cheery voice called out from deeper within the store. "Anything I can help you with?"

"Hello. Yes. Actually, we'd like to speak to the owner." Gideon got straight to the point.

"That's me." A thin, middle-aged woman appeared from behind a counter carrying an armful of flowers, reminding me again of home. Her hair wasn't as black as Fern's, but her delicate features and friendly smile exuded her love of flowers, just like my sister's.

"Wonderful. We need to track down the person who placed this order with your shop." Gideon reached behind him, snatching the plant from my hands.

"Oh, yes. Such a lovely specimen!" the woman gushed. "Very rare. Was there a problem with the plant?"

"No," Gideon answered, "but we need to obtain the name and hopefully the address of the person who placed the order." Gideon smiled wide, and I wondered if he was using his fae charm to help loosen the owner's tongue.

The woman's face was apologetic. "While I can't give you an exact name or address, I can tell you the order came from overseas."

"Really? Whereabouts?" Gideon asked.

"Essex, England." She smiled proudly. "We don't usually get a lot of foreign customers, so that one's easy to remember."

I held my breath, waiting to see what Gideon would do next. Essex was home to the original gate and the largest fairy portal in the world.

"Thank you for your time. It's much appreciated." He turned on his heel, shoving the plant back into my hands before striding for the door.

"Happy to help!" the shop owner called out as we rushed to leave behind him.

"So, what does this mean?" I asked.

"It means we're going to England."

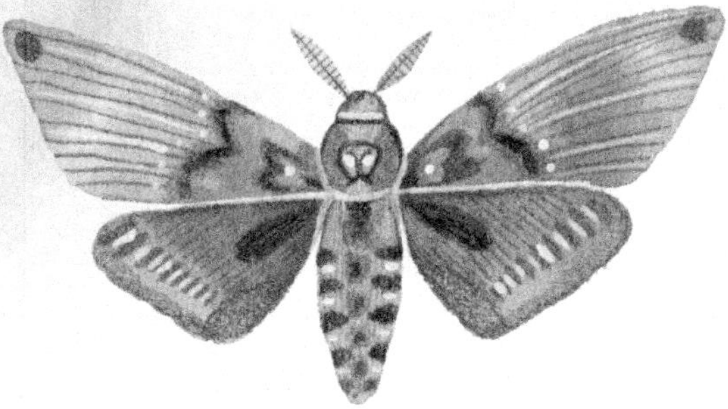

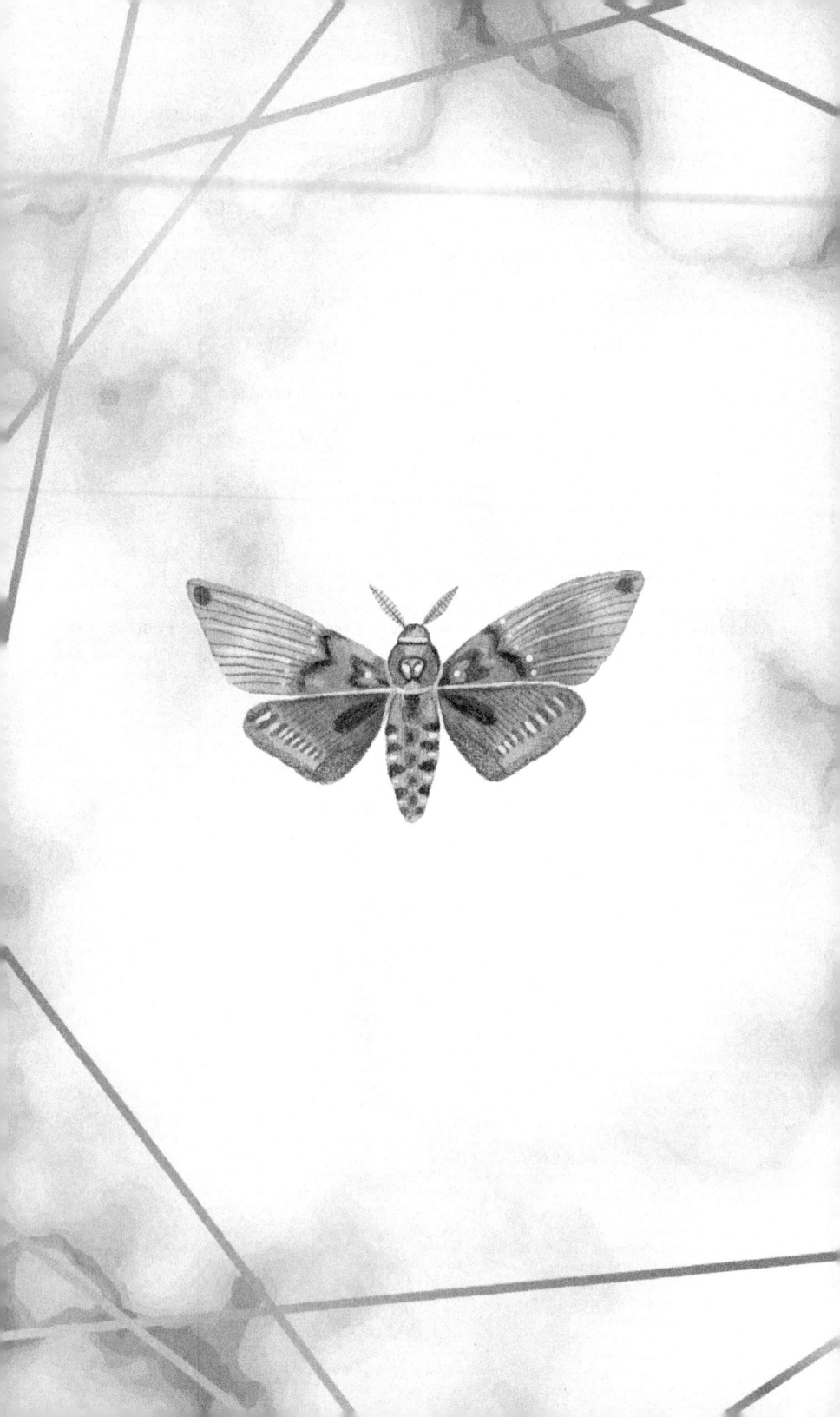

Eleven

It took a few seconds for Gideon's words to sink in. "What? No! There's no way I'm leaving the country with either of you!" I proclaimed.

Bennett dropped his head, plunged his hands into his pockets, and proceeded to stare at the curb outside of New Haven Blooms while I continued to freak out.

"Unfortunately, I'm afraid you don't have a choice." Gideon interrupted my emotional spiral with an unwavering stare as three plane tickets snapped into existence between his fingers. "You knew the drill when you agreed to come. We need your help to find the book. Especially if you want to save your shop."

At the words *your shop*, my chest tightened.

Our family of witches was one of the few covens tasked centuries ago with protecting the fairy portals around the world. And while the original gate stood in Essex County, England, the portal at home—below our treasured shop in Essex, Connecticut—was the second most important of all, tying directly into the ley line that ran beneath the entire East Coast. Our homey little town in Connecticut was the spitting image of its European predecessor, and no matter where you wandered, all roads led to the town dock and the adjacent Connecticut River Museum. It was just another thing I loved about its small-town vibe. Filled with quaint stone buildings, white-washed brick and lap-sided houses, Essex was a quintessential East Coast town, boasting manicured lawns and white picket fences. And I, for one, could never see myself anywhere else in the world.

"I need to call my mom." Walking away from them both, I dialed home.

"Aster, hi. I need to talk to Mom... Yes, I'm fine, but can I please just talk to Mom? Thanks." I waited patiently as Aster called our mother to the phone.

"Hi, baby. What's going on?" My mother's voice soothed me instantly.

"Gideon says we need to go to England. And... I'm scared." My voice hitched.

Mom took a deep breath. "Honey, you'll be fine. Gideon is a good man, and I trust him. You should, too."

I looked over my shoulder, taking in the mysterious fae. With his glamour in place to hide his pointed ears, his dark hair was spiked in the front and smooth on the sides. His black denim jeans looked modern, and the way he wore his button-up shirt—rolled up at the sleeves—made him appear casual and normal. But I knew the truth... Underneath all that façade there was nothing normal about him.

"Okay, thanks, Mom. I guess I'll talk to you soon."

"Sounds good, honey. Just stay alert and don't leave Gideon's side. He'll protect you if anything goes wrong. Take care, sweetie."

The line went dead and my momentary calmness died with it. Why did Mom have to say that? *"If anything goes wrong..."* Now, I was certain it would.

"All set. Our plane leaves in three hours." Gideon shoved his phone in his pocket and smiled as if nothing was wrong—as if my world hadn't just shifted again.

I'd never flown before, and I didn't understand why we had to now. "Don't you have a more *magical way* to do this?" I whispered to Gideon as we walked toward the security gate in the airport, our magically produced passports clutched tightly in our hands.

"That much power would be hard to conceal, so no, I don't." Gideon looked down at me with kind eyes. "It will be okay, Lily. I won't let anything happen to you."

His words seeped into my soul like warm honey, and I wondered if he was using a bit of his power now to keep me calm. If so, I'd have to thank him later.

Stepping through the checkpoint, I retrieved my bag and followed Gideon and Bennett down the corridor to our gate.

Heading to Essex, England was a dream of a lifetime for many witches. To see the original fairy gate and spend time exploring the origins of our familial duty to protect it… I had to admit, I secretly couldn't wait to get there, even with my trembling nerves.

Boarding the plane went smoothly enough, but the moment the flight attendants finished their announcements and the engines began to rev, my fear shifted into high gear.

"Hey, it's all good. Don't worry." Bennett placed a hand on my vigorously bouncing knee, yanking it back when I jerked away with a shocked gasp. "I was just trying to say that I've flown tons with my team, and there's nothing to worry about."

I took a deep breath, grateful for his words and effort. "Thank you. I'm sorry I'm so jumpy. This is all just… a lot."

Bennett bobbed his head and smiled, then jerked his chin toward the window. "See? We're already on the way."

I turned to the small oval opening and all my fears fell away. I couldn't explain how soaring through the sky felt so right, but somehow it did. Silver-lined clouds shimmered in the moonlight, reflecting their magical glow against the outside of the plane. "This is beautiful," I whispered.

I didn't turn around, but I heard Bennett's reply. "Yes, it is."

Thankfully, the plane ride was smooth and uneventful, though dreadfully long. Now, with only a few more seconds left inside London's Stansted Airport, I couldn't wait for my feet to sink into the earth again.

Peering through a thick drizzle into the gray sky surrounding us, I smiled wide, utterly content as Bennett loudly voiced his despair.

"Are you kidding me?" He flung out his arms, shaking off the rain.

"What did you expect? It's England," Gideon supplied flatly.

Yanking my jacket collar tight, I followed my companions onto the frigid street. With this being my first trip away from home, I hoped it would be enjoyable. Seeing as this was my favorite type of weather, things were off to a good start. Then again, we were there to look for a rogue witch's magical book to stop the fairy realm from leaking into our own. So yeah... good times all around.

"Where do we go from here?" I heard Bennett ask.

"The flower shop owner said the plant was purchased from a florist in Essex, so let's find a phone book and narrow down the search," Gideon replied.

"On it." Bennett pulled out his cell phone and did a quick online search. "There are eight flower shops in the city, with the first being only a block away from the train station."

Gideon held up his hand and suddenly a black car pulled to a stop right in front of us—an actual hackney carriage, from what I'd learned from the plane's inflight magazine. "No trains for us." Gideon smiled. "Let's get out of this rain." He held open the taxi's door, sliding in beside me as Bennett ran through the rain and jumped in from the other side.

"Where to?" the driver asked, his accent exactly as I imagined.

"Rosie's Roses in Essex, please," Bennett replied.

"Oh, that's cute." I enjoyed the play on words, and it didn't hurt that she was named after a flower, just like me and my sisters.

Forty-five minutes later, we pulled up to a quaint strip of brick buildings, a white sign displaying Rosie's logo above the middle one.

"Please wait here." Gideon handed the taxi driver some money before stepping out and jogging for the shop's front door.

[71]

Bennett and I followed him inside and I was immediately hit with the scent of burning incense, reminding me of Daisy's shop. My chest tightened at the thought of home.

"Hello. Can I help you?" a soft voice rang out from behind the counter.

I looked up to find a sweet old lady with silver-blonde hair wrapped up into a perfect chignon. I assumed this was Rosie.

"Hello. Yes. We're looking for the shop where this plant originated." Bennett held up his phone, displaying a picture of the purple plant on the screen.

"Oh, my. That's a unique beauty. But no. We don't stock anything like that here."

Thank goodness. For some reason, I really hoped she didn't have anything to do with this.

"Do you know of any shops that do carry these types of rare plants? I asked.

Rosie looked at me and shared a sweet smile. "No, honey. I don't. We may be a small town, but we don't exactly get together and talk plants... anymore."

"That's too bad." I shrugged.

"Yes, well, it's not for lack of trying. We used to do things like that, until a large garden center moved into town. After that, everyone felt the pressure of competition and our tight-knit floral community all went their separate ways."

"Sounds like the garden center should be our next stop," Bennett whispered.

"Exactly what I was thinking," Gideon murmured under his breath.

"Rosie, thank you for the information." I dipped my head. "You have a lovely store here, and I have no doubt it'll continue to do well."

"Thank you, dear. That's kind of you to say." She gave us a friendly wave as we left.

After giving our next destination to the taxi driver, we rode across town in silence.

Staring out the window, I found the landscape to be exactly how I'd imagined it—rolling hills, white-washed stone houses, sprawling fields with livestock roaming the land. I took a deep, contented breath and finally admitted to myself… I was glad to be on this adventure.

"Here we are." The driver pulled up and stopped outside a large one-story, gray brick building located in the middle of nowhere.

Literally.

There was nothing around except for the building itself and the gravel parking lot on which we were currently parked. No rows of neatly maintained shrubs or manicured trees like you'd expect to see. A nursery this large back home would have been welcoming and lovely, but instead—even *without* the current weather conditions—there was something gloomy and foreboding about this place.

"What's the name of this store?" I asked, seeing no visible signage out front.

Bennett shrugged. "I'm not sure. It's only listed as 'Garden Center' on the web."

"That's odd." I looked to Gideon for confirmation.

Exiting the taxi, Gideon stood stock-still with his hands clasped behind his back.

"What is it?" I followed him out of the car.

"I can sense magic here. This is definitely the place."

I looked at Gideon and suddenly wondered how *his* magic worked. Obviously, he could sense all kinds of things since he pinpointed all our magics, plus Bennett's, right from the start.

"Are we in danger?" I took a step back, angling myself behind his broad frame.

"No, I don't think so. The magic here is twisted, but it's not fairy-based."

"A witch, then?" Bennett guessed as he came to stand beside us.

"I think so, but one from here in this realm."

"So, it could be the person working for the fae crone, then?" Bennett assumed.

"Possibly. But by choice or by force, I'm not sure yet. That's what we're here to find out." Gideon waved off the taxi driver then marched toward the solid wood door and twisted the antique brass knob, entering the building without a second thought.

Reluctantly, Bennett and I followed him inside.

Twelve

Creeping behind him on the balls of my feet, I followed Gideon, nervous about what we would find. I hoped all could be revealed and dealt with easily, but I knew down deep that was never going to happen.

Inside, the large open space was lined with flowers on growing tables, exactly like the nurseries back home, but there was no one here to greet us, which made a tense situation even more eerie. After scanning the space, Gideon used two fingers to signal us to fan out. Bennett went left and I veered right, weaving my way between two rows of hydrangeas.

The colors were vibrant and the plants looked healthy, but as I continued further into the garden center, the offerings became less vibrant and more oddly shaped.

Finally emerging at the end of our respective rows, we met up again in front of a single wooden door which sat square in the center of a solid brick wall.

"I don't like this," I whispered.

"Me either." Bennett moved close, his arm brushing against mine.

"Don't worry." Gideon lifted his chin. "I can handle whatever we find." Using a bit of his magic, he unlocked the door and disappeared inside.

"Well, hell." Bennett grabbed my hand. "Come on. I've got you."

I tiptoed through the door and gasped when the room came into view.

Glowing purple flowers filled the gigantic space, all pulsing with magic from the fairy realm.

"Guess we found our supplier." Gideon stood at the head of one of the grow tables with his arms crossed over his chest.

"What do we do now?" I asked, unclear where to go from here.

"We locate the owner and find out exactly what's going on." Gideon waved his hands in the air and the magic-laced crop wilted and died. "We can't take the chance of these falling into the wrong hands," he explained.

"What do you mean, the *wrong hands?*" I asked, unable to imagine anyone else involved.

Gideon turned to face me. "I mean, I don't think it would be a good idea if any more of these were sent out to trigger other portals. Do you?"

I shook my head. "No, of course not."

"Then let's keep going." Gideon marched toward the next door ahead of us, repeating his spell to gain entry once more.

Nudging my shoulder, Bennett gave me a kind smile, and I had to admit it helped. I was grateful for his presence. So, with Bennett by my side, I followed Gideon through the door and into the next room, ready or not.

A cold, dense fog surrounded us the moment we stepped inside. "Gideon?" I called into the void, unable to see.

"Give me a moment. I'm trying to clear it." His voice echoed from up ahead.

"Bennett?" I whispered, hoping he was still close by.

"I'm right here." A light brush against my hand brought a flush of relief, but I was barely hanging on by a thread. Being this far away from home, for the first time ever, and with two people who were practically strangers, was quickly draining any earlier excitement I had about our little adventure. Now, fear was the only emotion rising inside me as I tried to think about what Mom and Aster had said… that I could trust Gideon.

I called out again. "Gideon?"

Silence.

"Bennett?" I reached out, grateful to feel him still beside me.

"Over here," Bennett called back from somewhere up ahead.

Oh, Goddess. Screaming, I yanked my hand away from whatever was touching me and ran into the fog. Hard claws grabbed at my arms and legs, digging into my flesh the farther I ran. Collapsing onto the ground, I wrapped my arms around my legs and felt the ooze of blood beneath my fingertips. "Bennett, Gideon, where are you?" I cried miserably.

Their voices sounded even farther away now, swallowed by the mist. I had no idea where I truly was. Still inside the garden center? Somehow outside in the deteriorating weather? Or worst yet—caught in the witch's lair?

"Hang on, Lily! I'm coming." Bennett's voice broke through, sounding a fraction closer.

Tears streaked my cheeks and I started to shake, fear overtaking me. I wasn't prepared for this kind of thing. Even with our task clearly laid out, Aster made it sound like a walk in the park, something I should try to enjoy. But this? I knew I never should've left home.

"Lily, keep talking. I'm coming to you," Gideon called back from a distance, making me wonder how we'd gotten so far apart.

"I'm over here, and I think there's something else in here, too."

"Don't move. I'm coming." Gideon's voice was steady and calm.

"Bennett?" I yelled, wanting to make sure he was still okay.

"I'm here, but I'm stuck in some kind of bramble, I think."

"One more second…" The fog parted at Gideon's voice, followed by a scrambling noise all around us that I didn't even want to consider the origins of.

"Oh my God, Lily! Are you okay?" Bennett came running toward me at a breakneck pace now that the room was clear. We were still inside the garden center in another large room, but this one had groves of thorny trees and thick brambles planted throughout. "Lily," Bennett breathed, my name barely a whisper on his lips.

Hopping over a tangle of gnarly roots, he dropped to his knees beside me. "Are you okay?" he asked again.

A shaky breath rattled free from my chest. "I'm… I'm not sure. I felt something grab me, and I think I have a cut on my leg."

Bennett looked down, and as I pulled my quilted skirt to my knees, his eyes went wide.

I didn't need to follow his gaze to know it was bad. The throbbing was worse, and the trickle of blood was still flowing and wet. "How bad is it?"

Bennett didn't respond, but he put his hands over the cut to stop the bleeding.

I flinched at his touch, the pain increasing as my mind ran wild.

Had I been grabbed and sliced by the witch or one of her cronies, or was this simply a scratch from her infected forest? Either way… it wasn't good.

"Everything will be fine, Lily. I promise." Bennett's eyes met mine and for some reason, I believed him.

Warmth radiated up my leg just as Gideon rushed to join us. "Bennett. Lily. Are you both okay?" His eyes continued to scan the room.

"I'm fine, but Lily has a cut on her leg." Bennett pulled away, the warmth of his hands disappearing as he stood up next to Gideon.

"What cut?" Gideon peered down at me. "I don't see a thing."

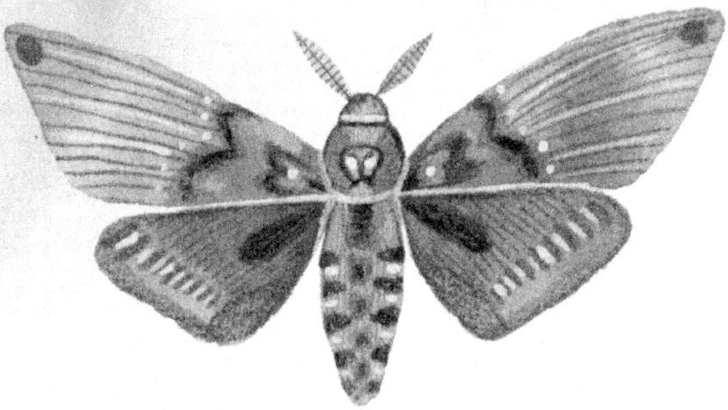

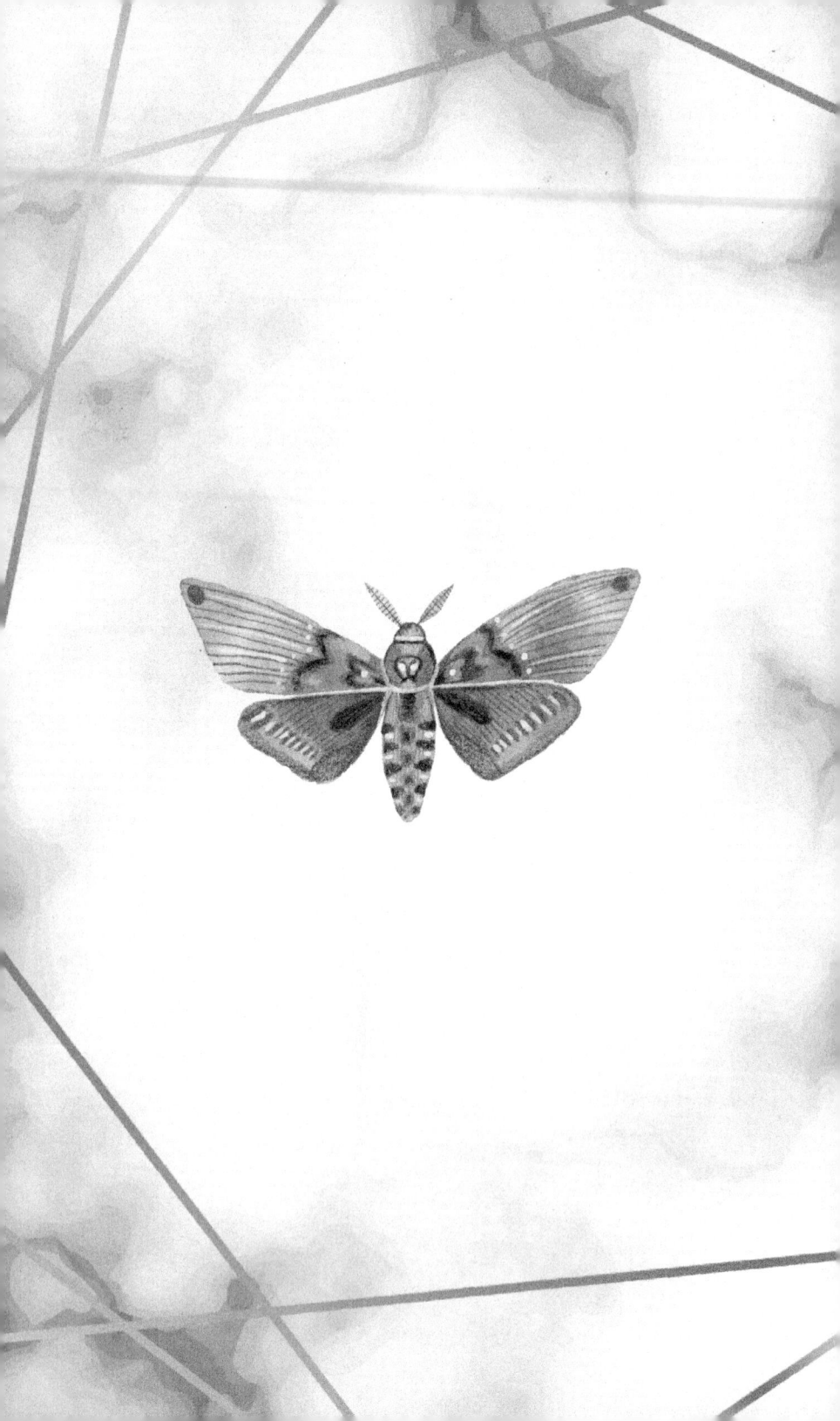

Thirteen

I ran a hand over my shin, feeling nothing but smooth skin. *What the hell?* Pushing the hem of my skirt out of the way, I turned my leg from side to side, looking for blood or at least a small scar. I saw nothing, though the lingering pain was still there. "How did you do that?" I looked up at Bennett in wonder.

Bennett stared at his upturned palms, clearly shaken. "I... I don't know," he stammered. "I don't think I *did* anything. I was just trying to stop the bleeding." He shook his head, disbelief painting his features.

There was no blood on his hands or my leg, and the cut I experienced was not only healed but had completely disappeared, as if it never happened at all.

"Looks like more of your fae magic is rising to the surface." Gideon stood over us, smiling wide.

"I didn't realize that would happen." Bennett remained frozen, still staring at his hands.

"Yes, well, the longer you're around anything fae-based, the more likely your latent abilities will begin to emerge."

"Okkaayy..." Bennett drawled. "But I still have no idea how I can even *be* fae. I grew up in Nebraska. Both my parents were normal... *human*, as far as I know."

"Well, as you can imagine, the fae bloodline goes back a very long time. In fact, your original ancestor could be centuries old by now."

Bennett spun to face Gideon. "What are you saying? That some ancient fairy relative of mine could still be alive?"

"Of course. Human lives are but a blink compared to ours. Why do you think there are so many tales of the Immortal Fae? It's because we live so damn long compared to humans, it seems like we never die." Gideon looked around. "Come on. Let's get out of here. We can continue this conversation later."

Bennett still looked shaken as he helped me to my feet.

"You okay?" I asked.

Bennett shrugged. "Guess so."

We followed Gideon back through each door in silence, exiting the front of the building one by one.

"What do we do now?" I asked. "There's no one here, and you killed all the fae-infused plants, right?"

"Right. But we still need to find this witch. That means you're up, Lily."

I looked around the empty lot, questioning what he meant. "Here? Now?"

"You said it yourself; there's no one here, and I think it's time your revelation magic shows us what's really going on."

I took a step back, gawking at the gravel parking lot. I knew he was right, but I wasn't ready. Before—in Bennett's dorm—I only had to concentrate on a single plant. But now, staring at this massive brick building and the sprawling land around it, the ache in my leg throbbed like the land itself was trying to poison any chance I had.

"I'm not sure I can. If this truly is the witch's den, the size of it and the amount of magic needed to conceal it may be too much for me to break through." I shifted on my feet, the crushed stones beneath me echoing like a gun shot into the wind.

I waited for Gideon to buck my excuse, but thankfully he remained quiet. Bennett, on the other hand, paced back and forth in front of the building, working out something of his own.

"Maybe we could do it together," he finally offered. "My fae magic might give you enough of a boost for you to cut through."

I looked to Gideon to gauge his reaction, and at the same time had a thought of my own. "Why can't you just do it?"

Gideon sighed. "For the same reason I couldn't transport us here from the States. If I use that much fae magic, it will be easily detected."

"Right." I rolled my shoulders and took a deep breath. "Okay, let's give this a try." Reaching for Bennett's hand, I let my magic unfold across the parking lot until an invisible light surrounded the entire building. "Now, Bennett."

I cast my intention into the ether, noting the tinge of Bennett's blue and purple magic surfing atop my own. Our magics played off each other's, the colors swirling like grease on water, creating a beautiful, pearlescent glow. As our joint effort reached its zenith, I blew out a breath, exhaling my intent of revelation.

Like a scene from a movie, the false façade faded away, crumbling to reveal the garden center's true state.

The building looked similar to the original, but only in shape and size. In truth, it was dilapidated beyond repair. Exposed holes and cracked bricks littered the front, revealing twisted branches and crawling vines protruding from within. It looked like an overgrown ruin left behind from ancient times.

"Now we're getting somewhere." Gideon's eyes traveled over the new scene, taking in things Bennett and I apparently couldn't see.

"What is it?"

"There's definitely a twist to the magic here, but I can't make out if it's coming from the witch herself, or if the crone has somehow broken through to influence things on her own."

"So, it may not be this witch's fault after all?" I looked back at the ruined building, hoping my assumption was right. For whatever reason, I couldn't stand the thought of any witch having something to do with a plot this evil.

"It's possible the crone may be controlling the witch to achieve her goal."

I spun around. "And what is that goal, exactly? Do you honestly think a crone of the fae world would care this much about a frickin' book?"

Gideon's eyes narrowed as if he couldn't believe what I was asking.

"I'm sorry. I just mean that if the book has been gone this long, I'm sure she's found ways to live without it. I don't understand why it would still be so important for her to get it back." I turned around and kicked at the rocks, clearing a spot for me to sit down. Dropping to the ground, I crossed my legs and stared at the dilapidated building again.

Moments passed before Gideon replied, his tone more cautious than I'd ever heard it before. "Lily, you remember what Aster said… This book has been mentioned throughout fae history as a tome of great importance. And like I explained, it's the only way to recast the spell that keeps the magic of your store in place and the fairy portals closed. And *I* need to find it so I can make amends." He paused, taking a deep breath "I'm the one who stole the book, and then lost it."

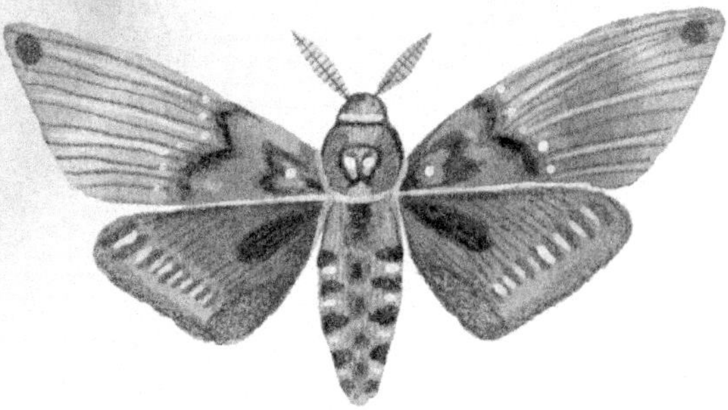

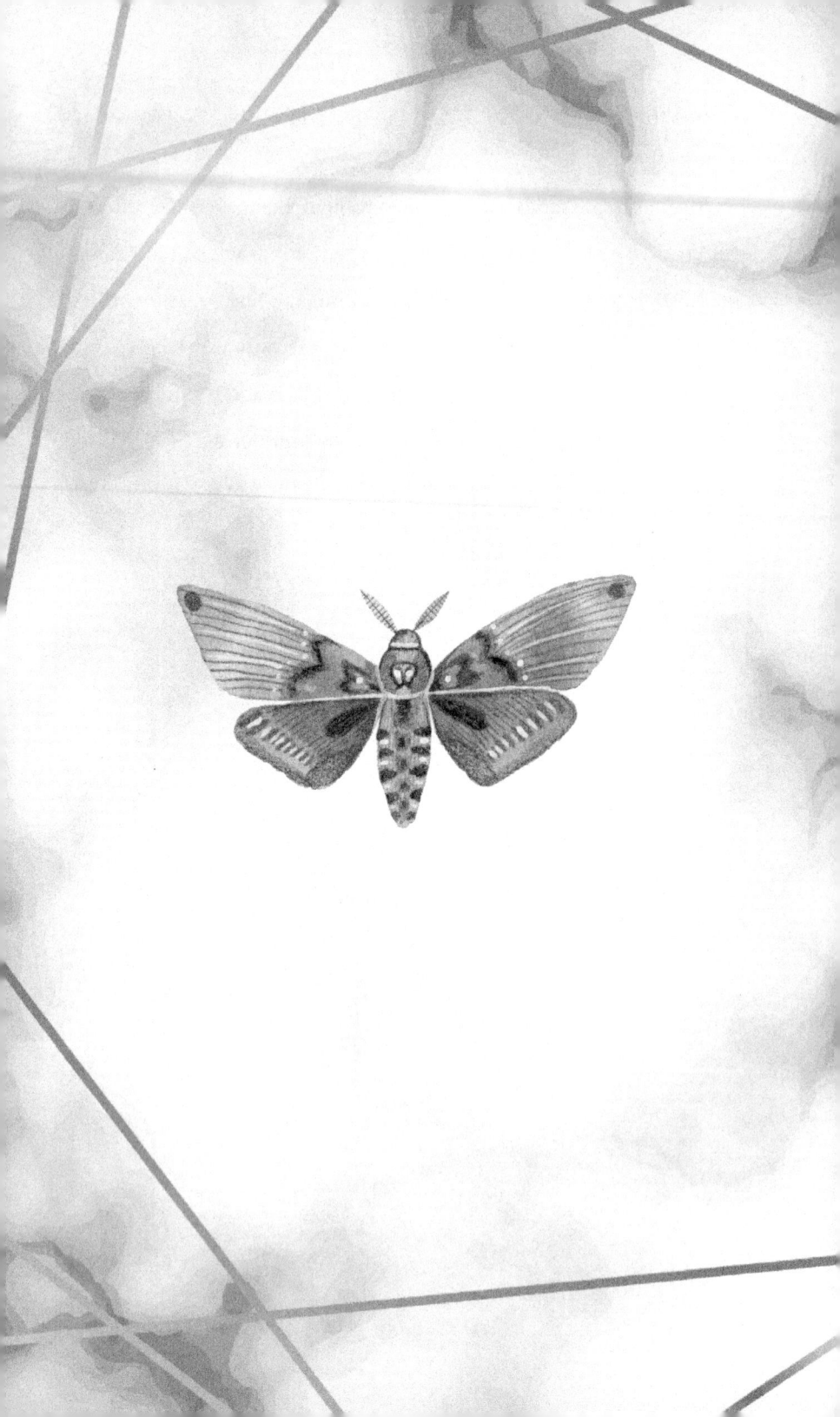

Fourteen

Wind whipped through my hair and gravel crunched beneath my feet as I jumped up to face the Dark fae. "So you *were* cast out for being a criminal!" I yelled. "I thought we could trust you!" I stomped in circles, fear and confusion swarming my head.

"Lily, please calm down." Gideon raised his hands but remained in place. "That's not what happened. I wasn't cast out... I was fleeing for my life."

"Yeah, because you stole their ancient book!"

"No. I mean yes... I *did* take the book... but only because I was trying to save someone else."

"What are you talking about?" Plumes of cold air flowed from my nose and mouth as I started to hyperventilate.

"Please calm down and let me explain," Gideon stated flatly.

Looking around, I realized there was no chance of a taxi happening by the garden center on its own. I snapped my head in Bennett's direction. "Get me out of here!"

Rushing to my side, Bennett reached for my hand, fumbling with his phone in the other.

Blue and purple lights exploded in the air, spinning around us as the wind whipped to a crescendo that lifted me off my feet. One minute we were standing in the vacant parking lot together, and the next, we were lying on the ground under a massive, leaf-less tree.

"Oh my God, what just happened?" Bennett sat up, but he didn't let go of my hand.

"I… I'm not sure, but I think you just transported us using your magic." I peeled my fingers from his and pushed to stand.

Rolling hills spread out in every direction, leaving us completely lost in a new and unknown place.

"No way." He shook his head. "There's no way my magic's that strong yet." Bennett stood up and waved his phone in the air. "I was just trying to call for another taxi," he looked at me with wide eyes, "… and help calm you down."

I paced around the large oak, teetering on the verge of panicking even more than I was before.

"Wait. My phone says we're still in Essex." Bennett showed me his screen with Google Maps displaying a red pin marking our current location.

"How far away is the garden center?" *And Gideon,* I thought.

"Um…" Using his fingers to expand and retract the map, Bennett searched for a few moments before admitting, "I don't see it anymore."

"What?" I leaned in, my shoulder pressing to his chest as I took a closer look.

"From what I remember, it should be right here—" He pointed to a spot somewhere between the town's center and the outlying place where were currently stood. "It should be there, but the location's completely gone from the map." His chest rose when he took a deep breath, lifting my shoulder from where our bodies still touched.

I took a step back. "Maybe your phone's just glitching. Try to restart it."

Staring out across the grass, I searched for any signs of life, imagining how green it would look if the sky wasn't gray. Thankfully, the rain had let up since the only shelter we had was comprised of the skeletal branches of this massive old tree. Lowering myself to the ground, I leaned back against the trunk, comforted by its sturdiness. Unfortunately, when I closed my eyes, all I could think of was the tree Mom used to take us to—the same one she used to summon Gideon.

King of Dark, King of Doom... I cut off the thought the moment it started. No way was I ready to face Gideon again, even if the full chant still deemed him as a friend.

Bennett's phone dinged back to life, pulling me from my thoughts. "Any luck?"

"No. The garden center is still missing from the map. But I think if we walk in that direction—" he pointed over the hill to our south, "we should reach the town in a few hours." He extended his hand to help me up, but I didn't take it.

Sucking in a deep breath, I closed my eyes again. My energy was drained from the stress of the situation and most likely a major case of jet lag, but for the first time since leaving home, I finally felt a moment's peace. "Can we just rest here for a bit first?"

Bennett slid down to the ground beside me, his fingers brushing against mine as he lowered himself onto the grass. "Sure. I'm in no rush."

I looked over and met his kind eyes, wondering how he could be taking all this in stride. If I just found out I was part fae and my magic had just activated for the first time in my life, I'd probably lose it. "How are you staying so calm about all this?" I asked. "I'm used to magic and I'm totally freaking out."

Bennett laughed under his breath. "If it makes you feel any better, I'm freaking out, too. But I didn't think it would help if both our emotions were running so high." He shrugged. "It's something I learned from playing sports. Sometimes, you have to let go of the fear to focus on what matters most in the moment."

Bennett's hand fully covered mine.

I opened my eyes to find him staring at me with a shy smile pulling at his lips. "Is this okay? It's something else I learned," he rushed on. "Physical touch has been proven to calm a stressed-out nervous system."

"Ah…" I wove my fingers through his. "That college education sure seems to be paying off."

Bennett smiled wide. "Why yes, I think it is."

Fifteen

"Psst... Lily." Bennett's low voice and a slight nudge pulled me awake. I had no idea how long we sat against the tree holding hands, but obviously it was long enough for me to relax and fall asleep since the sun was already making its descent. "I found a place where we can stay the night. It's just over that hill." His warm eyes swam into view as I blinked repeatedly, following his arm as he pointed to the west.

I scrambled up off the ground, pushing off the large trunk as my stomach protested at its lack of food. "Great. Lead the way." I wavered on my feet.

"Whoa, are you okay?" Bennett grabbed my arm.

I shook my head. "Just a little hungry and dizzy, I guess."

"Well, friends don't let friends hike dizzy. Here—hold my hand while we walk to the inn."

Friends, I thought. At this point, I guess it was true. The only friends I ever needed growing up were my sisters, which made this yet another new experience for me. "Did you say *inn*?"

Bennett shrugged. "Yeah. Once I realized you were asleep, I took off to explore a little to see if I could find someplace to stay since we wouldn't be able to make it back to Essex before nightfall." He paused. "And… I wanted to practice my magic." He slowed our pace but didn't release my hand. "I stayed close, but far enough away that I wouldn't hurt you in case I messed up."

His excitement to practice his magic was one I knew well. "How did it go?"

He shook his head. "Nothing happened. I couldn't get it to work at all."

I opened my mouth to ask another question but was hit in the forehead with a thick splatter of rain. Heavy drops fell sporadically, until they joined together to become a deluge.

Pulling me along, Bennett's fingers held tightly to mine. Running became arduous as the grass quickly turned to a muddy mess. Cresting the hill, I spotted a two-story inn in the meadow below, its old-world charm reminding me of every European pub I'd seen on TV. A large wooden sign hung over the door with a carving that looked exactly like the huge tree we just left behind. The words *Sessile Oak Inn* wrapped around the design in a circle, giving name to where we'd be spending the night. Other weathered wood buildings littered the outer edge of a small grove of trees with the quaint inn built squarely in the middle.

Shivering and wet, we eagerly made our way to the front door. "I already booked us a room, but figured you'd want to eat first."

Bennett smiled as we stomped the mud from our feet at the front step.

My stomach growled again, confirming his assumption was right. "That sounds great." Pushing through the thick door, I dropped Bennett's hand and meandered towards the first open table I saw.

Shuffling in our direction, an elderly man neared our table, a twisted cane aiding his every step. "What can I get ya?" His brusque tone immediately put me on edge.

"Hello. May I have a menu?" I asked politely.

He squinted suspiciously. "What for? Today's specials are either haggis or our famous bangers and mash."

"What makes them famous?" I asked, because there was no way I was eating sheep organs.

With a huff, he pointed to another carved tree that hung over the bar. "The Sessile oak. You must have seen it on your way here. Its timber is used for cask-making, and it gives our wine, spirits, and sauces a particular flavor the fairies seem to like."

Bennett and I both froze. "I'm sorry. Did you say fairies?" I looked back at the sturdy oak carving, its mangled branches captured perfectly in the wood. I shook my head, flabbergasted and imagining myself a modern-day Rip Van Winkle waking up beneath the real thing. "I'm sorry to pry, but you believe in fairies here?"

Our waiter—if you could call him that, cursed under his breath before dropping into the extra chair at our table. Rubbing his leg, he leaned forward conspiratorially, lowering his voice. "In this part of the world, you bet we do." His breath stunk of liquor, and I wondered if he was the owner of the establishment in which we currently found ourselves.

I should have held my tongue, but I pushed on. "If you don't mind, I'd love a plate of your famous bangers and mash, but I'd also love to learn more about your fairy beliefs." Bennett gawked at me with wide eyes, earning him an innocent shrug. "What?" I whispered.

Assuming Bennett would want the same thing, the old man yelled our orders across the room. Pots and pans clanged in the back as a cook we couldn't see grumbled his response from the kitchen. With his leg outstretched, our host proceeded to load a pipe he pulled from his shirt pocket. The scent of warm tobacco permeated the air, lulling me into a welcome state of calm.

"Fairy lore has always been a part of our lives here," he grumbled.

"Here, as in your inn specifically, or is this something that's openly discussed in this part of the world?" I pressed, hoping he'd humor me with a drunken conversation.

"Well, I'm not sure I can speak for the rest of the world, but around Essex, Cornwall, and Devon, we all learn to put out gifts and craft our protections from a very young age."

"Protections?" Bennett asked.

"Fairy wards." The old man coughed. "You won't find a house in these parts without some bells, rowen wood, iron, or freshly baked bread." He shifted in his seat, digging something out of his pants pocket. "As a boy, I wasn't even allowed out of the house unless I had a piece of dry bread with me. It's how we were taught." He tossed a crumbling sample onto the table between us as proof of his convictions.

"But why?" I laid a paper-thin napkin in my lap. "Offerings and protections make it seem like you're scared of the fairies."

A huff escaped the old man's lips. "With good reason! British fairies aren't your happy-go-lucky pixies with purple and blue wings, girl. No…" He shook his head. "They're devious and will happily trick you into a sexual frenzy while they steal away your kids."

"What?" I exclaimed, earning us a few frowns from the hardened faces occupying the pub.

A middle-aged woman with scraggly hair—the only other female I saw in the room—set two large cups of ale down on our table, then slid up a chair to join us. "Oh, yes… fairy changelings are a well-known part of European lore," she took over the story. "That is to say, abducted human children who are exchanged for fairies. Everyone here knows about it and protects against it. And did you know English fairies are either Light or Dark, not Seelie or Unseelie?" She nodded proudly. "That's Scottish, in case you're wondering, but all are dangerous given the right circumstance."

I swallowed hard. "No, I guess I didn't know that, either." *Damn.* Apparently, there was a lot I didn't know. Growing up protecting the portal was one thing, but living in actual fear of having your children stolen on any given day wasn't how me or my sisters were raised… thank the Goddess.

I looked at Bennett, wondering what his take on all this was and frowned when I saw his face. He'd sunken back against the hard wood chair and crossed his arms. "What's the matter?" I asked.

He shook his head and whispered, "Tell you later."

The woman continued her story with no further prompting from me. "The oldest fairies on record in England were first described in the thirteenth century. And I'm sure you've heard of Morgan le Fay." Without waiting for confirmation, she continued. "It's said that European fairies haunt specific locations and are known to lead travelers astray using will-o'-the-wisps. That's why this inn's built in a grove made up of the Fairy Triad."

I shook my head, confused. "I'm sorry. You've lost me again. The Fairy Triad?"

"The Fairy Triad is made up of the three types of trees that offer the most protection against the fae. Oak, ash, and hawthorn." The old woman wagged her finger and me and Bennett. "But be careful around the ash trees. While they offer protection, they can also be a gateway between the worlds."

A large, hulking brute entered the room, placing our plates on the table and saving me from forming a response. It was a good thing, too, because I didn't have one. Changelings, gateways between our worlds... It almost seemed as if these locals knew more about my familial duty than me, and that left me speechless.

"Come now, you two, don't scare our guests with your wild tales." The beast of a cook nodded at the man and woman, effectively chasing them off.

Releasing a puff of smoke, the old man caught my eye as he stood. "They may be wild, but that doesn't mean they're not true."

I took a large gulp of ale from the cup, swallowing hard. "Yes, well, thank you for the conversation. I'm sure I'll feel better after this nice meal and a good night's sleep."

Bennett leaned in close as the others retreated into the small crowd. "Before we go up, I need to tell you something."

"What's that?"

"The last room they had available only has one bed."

My eyes snapped to his. "Excuse me. Did you say *one bed?*"

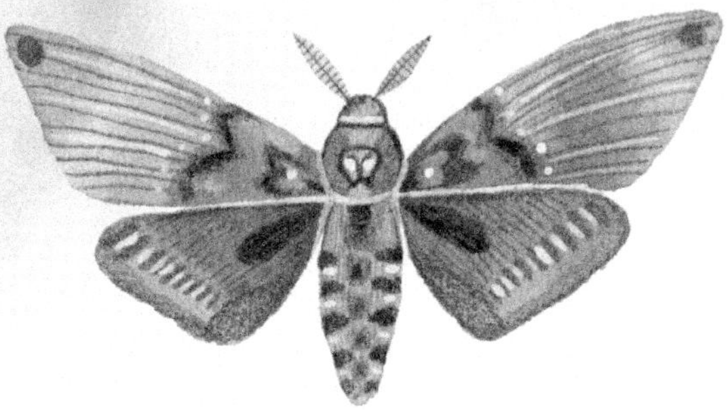

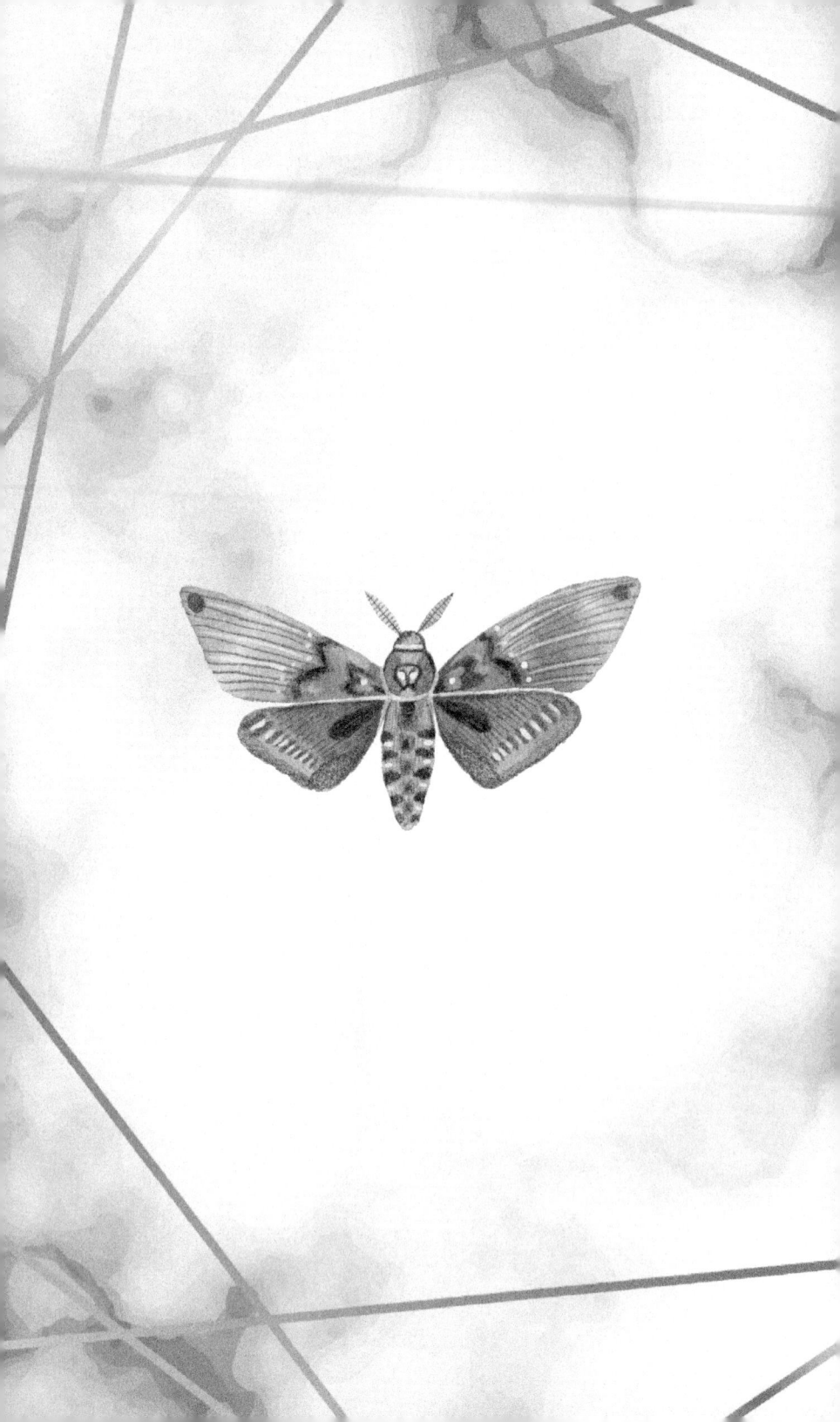

Sixteen

After a delicious meal of sausage, vegetables, fresh bread, and apple crumble for dessert, Bennett and I retired to our room. *"The last room they had available only has one bed."* Bennett's words lingered at the forefront of my mind as we climbed the stairs.

"So, um… which side do you prefer?" Bennett stood in the corner of the tiny room, shifting uncomfortably on his feet with his arms crossed over his chest.

I glanced at the narrow bed pushed against one wall. "The inside, I guess." I crawled across the squeaky bed and dove beneath the covers, fully clothed. Easing down, Bennett pulled back the patchwork quilt and climbed in beside me. Rolling to face him, I propped my head in my hand. "So, are you going to tell me what was wrong downstairs?"

Bennett turned onto his side to face me. "I don't know. When that woman mentioned changelings being a thing around here, it made me think."

"Think of what?"

He hesitated. "That I might be one… a changeling." His gaze fell to the bed and a heaviness settled between us.

I'd never heard of a changeling before tonight and had no idea if there was a way to find something like that out. "Maybe we could ask around more about it in the morning," I offered.

Bennett rolled onto his back, raising his arms to rest them behind his head. "I don't know. Honestly, I'm not sure if I even want the truth. I grew up happy. I love my mom and dad. But I don't know... all this fairy stuff is starting to make me think."

I couldn't blame him. Things had been pretty overwhelming since the garden center. "Well, if there's anything I can do—" I refused to think about Gideon and the answers he probably held.

"Thanks. Maybe one of your revelation spells could show me something when I'm ready."

"Sure. I'd be happy to try and help."

Bennett closed his eyes, and silence filled the room despite the storm still roaring outside. The slap of rain and the creak of branches became the soundtrack of our night. Speckled moonlight broke through the clouds, spilling into our room through one tiny window in random waves. My eyes roamed over Bennett's form. I was terrified to move—worried I'd rouse him and bring the fact that we were lying in bed together into stark relief. Me and Bennett was something that couldn't happen.

I jumped, shifting the bed when a loud crash sounded in the distance, followed by something heavy falling outside.

"Are you okay?" Bennett asked.

I nodded, even though he couldn't see me in the dark.

"Lily?"

"I'm okay." I tried to keep my voice even. Something about being this close to him made it impossible to ignore how much my life was changing—how much both our lives were changing. All because of the fae.

I rolled onto my other side, away from Bennett and facing the wall. There were only inches between us, but it felt like so much more. A crevasse of fear and uncertainty, of past experiences neither of us knew anything about.

"Good night, Lily," Bennett whispered into the dark.

"Good night, Bennett." I closed my eyes, wondering what he was thinking and if any of it had to do with me.

He shifted slightly, bringing our bodies closer together. I smiled, convincing myself that it did.

Soft sunlight filtered through the small window across the room, pulling me awake. The rain had stopped, but the wind still whipped outside, shaking the trees in a rhythm that made me want to fall back asleep. Gentle breathing sounded beside me and I suddenly remembered I was lying in bed next to Bennett.

I slowly turned my head to look at him. He was still lying on his back with one arm propped behind his head, but his other hand was stretched out toward me. Mere centimeters separated his fingers from my waist. The image of it did something weird to my insides. This was the closest I'd ever been to a boy, and with his eyes closed and his chest rising with every breath, he looked like a vulnerable kid. My heart began to ache.

My fingers crept toward his of their own volition. His skin was tan and warm. The bed stirred, and I looked up to find his eyes on me.

"Morning." He smiled.

I yanked my hand away, shifting further until my back hit the cold plaster wall. "Morning."

Stretching like a cat in the sun, Bennett ran a hand through his sleep-tousled hair, smoothing it immediately back into place. *Oh, Goddess... my hair.* Covering both sides of my head with my hands, I worked my fingers through my wild red tresses, praying they would follow suit.

"Did you get any sleep?" Bennett asked.

"I think so." His words from last night reentered my mind. *"Maybe one of your revelation spells could show me something when I'm ready."*

"So, do you want to talk to the locals about the changeling stuff again before we leave? Or do you want me to try a spell back under the fairy tree?" I didn't know why I thought bringing it up again first thing in the morning was a good idea, but when Bennett stood up from the bed and looked back down at me, there wasn't an ounce of vulnerability left.

"No thanks. I'm good." His eyes were cold, and the timbre of his voice hit a nerve inside me I didn't fully understand.

"Bennett, I'm sorry. I didn't mean to upset you. Are you okay?"

He shook his head and pulled on his shoes. "I'm fine. Let's just get going. It's gonna take all day to walk into town."

I rolled out of bed and awkwardly prepared myself for the day, yanking my shoes on and smoothing my sleep-wrinkled clothes the best I could. Following Bennett down the stairs, we were greeted with the aroma of freshly brewed coffee. I couldn't have been more grateful.

"This smells delicious." I thanked the same woman from last night and lifted the cup to my lips and took a sip. The smooth liquid slid down my throat, warming me from the inside out. I looked over at Bennett and offered a small smile, hoping our issue from before could be chased away with a couple cups of coffee.

"You're welcome. How did you sleep?" the gruff waitress asked.

An image of Bennett's hand reaching for me popped into my head, stilling my response. Luckily Bennett answered for us both. "We slept fine. Thank you." He lifted his cup in the air. "And thank you for the coffee as well. We'll be on our way shortly."

"No time for breakfast, then?" She turned back toward the bar and kitchen located somewhere behind it. "Fergus is preparing a fry-up with some beans on toast."

Bennett looked at me, but all I could do was shrug. Of course I wanted to eat, but after upsetting him once today already, I wanted to leave the decision up to him.

"Thank you. Yes, there's always time for breakfast." Offering our host a charming smile, Bennett took a seat at a table near the window and proceeded to ignore me as he stared outside.

I joined him, scooting my chair up to the table precariously as I continued to drink my coffee in silence. Movement caught my eye and I looked out the window to find a shepherd herding his sheep past the pub. "I can't believe we're really here." I took another sip of coffee and looked up to find Bennett's eyes once again plastered on me.

Seventeen

Breakfast was delicious, but the underlying tension between us wasn't something I enjoyed. Bennett stared at me sporadically throughout the meal while I attempted to make small talk with the waitress whenever she drifted by. By the end of it, we'd only shared a few words, and before I was finished eating, Bennett stood and waited impatiently by the door.

I nodded at the waitress. "Thank you again for your hospitality. We truly do appreciate it." I waved goodbye and headed out into the frigid morning air.

"What's your problem?" I demanded the second we were out of earshot.

Bennett didn't stop walking or bother to answer me as we pounded our way back up the hill. Cresting the top, I noticed the fairy tree in the distance.

"This way." Bennett turned south and started walking again.

"No." I crossed my arms over my chest. "I'm not taking another step until you tell me what's wrong. Did I really make you that mad? I was only offering to help!" I rambled.

Bennett finally stopped but didn't turn around. "I'm not mad at you, Lily. I'm just confused."

"Confused about what?"

"Everything." He kicked what was probably an imaginary rock, as there was nothing lying in the grass surrounding us. "I know this is your first time away from home, but at least you know who you are and what your life's purpose is supposed to be. Now, after learning about all this... I have no idea about any of that!"

I eased up beside him. "Bennett, I'm sorry. I know the shock of all this must be rough, but that's why I was trying to help. Whether we talked to the locals more or tried a spell... I only wanted to bring you some answers. That's all!"

Bennett looked down at me with tears in his eyes. "That's the thing, Lil... I'm not sure if I even *want* the answers."

The sad lilt to his voice and the sound of my shortened name coming off his lips almost shattered me. "I don't understand," I whispered.

"Like I said last night... I've lived a happy life. Have great parents. Love playing ball and going to school. And just because I'm here and there's some ancient magic awakening inside me, it doesn't mean I want any of those things to change."

That, I understood.

"I'm scared too, Bennett. I have no idea what we'll be facing through all this, but at the same time, I'm happy to be going through it with you." A shy smile pulled at my lips. "Let's just focus on finding this stupid book, and then we can *both* go home."

Bennett nodded and wiped his eyes, and together we started forward again.

Walking through the wet grass, we slipped and slid our way over the hilly terrain. Bennett checked his phone again, and while the garden center was still missing from the map, we were on track and headed toward the main town of Essex as planned.

"Hey, do you mind if I ask what happened when you went off to practice your magic before? I mean, if you don't want to talk about it, I totally understand." After our earlier exchange, I wasn't one-hundred percent sure where he stood on the magic part of things.

He shrugged off my concern. "It's fine. At the time, I figured I should practice and figure out how in the world I even transported us like that, but when I tried it again, nothing happened."

"Really? Nothing at all?"

"I mean, I could feel the magic within me starting to stir, but I couldn't duplicate the way we jumped no matter how hard I tried."

I looked at the ground. "Well, the last time it happened, we were holding hands. Do you think that would make a difference?"

Bennett didn't reply, but after a moment's pause, he reached down and wound his fingers through mine. Soft energy blossomed in my chest, rising to meet his as we walked on hand-in-hand.

"I think it's worth exploring."

When Bennett squeezed my hand, I couldn't hold back the smile that burst onto my face. "Okay, cool. Let's stop and try it here."

Turning to face each other, I took Bennett's other hand and asked, "Do you remember what you did, or what you were thinking when it happened?"

"I really don't. All I was thinking about was getting you away from Gideon like you asked, and then, boom! We ended up in a completely different place."

"Okay, this time, why don't you focus on getting us over there?" I pointed further up the trail we were cutting through the hills, thinking if he could see the destination this time, it might make a difference.

"Okay." He squeezed my hands. "Should we close our eyes?"

"Um… sure, if you think it'll help you concentrate."

"Yeah. Okay." Bennett closed his eyes, and I followed suit.

His hands were soft for a baseball playing botanist, but I could feel his nervous energy through the small twitches his body made. "Calm down. Just breathe," I offered.

After a few deep breaths, his nerves receded and our magics rose to the surface again. Gentle waves of his energy mingled with mine, creating a fae-witch connection that seemed to make us both stronger. Another moment passed, then I felt a shift in the air.

I opened my eyes and laughed. "You did it!" We were standing in the exact spot I'd pointed out to him.

His eyes were wide with amazement. "Wow. I guess I did! But I still have no idea *how* I did it."

"You can't pinpoint anything at all? Like a thought, or a wish even, that you simply wanted it to work?"

He shook his head slowly. "Not really. I just did what you suggested and took a few deep breaths to calm myself. That was it."

I looked down at our still-joined hands. "Maybe it really does only work when we're touching each other." A flush ran through me, reddening my cheeks.

Bennett's breath hitched as we locked eyes. "I guess that's something we'll have to keep researching."

I held his gaze and grinned. "I guess it is."

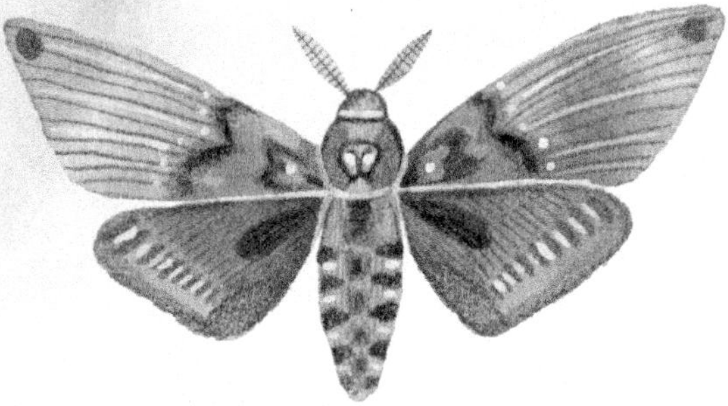

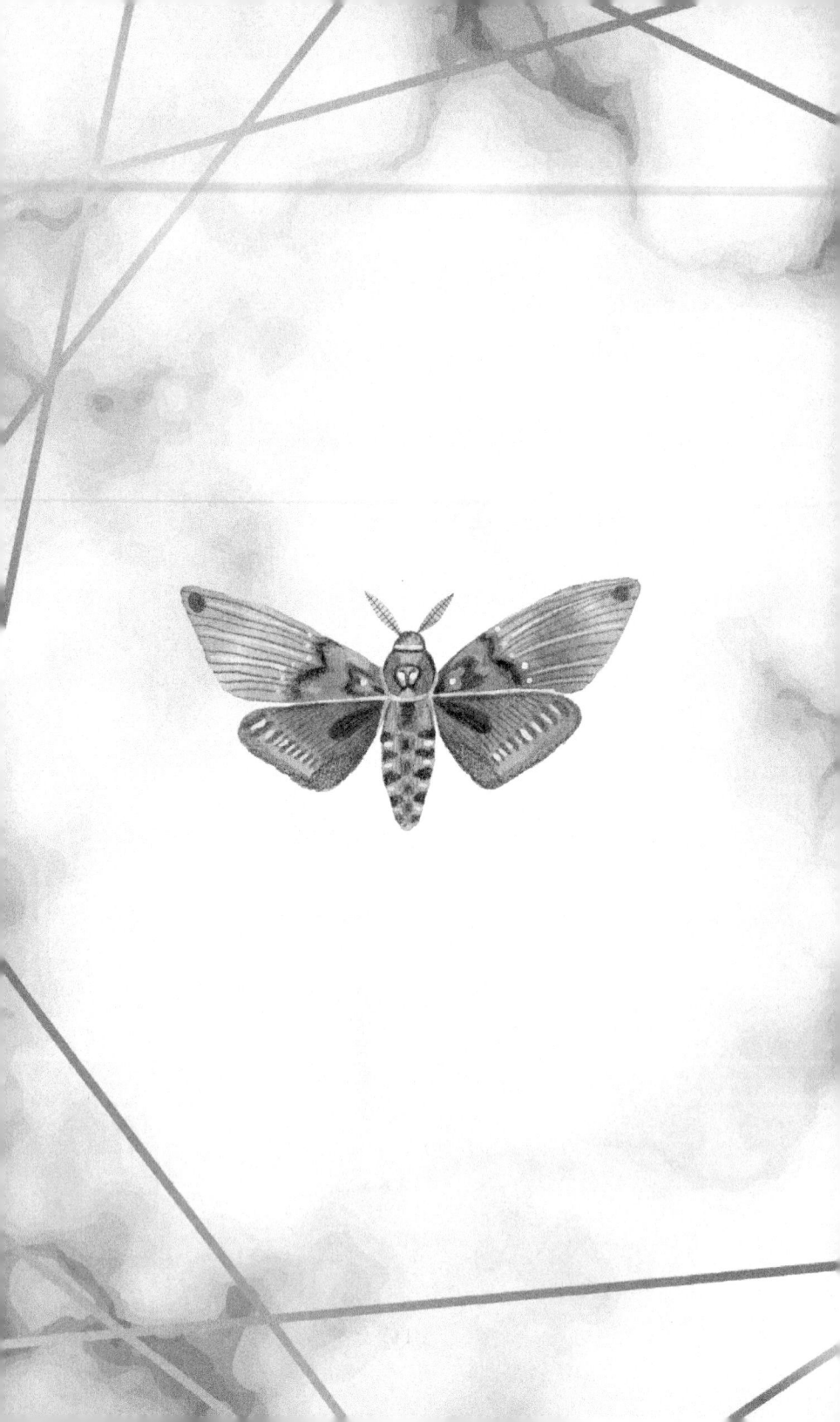

Eighteen

We made it half-way to town by testing our combined magics over and over. But as with anything else, spending too much energy took its toll.

"We can rest here." Bennett led me to a stone wall that ran along the edge of the field we were currently traversing.

Sinking down to the ground gratefully, I let the cool stone catch my weight as I leaned my head back and closed my eyes. "I didn't realize how drained I was until right this moment."

"Yeah, me too." Bennett sank down beside me. "Here. Have a drink." Bennett passed me a water bottle he pulled from his pack, and I gladly took a sip.

"Thank you," I said, passing it back.

"Hey, can I ask you something… about Gideon?" Bennett's voice was soft and tentative.

"Sure, I guess."

"What makes you think he was lying?"

I thought back to the first time I'd seen Gideon, walking into our living room behind my mom. "After you showed up at our house, my mother cast a spell to see if we could gain insight into who was involved with all this. The result was a vision of Gideon, even though my sisters and I didn't know it at the time."

"Are you serious?"

"Yes. But it's still confusing, because my mother is the one who brought him in to help. She said we could trust him." I hung my head.

"But you don't believe her?"

I shrugged. "I did at first. But originally, he told us he was *cast out* of the fairy realm, so when he admitted that he'd fled and he was the one who took the book… I don't know. I guess I panicked because of my initial reservations."

Bennett handed me his water bottle again. "Makes sense. But if your mom agreed to let you go with him, it's hard to imagine he'd be the one behind it all."

"Like I said… confusing." I took another sip and returned the bottle.

Bennett lifted it to his lips, draining the last of the water, then stowed the empty container in his pack. "I know we're headed to town, but don't you think we should keep looking for the book out here first? I mean, Gideon said it himself—we can use my magic to track the book's signature, and your magic to break the spell."

I looked across the landscape, enjoying the peacefulness of the area. Something about the rolling hills felt like a green wave, cresting and carrying me toward my destiny.

"Sure. I guess we can try."

Bennett shifted on the ground, turning to face me as he crisscrossed his legs. "Okay. So, what do I do? How do I track the book?"

Eyes wide, I pulled back. "I don't know."

"Well, you're the witch. I figured you could give me some pointers." He grinned playfully.

I wasn't sure how to track the book, and only knew one way my magic worked. "I'm not sure if it will work the same for you, but I basically close my eyes until I feel my magic waking up inside me. Then, I just ask it to find what I'm looking for and the magic does the rest."

"Sounds easy enough." Bennett closed his eyes, which I took as my cue to be quiet.

Sitting silently, I watched him concentrate, taking in every nuance of his face. My eyes roamed from his disheveled brown bangs to his angled features, concentrating lastly on his perfectly shaped lips. An image of us lying in that room at the inn together flashed across my mind, making my fingers ache to touch him again. I knew he felt when I reached out for his hand back in that bed, but he never said a word.

I wondered if he would now.

Reaching out, my fingers grazed his upper arm, sliding down his muscles until my hand covered his. He didn't open his eyes, but heat bloomed in my chest when a quirky smile pulled at his lips.

I smiled back, even though he couldn't see it, and let my magic blend with his. Focusing on the idea of the book, a grainy image formed in my head. An old tattered tome with two metal clasps took shape in my mind's eye.

"Do you see that?" Bennett said aloud.

"I do."

Bennett shifted again and reached for my other hand.

Fully focused on the image, I asked my magic to reveal where it was.

Blue and purple energy swirled around the vision, and in the next moment a picture of Gideon fighting a witch came into perfect view.

"Oh, no!" I pulled back as we both opened our eyes. "We left him to fight the witch alone."

"Shit." Bennett scrambled up off the ground and pulled his phone out of his jeans pocket. "Dammit. The garden center still isn't showing up on the map, but we have to get back there."

"Do you think we should try jumping again?" Placing a hand on the cold stone wall, I pushed to stand, not sure I wanted to follow through with this idea or not.

"Yeah, I think so. But it only seems to work when we're holding hands." Bennett shrugged.

"I've noticed," I said, smiling back.

Taking my hands again, Bennett closed his eyes and prepared to jump us back to Gideon as I simply held on and hoped we didn't die.

The same lights surrounded us again, spinning in a vortex that lifted us off our feet. In the next moment, we were standing at the edge of a gnarly forest made up of fallen trees and twisted branches.

"Where are we?" I whispered.

Bennett looked just as uneasy as I felt. "Not sure. I just cast my intention to take us to Gideon."

A loud crack sounded from the forest at the same instant a white light exploded from somewhere deep within.

"That way." Bennett took off without an ounce of hesitation.

"Wait!" I yelled, not ready to stumble into the middle of a supernatural fight. "What if we distract him? Maybe we should wait here to see if he's found the book."

Bennett shook his head. "What if he needs our help? I don't want to give the witch the chance to escape with the book again."

Damn. He had a point. "Fine, but let's go slow and be quiet. I want to see what's *really* happening in there before we put ourselves in harm's way."

Bennett nodded, reached for my hand, and led me directly into the heart of the witch's forest.

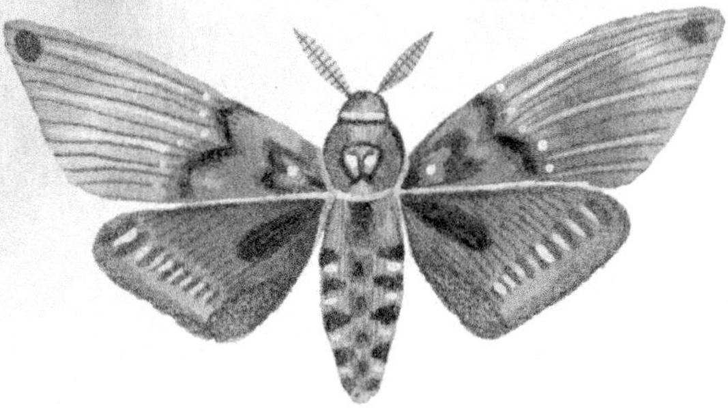

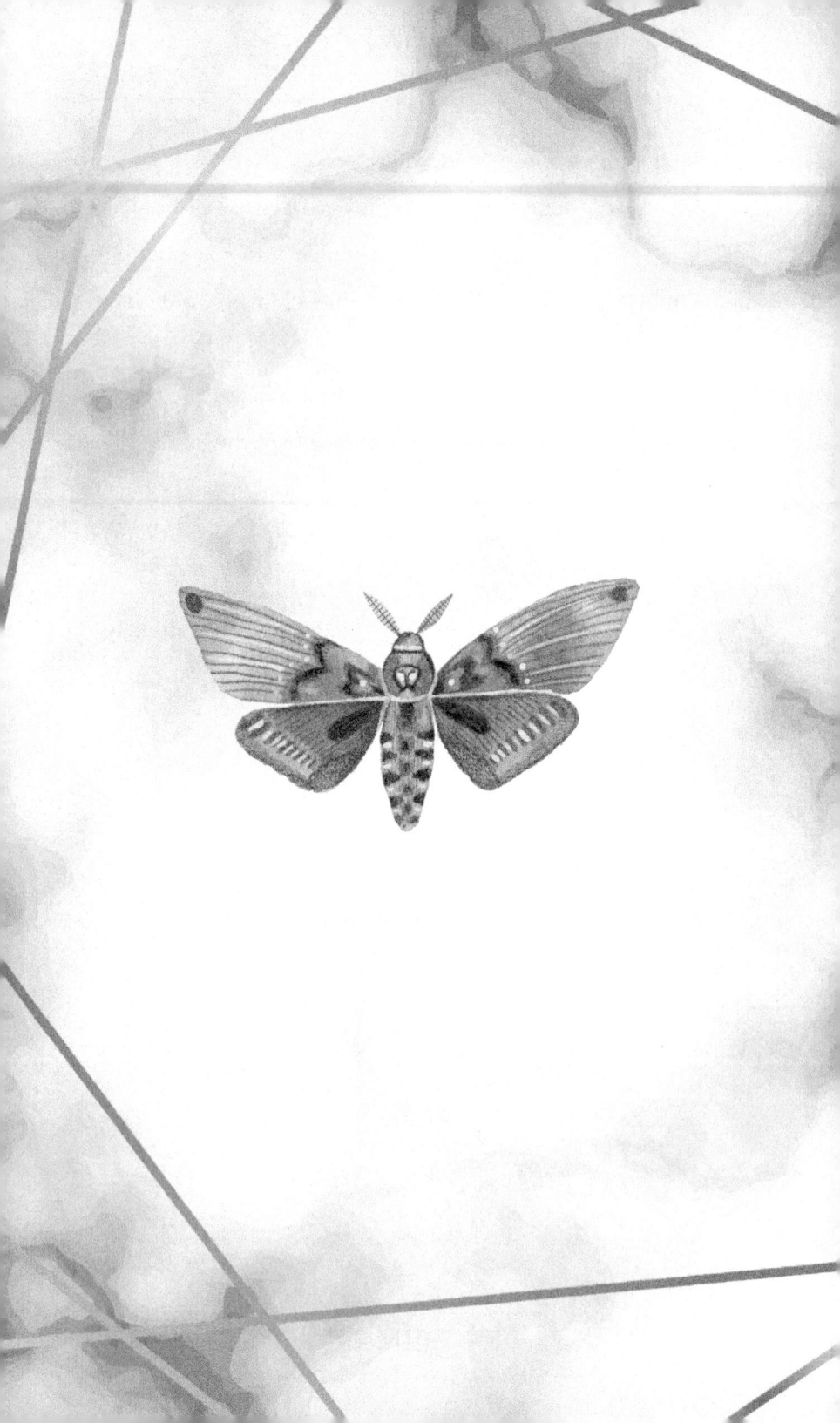

Nineteen

Branches snapped beneath our feet as we worked our way to the center of the forest. The sun had begun its descent, the air already starting to cool. Dusk settled around the trees in a tinge of pinks, purples, and blues, making the tall trunks look like paintbrushes ready to decorate the sky in cotton-candy plumes.

"Here. Put this on." Bennett pulled a sweatshirt out of his bag and handed it to me. "The sound of your teeth chattering is going to give us away," he teased.

I rolled my eyes. "Geez. Sorry I wasn't prepared to traipse through a haunted forest in the freezing cold."

"It's okay. I forgive you." A playful smile lit up his face, and I suddenly wasn't cold anymore.

"What do you think you'll do after all this?" I asked randomly.

"What do you mean?" Bennett pushed forward, leading the way and snapping off the protruding limbs and thorny vines that continued to hinder our path.

"I mean, will you just go back to Yale like nothing's happened, or has learning all this changed things for you?"

An eerie silence settled over the forest, and I knew I'd said something wrong.

"I'm sorry. You don't have to answer," I whispered.

Bennett turned to face me with a finger pressed to his lips. "Something's wrong."

In the distance, a bright light seeped from beneath the trees' gnarled branches. Crouching down in a thicket of mangled brush, we listened like our lives depended on it… because they probably did.

Not a single sound penetrated our hiding place—no leaves rustled in the wind, no animals scurried away into the night. Absolutely nothing made a sound, except for me.

I slammed a hand over my mouth, trying to hold in my panicked breath when the white light flared again, closer this time and directly ahead of us.

"Come on." Bennett grabbed my hand and we inched forward together, carefully minding our steps.

A wider path emerged and we slowly crept toward the unknown.

"It's about time you two showed up." Gideon stepped onto the path in front of us, his voice holding an air of playfulness.

Standing upright, I glanced past the Dark fae and saw an entire coven of witches gathered around a fire. Dressed in all white, the witches held hands, creating a semi-circle around their communal blaze. This was the light we saw from afar. Not a fight, but a ritual.

"Yes, well, it's not like we had any idea where to go," I snapped. Gideon's answering smile was full of pity, which pissed me off even more. "What's happening here? Who are all these witches?" I wasn't about to discuss why I ran away, or whether I felt like I could trust him now or not. No, this was about getting on with our task so we could go the hell home.

"Lily, Bennett... meet the Acrucian Coven." He stepped aside and all thirteen witches bowed their heads.

"They, like your family, guard the main portal here in Essex. After you left, I sought them out to see if anything had been amiss." Gideon held out his arm, gesturing for us to join him in a large tent set off to the side.

I followed him away from the circle but kept sneaking looks behind me, studying the awe-inspiring gathering of witches. "Why are they chanting?" I asked as soon as we were inside the large canvas structure.

"Because something *is* amiss." He pulled out two cushions for us to sit on while claiming the only wooden chair in the space. "I found them like that when I arrived. They said they've been chanting to maintain the portal's locks for weeks—alternating in groups of six two times a day with the high priestess never leaving."

"What? How is that possible?" I asked.

"Apparently, they're more powerful when they're all together. They let her siphon off some of their energy so she can continually maintain the wards. They started having problems with breakthroughs about a week ago."

Bennett looked at me with raised brows. "Breakthroughs?"

"Don't worry. There are no Morphineas here, but other fae creatures have slipped through. More importantly, Sybil, their high priestess, says there's a dark energy seeping out that she simply can't contain."

"The crone," I surmised.

"Yes, we think so. After you left, I searched the garden center again, but there was no sign of a human witch. And after speaking with Sybil, I have no doubt the crone's energy has been causing these issues all along."

I looked around the yurt-like tent, taking in shelves of ingredients and foreign herbs hanging from the bowed rafters. "Did you ask them about the book?"

Gideon dropped his head. "Not yet. With Sybil constantly needed at the portal, I haven't been able to speak to her alone."

I looked back toward the witches in confusion. "What do you mean, *needed at the portal?* Where is it, exactly?"

In that moment, the fire flared, shooting more white-hot light into the sky.

"It's there. On the ground... under their sacred fire."

Holy shit. The fire was like our metal gate, protecting the portal beneath it.

"I've never seen anything like that," I marveled. Though, to be fair, I hadn't seen much of anything beyond our shop and town.

Suddenly, all I could think of was my sisters and my mom. I wondered if they'd ever gathered in the basement, holding hands, and used their magic to secure the portal like this. It was something I hadn't personally witnessed, but that didn't mean it couldn't have happened before I was born. I imagined Fern and Iris's long black hair swaying softly in time with their chant. Aster without her glasses with her head tipped back, soaking in all the energy. Daisy's witch hat would have remained in place as she anchored them all with her grounding force. And Mom—our high priestess—singing the loudest as she secured our ancient duty for another hundred years...

Whoa! Where did all that come from?

"Yes. Witches have been secluded here for centuries, protecting the passage between your world and mine." Gideon's words pulled me from my thoughts.

"And yet they can't find a missing book or stop the fae crone?" My shitty response was aimed more at Gideon than the Acrucian witches, but still, I felt bad the moment the words left my lips. "I'm sorry," I said loud enough for the witches to hear.

Gideon's eyes held a hint of sadness, and I knew he could see right through me.

I was tired of running around, feeling completely useless. We still had no clue about the book and couldn't figure out exactly how Bennett's magic was working either. Honestly, I didn't know why I was here.

"Lily?" a soft voice sounded behind me. I turned and came face to face with the most beautiful person I'd ever seen. She reminded me of my mother, but with soft red waves similar in tone to mine, falling past her shoulders like a gentle lava river flowing against her white dress. Her lavender eyes sparkled when she smiled. "My name is Sybil, and we're glad you're here. Join us, and perhaps we can help answer some of your questions."

With a nod from Gideon, Sybil took my hand and led me into her coven's circle.

White-hot fire grazed my legs as I took my place. Sybil stood beside me, holding my hand, her skin as cool as stone. I listened for a while, learning their chant, but when I was about to join in, Sybil broke their rhythm. "We welcome Lily from the land apart, and honor her with our magic."

My head flew back as a burst of lightning surged through my body. I stared into the ethos through blind eyes, witnessing a vision as if I were really there—

Gideon stood in a throne room made of white marble. In the corner, the crone writhed deep within the shadows, hiding away with her book. A blade, a cry, and a rush of activity filled the scene as Gideon bolted for a portal, desperate to save a baby's life.

Shocked back to the present, my eyes cleared, and with them, any doubt of Gideon I still harbored faded away.

He was telling the truth.

Twenty

With the vision gone, I could finally see clearly. Gideon truly was a friend, and I owed him an apology.

Returning to the tent, I lifted my chin, hoping he could read the sincerity in my eyes. "I'm sorry I doubted you."

His features softened. "You have nothing to apologize for. I understand this is a lot… leaving your home, finding out about me. But you can trust me, Lily." He laid a hand on my shoulder. "I would never let anything happen to you."

I smiled up at him. "I know that now."

"So…" Bennett extended his arms, bringing his hands together in an awkward clap. "How are we going to ask Sybil about the book if she can't leave the circle for more than a few seconds?"

"Right," I said, happy to get back on track. "What if I take her place while she comes and talks to you?" I shrugged. "Not that I feel worthy, but if my magic is strong enough to reveal the book, I think I could be her stand-in for a minute or two."

Gideon's brow creased as he thought for a moment. "Let me go ask her."

I nervously shifted on my feet. *What have I done?* I had no idea what level of power Sybil had, and yet, I tossed myself into the fire... literally. I watched as the Dark fae whispered to the light witch. Their contrast made an odd giggle burst from my lips.

"What's so funny?" Bennett asked.

"I don't know." And I didn't—at this point things were so wildly off-kilter, I think my mind was just trying to protect me. As such, the only thing I could muster was a laugh.

Gideon returned to the tent with a sour look on his face. "She doesn't think it's a good idea." When I snapped my head in the witch's direction, he continued quickly. "Not because she doesn't think you can do it, but because she's not sure how your magic will react with theirs."

"What do you mean? They just welcomed me with a shot of their magic straight into my veins!"

"Yes, but that was *them* giving *you* their blessing. Not you using *your* magic to interact with *theirs*."

I saw his point, but still, it stung a little. "I understand. What do you propose instead?"

"Sybil has noticed an ebb and flow to the crone's energy. It spikes and wanes. The next time it lessens, she'll come talk to us then."

"Sounds reasonable," Bennett offered.

"Sure. That'll work, I guess." I shrugged, unsure if removing the high priestess was a good idea or not.

"What do we do until then?" Bennett asked.

Gideon pointed to some bed rolls stacked up in the corner. "Get some rest. She said she wouldn't be able to join us until morning."

I eyed the sleeping material, remembering Bennett's warm body as we laid next to each other in the single bed at the inn.

"Um, yeah… okay." I awkwardly yanked the top roll from the pile and hastily shook it out. Climbing in as fast as I could, I pulled the top blanket up to my chin and shivered in the cold bedding.

Bennett tried to hide his grin, but I noticed it as he spread his blankets out right next to mine. "Figured the proximity could help keep us warm."

"Thanks." I couldn't contain my answering smile.

Gideon settled on the other side of the tent, taking two whole rolls with him to complete his pallet on the floor.

The night air made for good sleeping, and with the witches' melodic chant wafting in on the chilled breeze, I was lulled to sleep in a matter of minutes.

Wisps of shadows, cackles in the dark, skittering creatures across the floor—anything terrifying my brain could conjure woke me from a dead sleep with a strangled cry.

"Jesus!" Bennett cussed, reaching out for my arm. "Are you alright?"

The feel of his hand on my skin grounded me quicker than any meditation could. "Yes. Thank you. I just had a bad dream." He pulled his hand away and I flinched. "Do you mind holding onto me?" The question felt like it came out of someone else's mouth, even as the words still lingered on my lips.

"Of course not."

I started to balk, then realized he was answering my question of whether he minded or not. "Thank you. It helps to ground me."

"What does that mean? To *ground* you? I've heard people say it before, but I'm not sure what it is," he whispered.

I squinted into the darkness, trying to meet his eyes. I kept forgetting how innocent he was in the world of magic and lore. Before stumbling into our shop, he had no idea about witches, fairies, or the magic contained within him.

"It's a way for us to keep our energy balanced. Like the phrase, *Keep your feet on the ground and your head out of the clouds*, but more literal. Our magic stems from the earth, so if you can find an anchor of some sort, it'll help keep you… well, *grounded*." I couldn't think of a better explanation in the moment as his thumb absently rubbed tiny circles on the inside of my wrist.

"I think I get it. Sometimes before a game, our coach would have us do some breathing exercises to release our nerves."

"Yes. It's basically like that… but can be more effective if touch or a physical object is involved," I added in a rush to justify my needy request.

He gave my arm a light squeeze. "I can understand that."

Smiling like an idiot, I closed my eyes when his thumb started to move again.

"Lily," Bennett whispered next to my ear.

Jolting upright, it took me a moment to remember where I was. Sunlight beamed down on the white tent, warming it enough to chase away the chill of the morning air.

"It's almost time." Gideon nodded toward the entrance of our temporary shelter and I watched as Sybil broke from her ranks.

Scurrying inside, she grabbed a blanket from the pile and tossed it around her shoulders. "I forget what a toll this takes until someone leaves the circle." Shivering, the borrowed energy that had been keeping her warm drained from her frail frame. "What did you need to ask me that you can't share in front of my coven?" Her eyes roamed the three of us suspiciously.

Bennett and I remained seated on the ground, letting Gideon take the lead.

"We're looking for a book that was lost a long time ago." He took a step toward her, lowering his voice. "A book from the fairy realm."

Creases formed at the corner of Sybil's eyes as she squinted. She began to pace the tent, muttering to herself, too low for any of us to make out her words. Suddenly, she stopped. "Yes. I believe we did have possession of it once."

I jumped up from my makeshift bed. "What? When? Where did it go?"

Gideon shook his head, probably embarrassed by my outburst and my "three W's" line of questioning. Thankfully, Sybil acknowledged my urgency and answered anyway.

"It was a very long time ago. So long, that I don't fully recall it. But there is a nagging memory of a book that's pulling at my core. As for where it went… I have no idea. That was long before my time as high priestess here."

Shit, I cursed internally. What the hell were we supposed to do now?

Twenty-One

As the leader of one of the most important covens on the planet, I expected more from Sybil. I felt bad thinking it, but after witnessing how my mom and sisters worked together in such a cohesive and peaceful way to craft their spells, Sybil's flippant attitude was quickly becoming an irritation.

"There has to be something we can do to try to help you remember," I pressed.

She lifted her cool lavender eyes from the bowl of soup she'd fixed for herself and stared at me blankly as she took another bite.

I threw my hands in the air. "I need to take a walk."

Gideon let me go, but Bennett followed—whether instructed or by his own accord, I wasn't sure.

"Look, I know you're frustrated, but I don't think you should push her like that."

"Excuse me?" *He was taking her side?* I stopped in a huff. "If you're only following along to irritate me, then don't. I just need some time to think."

His eyes sparkled. "Geez, I'm sorry my very on point and rational statement irritated you."

I couldn't help but smile at his playful tone. "It's okay. I forgive you," I repeated his earlier words back to him.

"Thanks! But before you bite my head off again, Gideon says we can't go past the boundaries of the coven's land."

I spun in a circle with my arms held wide. "And where, exactly, is that?" The same tall trees and thick brush we encountered on our way in surrounded us in every direction.

"He said there's some sort of energy barrier that we'll feel if we get too close." He shrugged. "Apparently, they lowered it last night when Sybil felt us nearby."

"Really? She can track people traipsing onto her land, but she can't remember or locate a book that used to be in her possession?"

Bennett stopped walking and crossed his arms over his chest. "Can you?"

"What?" I kicked a pinecone from the path and kept walking.

"Can you locate something you lost on a whim?"

I looked back, recognizing the challenge. "On a whim, no. But I could devise a plan and use my magic to do it. That's all I'm asking her to do, you know. Make a plan and use her magic."

His shoulders relaxed and he uncrossed his arms, catching up to me with a few steps. "I get it, Lil. Really, I do. But I'd think after standing in that circle for so long, operating on an energy that wasn't fully her own, she probably just needs a break."

His words stopped me in my tracks. I hung my head and dug my toes into the soft dirt. "I get it, too. I'm such a jerk."

Bennett reached out, taking my hands in his. "No, you're not. You're just frustrated and need a little patience is all."

"Yeah, well, that's one thing I don't keep in large supply."

"I noticed." He swung our arms back and forth between us. "How about we finish our walk by following the border's edge, then maybe, when we get back, Sybil will feel up to trying a spell or two?"

I looked down at our clasped hands. "Thank you. I'd like that."

Bennett released my left hand but kept a hold of my right as we continued down the woodland path. I told myself it didn't mean anything. He was probably just trying to be my anchor—keeping me grounded, like I'd asked him last night. But the way my magic reached out to his grew more noticeable with each and every touch, and I couldn't deny I was starting to like it.

The surge of energy and the mixing of our magic made me feel stronger than I ever had before. Wilder, too, which scared me a little. But not enough to let go of his hand.

"Hey, look at this." Bennett pulled me forward toward a fallen tree trunk the size of a Viking ship. Its cracked hull was full of ferns and tiny mushrooms that held the oddest glow.

Releasing my hand, Bennett bent down and plucked one of the colorful shrooms from its mossy bed. "For you. To remember me by."

I started to pull away, recalling Fern's lessons about all the poison mushrooms around our little town, but then I remembered Bennett was studying to become a botanist. He would never give me something that would cause me harm.

Reaching out, I took the tiny mushroom and used every ounce of my will power to refrain from making a 'this fungi is a fun guy' joke.

"Mushrooms are so interesting," Bennett declared, leaning closer to the fallen log for a better look. "Did you know the body of a mushroom is called mycelium, and that it can spread underground and take up hundreds of square miles?"

I shook my head. "No, I didn't know that." I looked down at the glowing cap in my hand and gasped in realization. If this mushroom's mycelium was that large, it was probably glowing because it came into contact with the fairy portal underground. "Shit!" I yelled, making Bennett jump.

I tossed the specimen onto the ground. "Don't touch any more of those."

His forehead was creased in confusion. "Why? What's wrong?"

I wiped my hands on my pants leg. "I think they're glowing because their main body is touching the portal."

Bennett gasped and edged away from the fallen log. "Like my eyes did, when I got close to yours."

"Exactly."

Bennett pulled off the flannel he'd layered over his t-shirt and scooped up a handful of the 'not so fun guys' into it. "I think we should show Gideon and Sybil."

"I agree with telling one of those, but I'm not sure about the other."

"What are you talking about?" Bennett tossed the question absentmindedly over his shoulder as he pulled more mushrooms from the deteriorated log.

"I'm saying we should show Gideon, but I don't want to show Sybil just yet."

"Why?"

"Because if this is her forest, and the portal is leaking magic into it... she probably already knows."

Bennett's eyes went wide. "Well, hell."

"Exactly."

By the time we returned to the camp, Sybil had retaken her place within the circle, leaving us alone to speak with Gideon.

"I'm telling you, something's not right here," I demanded for the hundredth time—at least that was what it felt like to me.

"Just because a few plants have a slight glow doesn't mean the portal is leaking magic into our world. And it certainly doesn't mean that Sybil is hiding anything." Gideon met my determined gaze with one of his own. "Lily, remember, I've been in your world a really long time, and if something this dangerous was going on here, I'd know about it."

"Okay, well, just because you've been in our world for a while, doesn't mean you know everything..." My words trailed off, uncertain how to fight his unflappable logic—because he was right.

As a powerful fae, if anything was amiss with the portals around the world, surely he would have felt it.

"Then how do you explain this?" I gestured to the mushrooms on the table, still wrapped in Bennett's shirt.

Gideon bent down and inspected them again. "I honestly don't know."

"Well, great. As usual, we're still in the dark."

Bennett's head snapped up at my statement. "Wait! Maybe that's it."

I spun around, anxious for his revelation.

"In a forest this dense and dark, sometimes organisms can develop a bioluminescence all on their own."

"I don't know what that means," I admitted.

Bennett shrugged. "I'm saying, the glowing could be a natural occurrence."

I gazed back at the pile of shrooms and hoped he was right. Because once again, I prayed a witch didn't have anything to do with what was really going on.

Twenty-Two

"Let me speak to Sybil about this," Gideon insisted, scooping up Bennett's flannel shirt that still held the luminous mushrooms.

"Fine." I flopped down onto one of the cushions. "But how can you be sure she's telling the truth in whatever answer she gives?"

Gideon's features hardened. "Don't worry. I can tell." He strode out of the tent with a determined gait.

"What was that about?" Bennett claimed the cushion next to me.

"I don't know. Maybe the Dark fae have a way to tell whether someone is telling the truth or not."

Bennett looked surprised. "What?"

I huffed, tired of repeating myself after having to do so with Gideon for the last twenty minutes. "Maybe he can tell by someone's tone if they're lying or not—"

"No, not that," Bennett cut me off. "You think Gideon is a Dark fae?"

"Um, yes." *Shit*. Had Bennett not heard him back at the shop?

"How can you tell?" he asked.

I thought back to the summoning spell Gideon entrusted me

with, along with the price I agreed to pay for the knowledge… *You'll be sworn to secrecy, unable to share my existence with anyone.* But surely that didn't include Bennett since he already knew about his existence, right? I questioned myself, struggling to find an answer, and decided to err on the side of caution. "Um, I can't say for sure. Just a feeling, I guess."

"Wow. Okay." Bennett scrubbed a hand over his face. "I know you had trust issues with him before. Is that the reason why?"

The question caught me off guard. "No, I was concerned that the story he originally told us didn't add up."

"But you trust him now, right?"

I looked outside the tent where Gideon was whispering to Sybil as she maintained her place in the circle. "Yes. I do." My vision had confirmed he was telling the truth. Now, I only hoped the high priestess would, too.

She met my eyes from across the circle, her features blank and unreadable as I held her gaze. I wasn't sure if she was testing me, but I felt my magic rise to meet hers.

"It will never be yours."

The same words I'd heard in our basement flitted to my ears, whispered on the wind with a promise of death.

I gasped, my eyes going wide as Sybil's did the same. In a flurry of hushed instructions, the coven closed its ranks around the portal as their high priestess made a bee-line for me.

"You heard it, didn't you?" she questioned as soon as she was within earshot.

"Yes." There was no point denying it, as she clearly heard the same thing.

"Was this the first time?" she asked knowingly.

"No, it happened at home before we left. The same words in the same menacing voice."

Gideon and Bennett looked back and forth between us, unaware of the danger in which we were possibly embroiled.

"Someone want to fill us in?" Gideon finally asked.

Sybil looked to me as if asking permission, and I nodded my agreement. Mostly because I had no idea how to explain what was happening.

"Someone from the fae realm has contacted Lily with an ominous message. Twice now, as a matter of fact."

Gideon's head snapped to me. "What did they say?"

I took a deep breath. "The same voice warned *'It will never be yours'*."

Gideon stiffened, his features hardening to the point of concern. Worry lines creased his usually perfect face and his eyes turned to pebbles of coal, dark and unyielding as he stared straight ahead.

"Gideon, please calm down," Sybil begged as his glamor started to fade.

Pointed ears, dark eyes, almost glowing skin—this was the Dark fae I recognized from my vision. Powerful and dangerous.

Bennett edged closer to me as if he sensed the same pulsing danger.

"Gideon, what's wrong?" I asked. "Do you know who the voice belongs to or what the warning means?"

He gave a single nod.

"Care to share with the group?" I pressed.

Sybil placed a hand on my shoulder before he could answer. "Let's give him some space."

I shrugged out of her grasp. "Why? I think I have a right to know, since they seem to be targeting me."

She pulled at my arm, less polite this time. "Lily, let's go. Gideon needs some time to calm down, and I have an idea that might help us find the book."

Her words were the only thing that tempted me away, because at this point, I was desperate to make *any* progress on this ridiculous search.

"Fine. Bennett, come on." No way was I leaving him with the Dark fae while he tried to *calm down*.

"I'm good. I'll be right here." Bennett squared his shoulders and crossed his arms.

"Um, no. You need to come with us." I placed my hand on his arm, his muscles tensing at my touch.

Sybil nudged me again as Gideon started to pace. "Lily, he'll be fine. Come on."

My gaze darted between the two men and I reluctantly released my grip on Bennett's arm. "I'll be right outside."

He nodded and stood his ground.

I followed Sybil from the tent with multiple looks over my shoulder to make sure everything remained okay. When we reached a clearing just behind the witch's circle, I spun and asked, "What the hell was *that* all about?"

"I believe the truth of the situation has become even more clear, but it's something that Gideon needs time to process."

"Why? What is he hiding?" I took a step back. "In fact, what are *you* hiding? We found the glowing mushrooms in the woods. Did you know the portal is affecting things in our world now?"

Sybil dropped her head. "Yes. That's why we've had to maintain a constant vigil as of late. As Gideon explained before, more and more fae energy has been leaking through. We've been on guard twenty-four hours a day since we first noticed it."

I thought back to the portal in our basement at home. The Morphineas were the first breakthrough we'd ever had, and that was where I originally heard the voice. "I need to warn my family!"

Sybil's kind eyes met mine. "They already know and are taking the same protective measures we are." She lifted a hand and touched my temple, a vision blossoming in my mind.

Mom, Aster, Fern, Iris, and Daisy all stood before our gate, holding hands. The pulse of the blue orb behind the metal throbbed incessantly while my family chanted together to maintain their hold.

The vision vanished as soon as Sybil removed her hand.

"I must get home! I have to help them!" I turned to stomp back into the tent, ready to abandon this quest when Sybil reached for my arm again.

"Lily, I know you're scared, but you have to keep going. If Gideon says that finding this book is the only way to put an end to all this, then that's what you need to do."

"How? We don't even know where it is, and so far, everything we've tried has turned up nothing. Absolutely nothing!" I yelled.

"That's why I think we should try something new." Full of patience, Sybil took my hand and led me to a nearby stump. It was tall and wide, standing about three feet tall with its top smoothed flat. Bits of sticks, herbs and crystals littered the top; I quickly recognized it as their altar. "I think it's time we did a spell to heighten Bennett's connection to the book," the high priestess suggested. "Once that's in place, you could piggyback on it and with your revelation magic, pinpoint its location."

I glanced back at the tent, thankful Bennett and Gideon appeared to be talking again. It was a good idea, and with help from the rest of the coven, I felt confident we could pull it off.

"Okay, let's do it." I beamed, excited by the potential of bringing this to an end.

Yet again, I should have known better

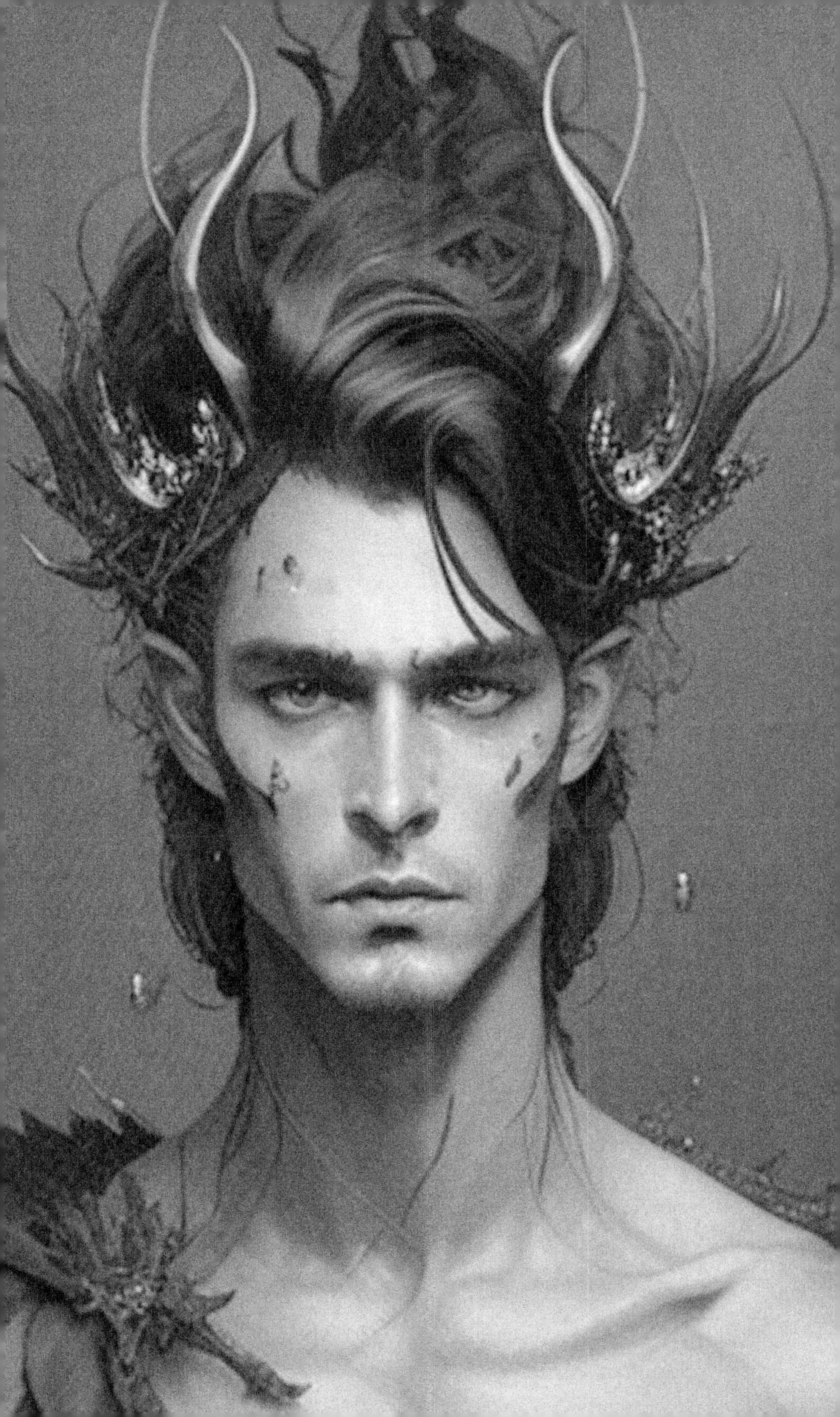

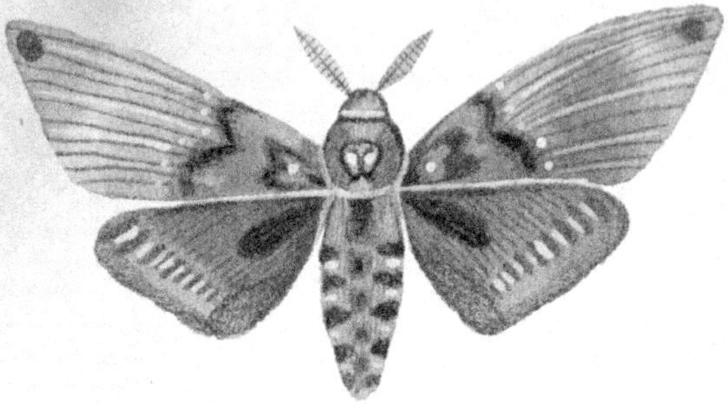

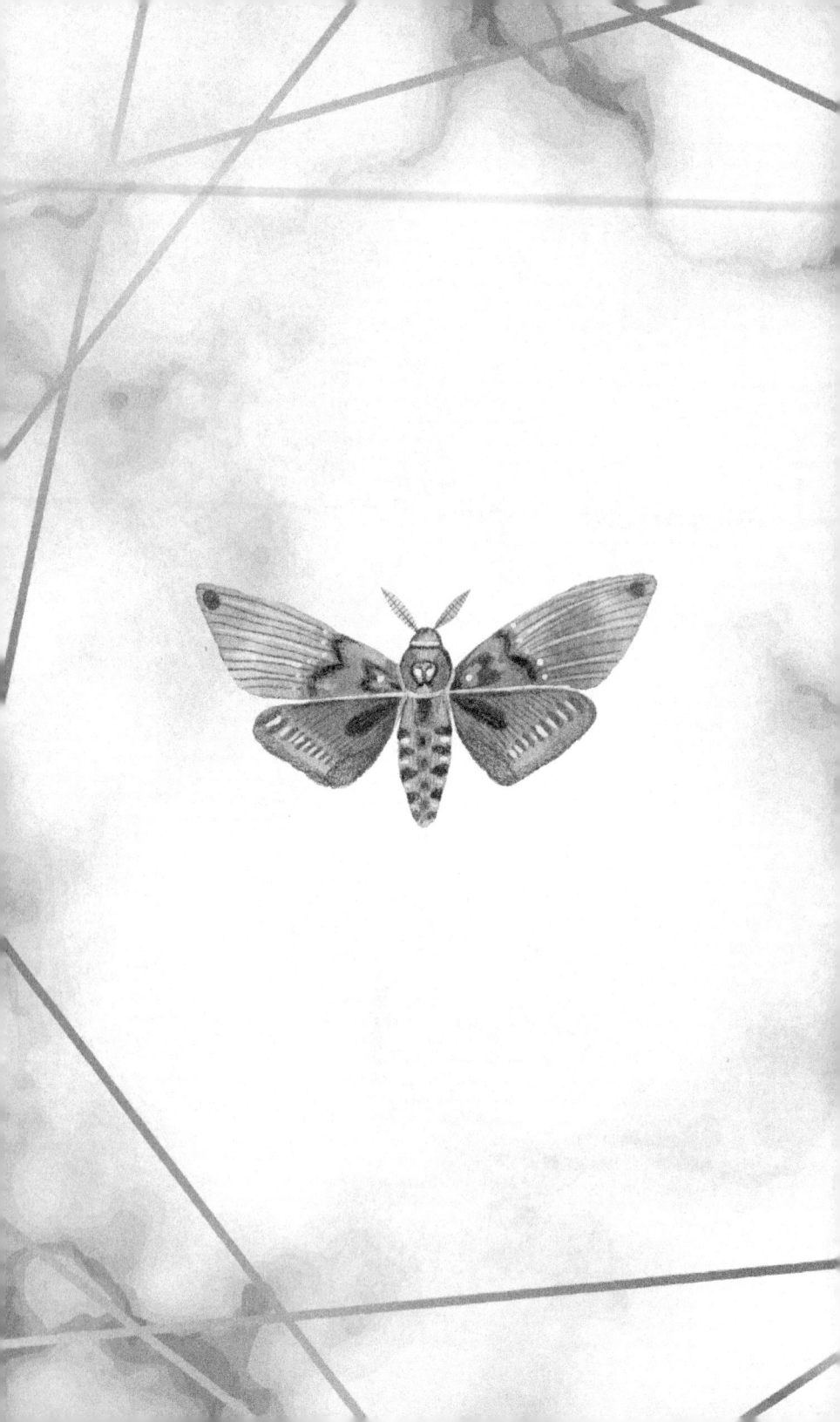

II

Mayhem

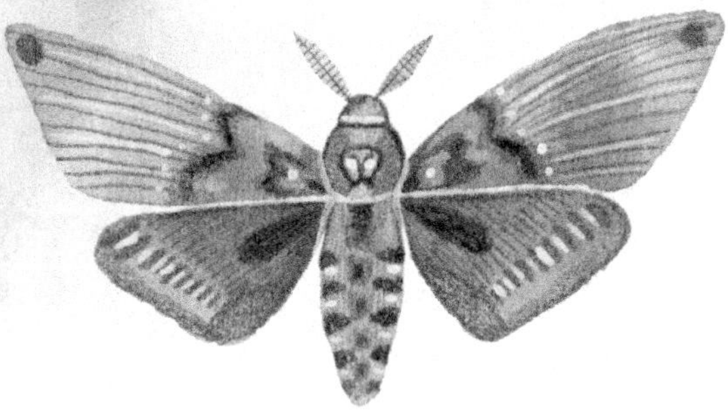

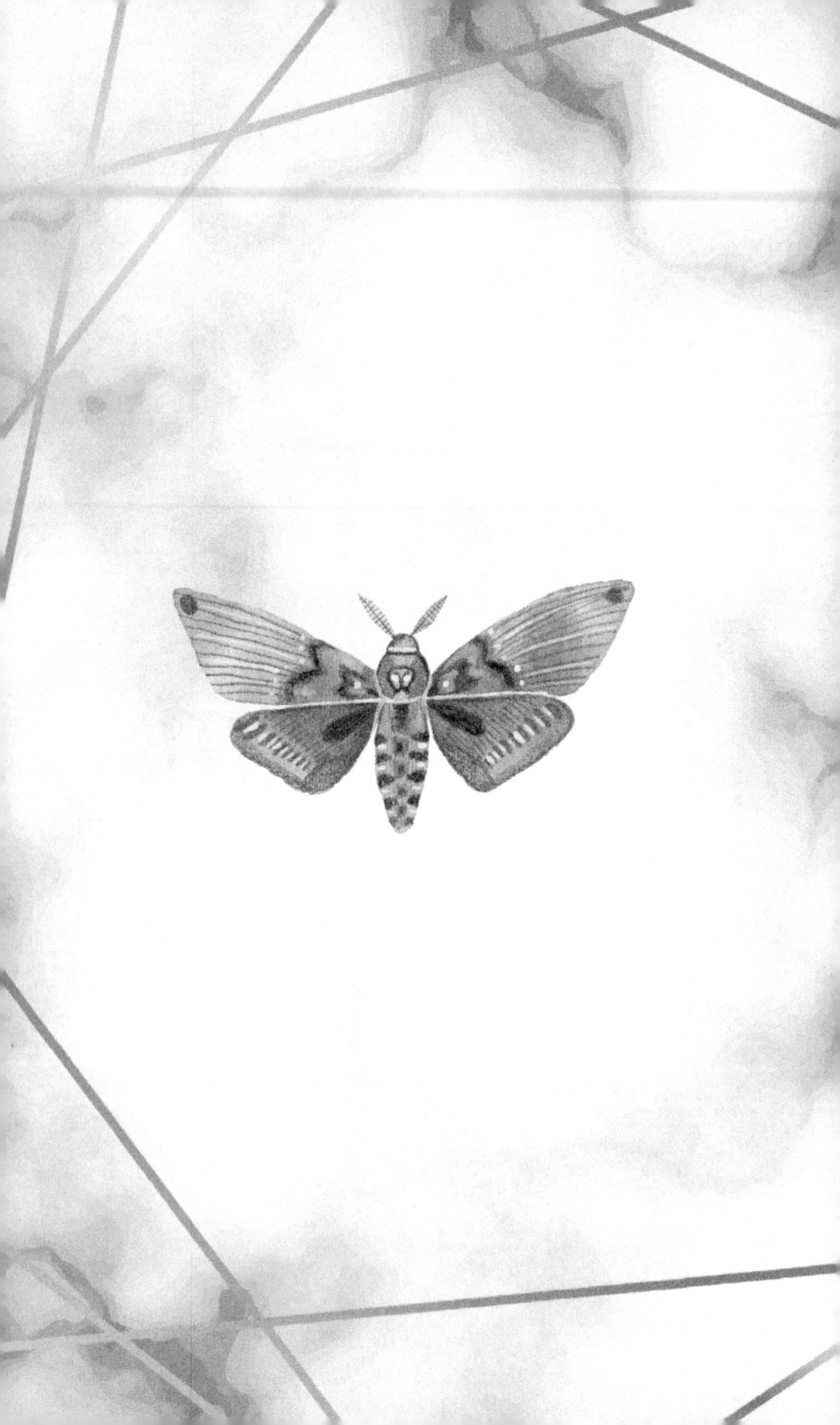

Twenty-Three

Sybil whistled and waved Gideon and Bennett over to join us. "We're going to attempt a spell to strengthen Bennett's connection to the book. Then, Lily will use her magic to locate its current whereabouts."

Bennett's eyes widened but he didn't say a thing, so I rushed to make sure he was on board with the plan. "Are you okay with this?"

He shrugged awkwardly. "Um, sure. At this point, I don't think we have a choice."

"I agree," Gideon added. "We need to obtain the book before the breaches get any worse."

I looked up at the Dark fae through squinted eyes. "Is there anything else you'd like to add? Like why you got all bent out of shape earlier?"

He took a deep breath. "Forgive my momentary lapse of control. Your news startled me, and I needed time to maintain the wards that suppress my magic."

"Oh, that's right… because if you were to use too much of your *true* magic, the witch would know where you are, right?" My tone was mocking, and I didn't care in the slightest.

He raised a brow at my obvious snark but answered my question anyway. "That's right. And it's something we cannot risk."

"Why... *exactly*?" I was done with all the secrets and games. "I think we have a right to know the truth before putting our lives on the line, don't you?"

Gideon took another breath and looked over at Sybil, who gave him a single nod in response. "You're right. You both deserve the truth."

Sybil gestured for us to take a seat on the smaller logs that encircled the altar.

Settled with Bennett by my side, we listened as Gideon began to explain.

"What I told you before was true. I fled the fairy realm with the witch's book because I was trying to save someone's life. What I didn't tell you was that I was fleeing from my brother Thadius, the Light King."

My mouth dropped open, but no words escaped.

"Which makes me the Dark King, if you hadn't already guessed."

Holy shit. I knew he was a Dark fae, but I had no idea he was the King!

"I must keep my powers suppressed because if I don't, my brother's witch, the crone, will be able to locate me and use that connection to blast the portals wide open, sending both our worlds into complete chaos."

Damn. That was definitely a good enough reason for me.

I asked the first question that popped into my head. "Does my mom know?"

"Yes. She helped me when I first escaped, and after that, we contacted all the high priestesses around the world and used the book to fortify their portals. Then, after things settled, I went into hiding, which was when the book was stolen."

"But how? If you were in hiding, how did anyone find you or the book?" I asked.

Gideon rubbed the back of his neck. "I left the book with your mother and oldest sister. They put a damper on its magic and transformed it into something else… something the crone wouldn't recognize even if she saw it."

"What?" I jumped up from the log, fuming, hurt, and utterly confused. "My mom and Aster have known about this the whole time?"

"About who I was and the book, yes," Gideon confirmed, shifting uncomfortably.

"And what about me?" Bennett cleared his throat. "Did they know about me?" The sadness behind his words pulled at my heart. He already assumed he was a changeling, and now, I think the truth of who Gideon was trying to save that night was starting to come to light.

"No. None of us had any idea about you, Bennett. I swear." Truth rang in Gideon's words, but I could tell Bennett didn't believe him. Honestly, I wasn't sure if I did either.

"We searched for the book when it disappeared from your shop all those years ago, but nothing changed. The portals stayed locked and no threats were detected, so we—" Gideon gestured to Sybil, "all agreed it was best to let the damn thing just disappear. If it was no longer part of the fae realm, then the crone and my brother were no longer a threat."

I stopped pacing directly in front of the Dark King. "Yeah, well, obviously that worked out just great, didn't it?"

Gideon had enough sense to drop his head. "Obviously, we made the wrong choice. I don't know how the crone broke through the portal without her book, but if we don't find it, things are only going to get worse."

I paced back and forth in front of the Acrucian Coven's altar, wanting nothing more than to call home and scream at my mom and sister. I knew, however, it wouldn't do any good. Gideon admitted that he'd sworn them to secrecy—an oath I'd taken as well.

I sighed and shook my head, trying to release my irritation and move forward. "Fine. Let's do this. How do we strengthen Bennett's connection to the book, and what exactly does the damn thing look like now?"

Gideon dropped his head again, clearly distraught. I couldn't wait to hear his next excuse.

"At this point, we don't know. Initially, they transformed it into a children's book, something cute and benign, but without constant monitoring, it could be anything by now, shifting to blend into its current environment."

My head dipped back, and I closed my eyes, exhaling a frustrated breath. "I thought you said my mom and sister suppressed its magic? If that was the case, how in the world can it shift on its own?"

Sybil answered this time with a firm cadence to her voice. "Because even with its magic suppressed, it's still a very powerful object from the fae realm." Her tone hinted at something else, but the look in her eyes made me hold my tongue.

I eased closer and watched eagerly when Sybil sauntered up to her altar and began prepping an herbal concoction in an old wooden cup. As a final ingredient, she added a pinch of the mushrooms Bennett and I had gathered. "Since they hold some of the portal's energy, they should help boost his connection," she explained.

"Just like the plant he received back home did." I nodded, happy I understood her reasoning.

She smiled. "Exactly. He just has to focus his magic on the book this time." Sybil motioned him forward. "Drink this and concentrate on finding the book."

Bennett took the cup but looked at me through narrowed eyes, unsure if we could trust the high priestess not to poison him.

"It's okay. I'll be right here. Once you get a sense of the book, I'll piggyback on that with my location spell." I hoped my words helped to settle his nerves, though truthfully, I was just as scared. I had no idea if this was going to work, but with self-righteous anger still stirring in my veins, now was the best time for us to try before I chickened out.

After downing the potion like it was a shot of alcohol, Bennett was immediately wracked with a vicious coughing fit, bending him at the waist. When he stood back up, his eyes glowed purple again.

"Reach out for the book, Bennett." Sybil's soft voice guided him.

Swaying on his feet, Bennett looked like a possessed cartoon. With his disheveled hair, purple glowing eyes, and tall, lanky features, it was hard to concentrate on the task at hand. However, when he lurched forward and grabbed me by the wrist, everything changed.

Twenty-Four

Spindly branches threatened to rip my skirt as we flew over the bare tree tops that stretched into the sky. A wicked wind whipped at my face, and when I turned my head, Bennett was hovering beside me. We were flying, or so it seemed, when I heard a distant voice barely reach my ears.

"Lily, focus. You're inside Bennett's vision. You're being shown the way to the book." Sybil's words guided me to fight the wind, so I turned my face back into it and tried to pinpoint something that looked familiar.

Nothing did.

Bennett's eyes remained purple, providing an otherworldly spotlight wherever he gazed. And though I knew it was a vision, I wavered in the air, certain I would fall out of the sky and crash to the ground at any moment.

Hills, trees, towns, and streets sped by at a blurring pace. I tried to keep my eyes open but simply couldn't without getting nauseous.

"Lily, look."

Several minutes later, Bennett's voice forced me to pry them open again. I gasped when the distinct buildings of the Yale campus swam into view. "Oh my Goddess. It's been near us the entire time!" I exclaimed.

Slammed in the back by a powerful force, my spine arched as we were yanked backwards through the sky. With the location revealed, our vision quest was over. Teetering on the verge of being sick, I wavered on my feet as soon as I felt the ground again. Opening my eyes, I found myself back in the forest, standing at the Acrucian's altar with Sybil and Gideon exactly where we left them.

"Did you find it?" Sybil asked eagerly.

I could barely move, but managed to shake my head ever so slightly. Bennett answered for us both.

"Yes. It's located somewhere on the Yale campus back in the States."

"But you don't know exactly where?" Gideon took a step forward.

"No, we were only shown the general location before we were pulled out of the vision," I added, finally able to catch my breath and settle my roiling stomach.

"Damn. I can't believe it's been that close this whole time!" Gideon paced around the altar, creating a circle all his own.

"Yes, well. At least now we can go home and regroup." I was anxious to get back to all things familiar. There were a few choice words I'd be sharing with my mother and Aster as soon as we arrived.

"It will never be yours!"

White flames shot into the sky, the coven's protective fire guttering and flaring. The voice that had haunted me from that first time in our basement was back and blaring loudly for everyone to hear.

Gideon ran toward the portal, pushing me protectively behind his splayed arms. "Sybil, get back in place with your coven!"

Sybil ran toward her fellow witches, but it was too late.

Blue light surged from the portal as a slew of strange creatures crawled from the gate. Glowing animals, fur-lined plants, even another onslaught of Morphineas crossed over into our world. In slack-jawed astonishment, all I could do was stand there and watch. I glanced to my left, searching for Bennett, and found him immobilized near the altar with his eyes glowing purple again.

"Bennett!" I screamed. "Snap out of it!" I was afraid his now-heightened magic was causing this new rip in the portal.

"This is not Bennett's doing!" Sybil shouted. "Someone on the other side is trying to break through."

Terror filled my veins as I stared into the roiling circle. The fire had weakened and was almost completely extinguished. The coven's protections were no longer in place, and I knew something bad was already on its way. The witches' chant grew louder and louder as they struggled to regain control, but in my heart, I knew it wouldn't work.

"Lily, we need you!" Sybil cried out.

"No!" Gideon shouted, holding me back with his arm still extended across my middle.

"Gideon, it's the only way," the high priestess pleaded.

My gaze darted between the two leaders, trying to decipher some unread intent they'd obviously chosen not to share.

Sick of their games, I pushed past Gideon's arm and raced into the circle, grabbing Sybil's hand. I focused all my revelation magic on the portal, hoping my witch's energy would provide the boost they needed.

Just then, all thirteen witches screamed in unison as a jolt of blue magic burst from my chest, surging through the circle and straight into their hearts. Gideon raced forward, yanking me back to break the connection. With a sudden crackle of silence that seemed deafening in its wake, everything went still.

"What the hell was that?" Bennett ran to my side, his eyes back to their stormy hue.

Sybil turned and knelt beside me, resting her hand over my chest. "Lily, are you okay?" she asked shakily.

Dazed, I tried to sit up, but Gideon held me in place, keeping everyone else at bay.

"Leave her be!" he barked at Sybil. "I told you *no*. I suggest you do not test me again."

"What's going on?" I mumbled. "I don't understand."

Sybil heeded Gideon's warning and slowly backed away, taking her place among the circle again and rejoining the witches' chant.

Fairy creatures had stopped emerging from the portal, which I thought was a good sign, but by the thunderous look on Gideon's face, I wasn't so sure.

"Rest, sweet Lily. I've got you. I'll explain everything once it's safe." Gideon's voice flowed over me in soothing waves, and my head bobbed in his arms as he carried me to the tent. Placing me gently on my bed roll, he smoothed back my hair and pulled a blanket up around me just as I began to drift into the darkness.

"It will be yours... Princess," a low voice whispered on the wind.

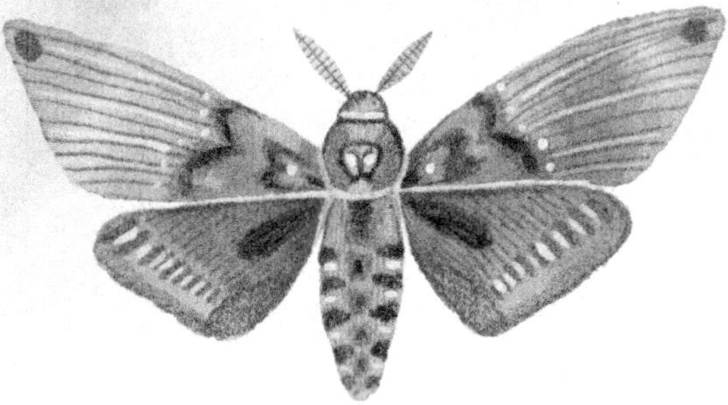

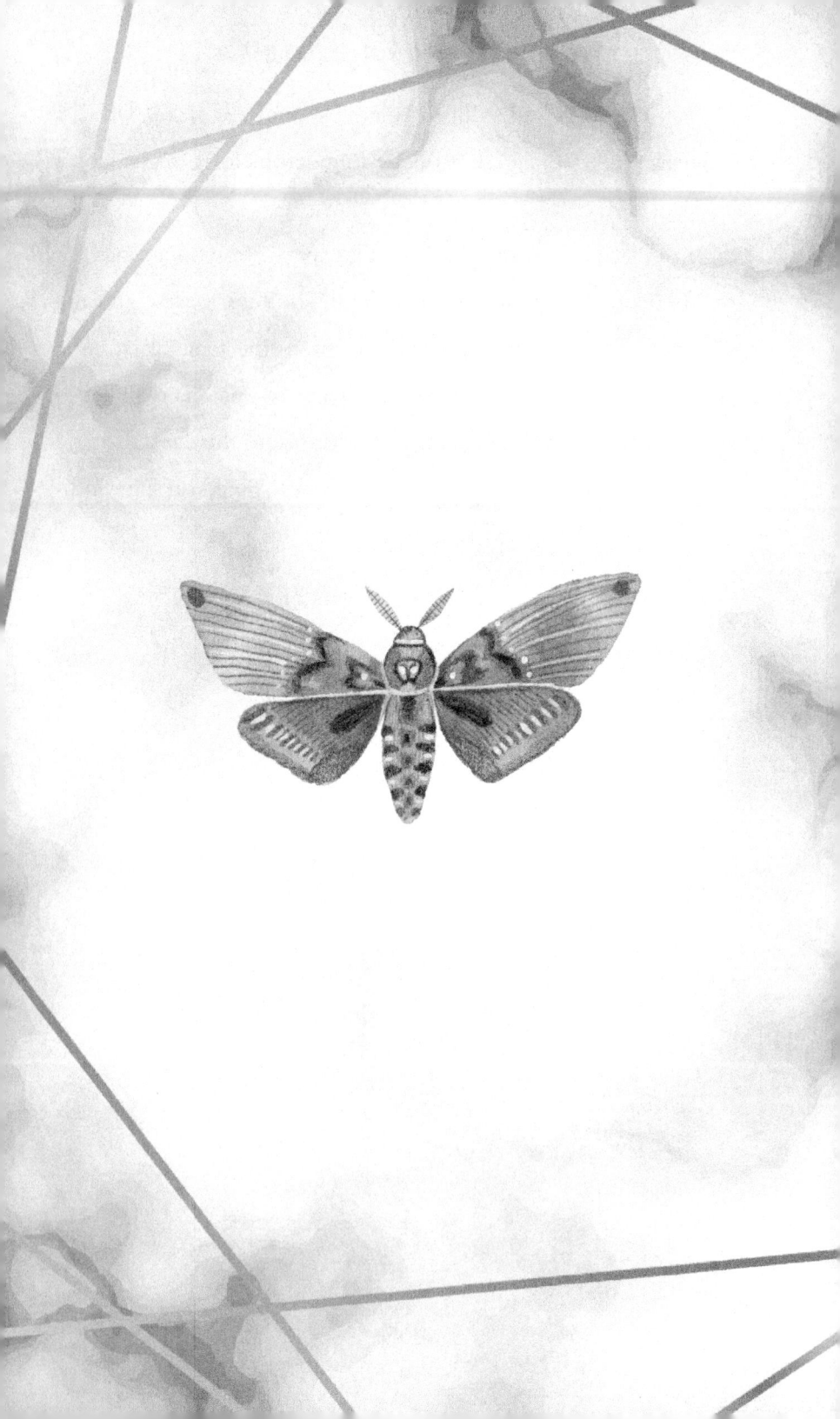

Twenty-Five

I woke to raised voices and tried to get my bearings through squinted eyes.

"I told you, under no circumstances were you to interfere!" Gideon's deep voice boomed from just outside the tent.

"And *I* told *you*, it was the only way," Sybil replied sternly but with far more control.

"She isn't ready yet," Gideon stated flatly. I knew in that instant, he was talking about me.

"How do you know? She's clearly had access to her hidden magic now, thanks to being around Bennett and you."

"That may be, but when she learns the truth, there will be no going back." The Dark King took an audible breath. "She'll never forgive us... *any* of us."

I listened intently, wondering what Sybil's next words might be, but when silence fell, I knew they were done talking—or more accurately, they knew I was awake.

Gideon ducked into the tent, looking far older than when I saw him last night. Worry lines creased his face and his fae ears were visible with no glamor currently in place. "How are you feeling?" he asked tentatively.

"Okay I guess, besides all the secrets you two seem to be keeping from me." I lifted my chin to Sybil who hid just beyond the tent's opening. "Please come in. I think it's time you both told me the truth."

Sybil shuffled forward, her steps delicate and fraught with concern.

I looked around the tent. "Where's Bennett?" I asked, surprised I hadn't seen or heard him yet.

"He's walking the coven's boundaries, taking note of where the creatures that escaped have gotten to so far," Sybil shared.

I sat up in a rush. "Is that safe?"

Sybil nodded but kept her distance. "He'll be fine. The portal is no longer flaring, so I sent one of my witches with him. Kressida will keep him safe."

Kressida. I had no idea which one she was, but the thought of someone else spending time with Bennett alone made my insides itch.

"On second thought, I think I'll join them first. We can talk about all this later." I pushed out from under the blankets Gideon had arranged on top of me last night and strode out of the tent. Looking back, Gideon and Sybil had already reengaged, speaking in hushed tones. I recalled Bennett's words back at the inn ... *Honestly, I'm not sure if I even want the truth.* That was exactly how I felt now.

The crunch of twigs and leaves beneath my feet created a rhythm that I happily stomped through the forest to, measuring my irritation against each step. I couldn't say for sure what the true source of my upset was—be it Mom and Aster's involvement with the book, Gideon's secret about being the Dark King, or the fact that I was jealous over a witch I didn't know spending time with a boy I'd only recently met. Regardless, I didn't like how any of it made me feel.

I knew the moment I returned to the tent and Gideon told me whatever truth he needed to share that my life would change, and I wasn't ready. Goddess, I could barely deal with the changes that had happened so far. Alone in the woods on another continent, far away from my mom and sisters or the warmth and safety of our magical shop... It was almost too much to bear. My heart ached for home.

Just then, a scream rent the air. I picked up my pace, running as fast as I could. I came upon Bennett and Kressida around the next curve in the path, surrounded by Morphineas and a group of tiny glowing animals.

"Stay back!" Bennett yelled, brandishing a stick at the invading creatures. Kressida stood behind him, pressed tightly against his back.

"Guess you found where everything fled." I picked up another stick to help him warn them off, completely ignoring the witch cowering behind him.

"Yeah, and look over there—" He nodded with a dip of his chin to some oddly shaped clumps at the base of an oversized yew tree.

The lumps were strange, but it was the tree itself that held my attention.

The trunk was at least twenty feet around with deep splits running up its middle. The canopy of bare branches swayed in the wind high above our heads, creating an eerie effect of skeletal arms stretching down to snag us straight from the ground. One minute I was staring at the ancient tree, and in the next, I found my hand laid against it.

Blue light burst from the center of the wood, sending the foreign animals scurrying into its core. A new portal pulsed before me and the world went completely still. An invisible force pulled at my guts, yanking me from my feet and into the fairy tree. Zaps of energy sparked against my skin as I fell through its swirling light, only to be dumped out with a hard crash as my bottom smacked onto solid ground.

I opened my eyes and closed them again, needing to make sure that what I saw was real. Squinting cautiously, I took in my surroundings before making a move. The landscape looked the same as home, but everything here glowed with a luminescence that could only be possible in the fairy realm.

"Ouch!" I cried out as Bennett and Kressida came tumbling through the portal, slamming into my back and tossing me face first into a patch of glowing green grass.

"Sorry." Bennett pushed away from me, then— "Holy shit!"

I righted myself and turned back to face them. Kressida was shaking, scrambling backwards on her hands and knees, while Bennett sat flat on his rear with his mouth hanging agape.

"How the hell did we get here?" he asked, as if I should have a clue.

"I don't know," I admitted. "I was looking at the fairy creatures you pointed out around the tree, and then… I was just here."

Bennett glanced around. "Wait. You don't remember touching the tree or creating a new portal in its trunk?"

"What?" I shook my head. "What are you talking about? First of all, there's no way anyone can create a portal out of thin air, and Goddess knows, if there was, *I* certainly don't have enough magic to do anything like that!"

Bennett stood and offered Kressida a helping hand.

An odd knot formed in my throat as she looked up at him with grateful eyes. He dipped his chin in a gentlemanly manner and I almost laughed. Ducking my head, I turned away. There were far more interesting things in the landscape ahead of me than the two of them.

Dandelion-like poofs filled the surrounding field, but instead of the white seed heads we grew up watching blow into the wind, these were bright pink and dotted with turquoise drops of florescent dew.

"Help!"

I turned around to see Kressida being yanked backward toward the large tree behind us. Its middle was filled with a green orb that pulsed like our blue portals back home. Bennett gripped both her hands with a panicked look marring his face. "Lily, help! She's being sucked back in!" I ran forward and grabbed her arms, trying to gain leverage against whatever was trying to pull her back to our world— at least I hoped that's where she'd go. "Hold on!" Bennett screamed.

Tears ran down Kressida's perfect face, making her light green eyes shine even brighter. I held on as tightly as I could, but when Bennett and I both started to lose our grip, we watched in desperation as fear turned to horror. Slipping from our grasp, one minute she was there, and the next she was gone—cast out of the fairy realm in the blink of an eye. Bennett and I ran for the portal, determined to follow her, but crashed into the yew tree's solid bark as the green orb shrank and disappeared.

"What the hell?" Bennett beat his fist against the tree trunk. "Why would it take her back and not us?"

"Because," a low voice declared, "she did not carry fairy magic in her veins like the two of you do."

I spun around to argue the wrongness of the statement, but lost my nerve when I came face-to-face with an enormous warrior fae.

Twenty-Six

With pointed ears, chiseled features, and a chest wider than both my legs combined—the warrior was at least seven feet tall. With no need for glamor here, his features glimmered in the waning afternoon light. Wild, dark hair and small antlers protruded from the top of his head, delivering an altogether stunning visage.

"My name is Alder," the fae greeted. "I need you to come with me." His leathers shifted as he took a step towards us.

"And if we don't?" Bennett asked, pulling me behind him until we stood with our backs flat against the tree.

Alder smirked. "You don't have a choice." The muscles in his arm rippled as he placed a hand atop the sword dangling at his side.

Pulling on a small wisp of my revelation magic, I asked, "If we go with you, where will we be taken?"

"Ferindale. The capital city of the Light Kingdom."

With a rightness I felt in my bones, I knew it worked... he was telling the truth. Not that his answer made me feel any better, but still... "Why would we be taken there?"

He cocked his head. "Would you rather be taken to Dartmoor instead?"

I remembered all that Gideon had said, chiefly that Dartmoor was the capital city of *his* Dark Kingdom.

"Yes. Maybe I would."

"Well, too bad. You don't have a choice." Alder stepped forward and prepared to draw his sword when I raised my hand.

"Wait! Stop. We'll go with you."

Bennett gasped. "We will?"

I nodded, not willing to risk either of us getting hurt.

"Fine." Bennett stepped forward and puffed out his chest. "Just keep your sword and your hands to yourself."

I smiled at the gesture, though the visual of it was hilarious to witness. Bennett was more than a foot shorter than Alder, but I appreciated the bravado.

"Sure thing. I'll even let you lead the way." Alder moved aside, gesturing to a path that wasn't there before. The tall green grass flopped down over the ground, parting like the Red Sea. And even though the shimmering rocks revealed beneath were bright purple, indigo, and pink, it reminded me of the yellow-brick road featured in *The Wizard of Oz*.

"I don't think we're in Kansas anymore," I whispered to Bennett as I took my first step into the mysterious, glowing world.

"How much further is it?" I asked, having practically worn through the bottoms of my shoes.

"You'll know it when you see it." Alder's snark had been building the entire way, and I was already over it.

I stopped, turned, and pointed a finger up at his face. "Look, big guy, we came with you willingly, so you don't have to be a smartass."

"Hmm… thinking about my ass, are you?"

I gasped, shocked silent by his teasing, but Bennett spun around and took a menacing step toward the warrior. "Knock it off. She's not *thinking* about you at all."

Alder barked out a laugh. "You sure about that, lover boy?"

Oh my Goddess, the nerve of this guy!

I grabbed Bennett's hand. "Yes. He's sure." I pulled Bennett around and we proceeded down the path, hand-in-hand, with Alder snickering at our backs. "Just ignore him," I whispered.

"Easier said than done," Bennett replied through gritted teeth.

I gave his hand a light squeeze.

As soon as we crested the next hill, Alder called out, "Ah, home sweet home."

There, in the distance, resting between two soaring mountain peaks, stood a sparkling white castle bathed in golden sunlight and surrounded by glowing, neon-colored clouds. White alabaster buildings enveloped the keep, comprising what I assumed was the city of Ferindale shining like a jewel far below.

"It's beautiful," I admitted, unsure what I expected the Light Kingdom to look like.

"Oh, yes. It's very beautiful." Though his words were agreeable, Alder's voice held a mocking air. With a shove to our backs, we were marched rather unceremoniously the rest of the way in silence until we reached a small door on the side of the main castle wall. Three knocks sounded by Alder's big fist, and the wooden door creaked open. "Here are the two I was sent for."

I snapped my head around, wondering who could have possibly known we were here. Before I could question our brutish escort, he shoved us through the door, gave me a flippant salute, then turned and walked away.

Any ounce of sunlight or the glittering glow we'd experienced thus far disappeared as soon as the door clanged shut behind us. Plunged deep into shadow, I gripped Bennett's hand as tight as I could. A spark of flame just in front of my face made me jump.

"This way." A hunched, elderly man with the scraggliest hair I'd ever seen snapped his fingers and suddenly my hands were bound with rope. Jerked forward by an invisible force, I shuffled to keep up, listening behind me as Bennett did the same.

"Where are you taking us?" I demanded.

"This way," the old fae repeated.

Led down the pitch-black corridor, we sank deeper into the heart of the white mountain. With every step I took, my magic seemed to recede further and further, settling deep inside me, just out of reach. By the time we arrived at our destination—a cold, damp cell at the end of the hall—I was shaking and freezing and unable to do anything about it.

"This way." Another tug by the grouchy fae, and Bennett and I were dumped inside.

The rattle of the metal door reverberated through my bones, sending a shock wave through me until I could stand no more. Dropping to the ground, I leaned against a rough stone wall, chilled further by its freezing temperature and solid, unforgiving texture.

"Are you okay?" Bennett's voice was tentative, like he already knew what a dumb question it was, as he lowered himself down beside me.

"No. I mean yes, I'm fine... but no. What the hell are we doing here? Why would they throw us in a frickin' dungeon? We haven't done anything wrong!"

"I don't know, Lil. But whatever the reason is, I'm terrified to find out."

"Me too, Bennett." I reached for his hand in the dark. "Me too."

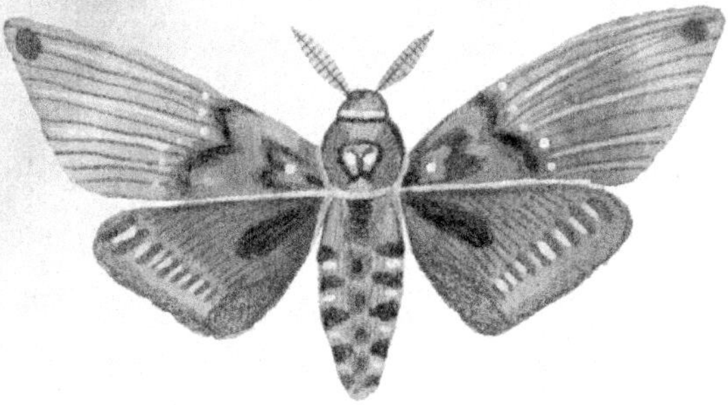

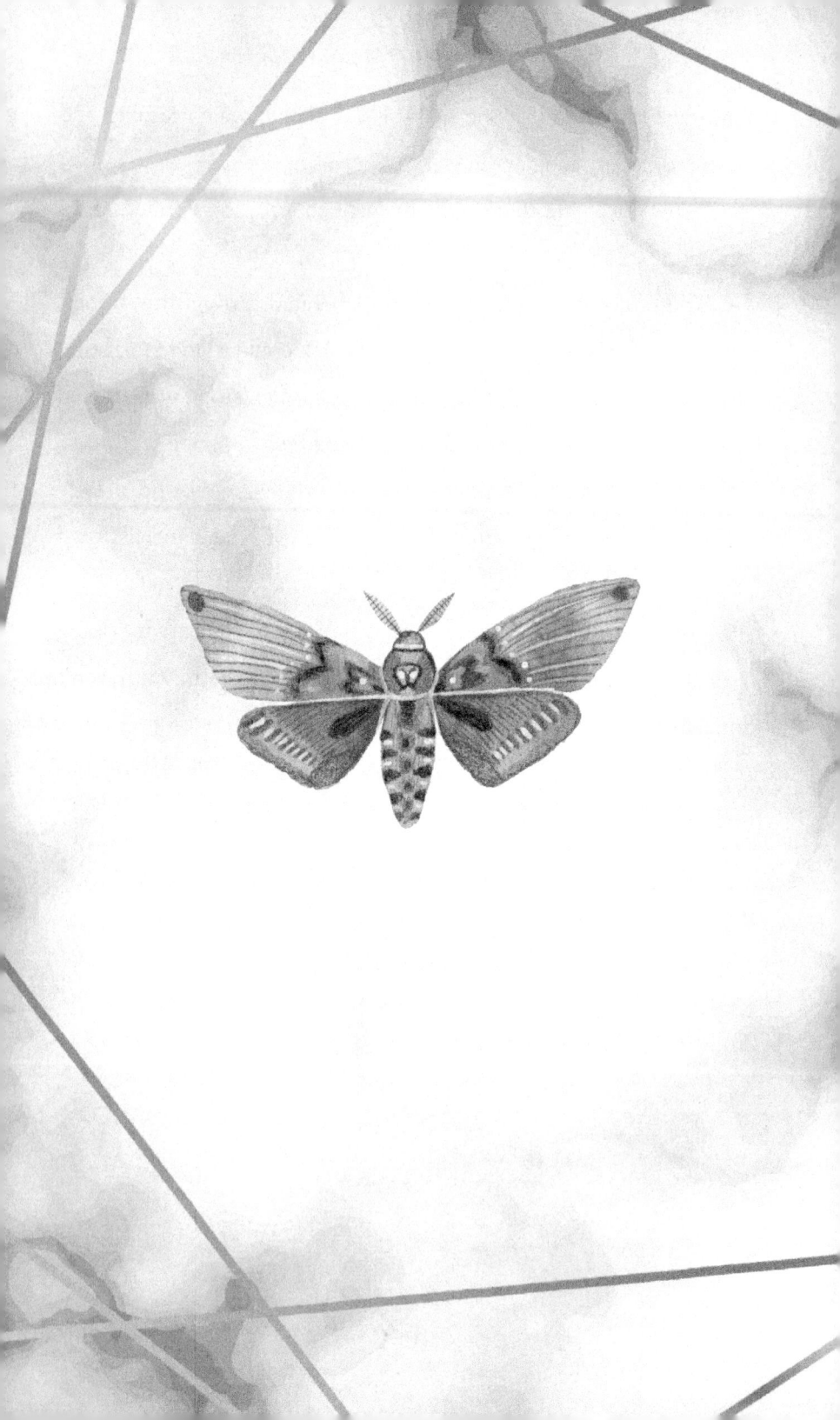

Twenty-Seven

"Here. You can finish mine." Bennett offered me his bowl again for the fifth day in a row. Left alone since our incarceration in the Light Kingdom's dreary dungeon, we'd only been fed once a day when the old prison guard brought us the same disgusting gruel.

"No, I'm good. You eat it. You need to keep up your strength."

"For what?" He scoffed. "We already know we can't break the bars, and there's no other way out of here. We both checked."

"Strength for whenever they come to take us out," I whispered.

Bennett huffed. "I don't know, Lil. That may be wishful thinking at this point."

I tossed my spoon down into the dirt. "Damn it, Bennett! Don't do that. I'm already scared enough as it is; I don't need you falling apart on me, too!"

"Sorry," he apologized, passing me his bowl and spoon in the dark.

Our eyes gradually adjusted to the stygian dungeon during that first night, and like he said, there was no visible way out. Only when the old fae carried in our food by torchlight were we able to see each other clearly.

We'd both lost weight, though it was only visible in our faces. Or perhaps that was just the fear and depression taking its toll.

"Thank you," I said, scooping up the last few bites. I'd wondered every day about the dangers of consuming fairy food, but after refusing for the first three days, neither of us had a choice if we wanted to survive.

"Do you want to try again?" Bennett asked.

"Yes. I think we should."

Scooting the bowls out of the way, we turned to face each other while sitting cross-legged on the dirt floor. Taking my hands, Bennett's thumbs rubbed the same tiny circles on the inside of my wrists like he had for the past few days as I patiently waited for him to teleport us out of here. After ten minutes, he released my hands and sighed, signaling his failure.

"Damn it. I'm so sorry. I just don't know what's wrong with my magic!"

I scooted back against the wall and pulled my knees to my chest. "I don't know for sure, but I think it has something to do with this place. When we were brought in, I felt my magic retreating. I haven't been able to grasp it since we were locked in here."

Bennett's voice was laced with bitterness. "Great! What the hell are we supposed to do without any magic?"

I smiled, though he couldn't see it. "Ironic, isn't it? You spent your whole life without magic, and here you are… wanting it back the second it's gone."

"Yeah, well, if it'll help get us out of here, I'll welcome it back gladly."

The door rattled, but I didn't bother looking up. I knew it would be the same surly guard coming to clear our bowls and leave us with one canteen of tepid water for both of us to share.

"Wow. Looks like you two could use some sun." Alder's voice was still full of snark, but I found myself happy to hear it.

"Offering to take us for a Sunday stroll?" Bennett's smart-ass reply made me laugh, but I truly did hope Alder was there to get us out.

"Not you, sweetheart, but the Princess here is getting a tour."

Alder extended his hand and I took it gratefully. "Don't call me princess," I added.

"Whatever you say, *Princess*." Yanking me to my feet, I fell against his chest.

Bennett cursed under his breath, but I still heard it and so did Alder. "Don't worry. I'll have her back before midnight."

With a clank of the cell door, we left Bennett behind. Alder led me down the dark corridor until we reached a wooden door. I shielded my eyes and walked into the sun, basking in its warmth like a newborn kitten.

"God, you really do look horrible." Alder grimaced and nudged my elbow, pointing to a trough of clean water built into the wall.

Grateful for more than a mouthful at a time, I rushed to the basin and cupped the water in my hands. I felt better the moment the bright liquid passed my lips. "Is this water magic?"

"Do you mean, is it magical water?"

I cocked my hip. "Same thing."

Alder shook his head mockingly. "No, it's not. If the water was magic, it would give anyone who drank it powers, but if it's magical water, it will only react to the fae."

"Then I guess I was right, because the water is obviously magic since it's making *me* feel better. I'm a witch… not a fae." I lifted my chin defiantly.

Alder grinned, his caramel eyes sparkling in the sun. "Whatever you say, Princess."

I crossed my arms. "Stop it."

"What?"

"Stop belittling me by calling me princess. It's fucking rude."

His eyebrows darted to his hairline. "Whoa! You kiss your mama with that mouth?"

I stopped short at his words. "Where in the fairy realm did you hear a phrase like that?"

"Who said I heard it here?"

"Are you saying you've been to my world?"

"Maybe." Once I scrubbed some water over my hair and face, he touched my arm again, nudging me to start walking forward. "And what do you think about that?"

"I think I'd like to know how you managed it. I thought all the portals had been sealed for centuries."

"And what if I was there before they closed in the first place?"

I looked the warrior up and down, trying to imagine him being hundreds of years old. "Nope. I don't buy it."

Alder laughed, the deep-toned cheeriness warming me from the inside out. "Fine. I read it in a book."

"A book? What book?"

He shrugged. "One brought over from your world."

"How did it get here?" I asked, following him along a clean, smooth street.

"I'm not sure," he replied flippantly. "Maybe a changeling had it when a switch was made."

I scrunched my face in disgust at such a barbaric practice. "A changeling? So that was really a regular thing?"

"A long time ago, yes."

I narrowed my eyes on his broad back. "How long ago? Exactly how old are you?"

"By your standards? One-hundred and eighty-two. By fae standards... twenty-six."

I did some quick math in my head. "So, it's like dog years? For each one fae year, it's seven human years."

Alder stopped walking and turned, grabbing me roughly by the arm. "Are you calling me a dog?"

I went stiff, scared for a moment, then— "What's wrong, puppy? Don't like it when someone calls you a name?"

Alder leaned down until we were nose to nose, his breath fresh and warm as it fanned across my skin. "No, Princess. I don't."

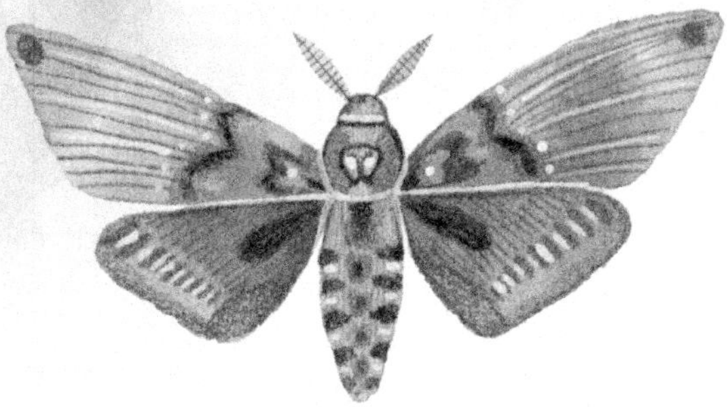

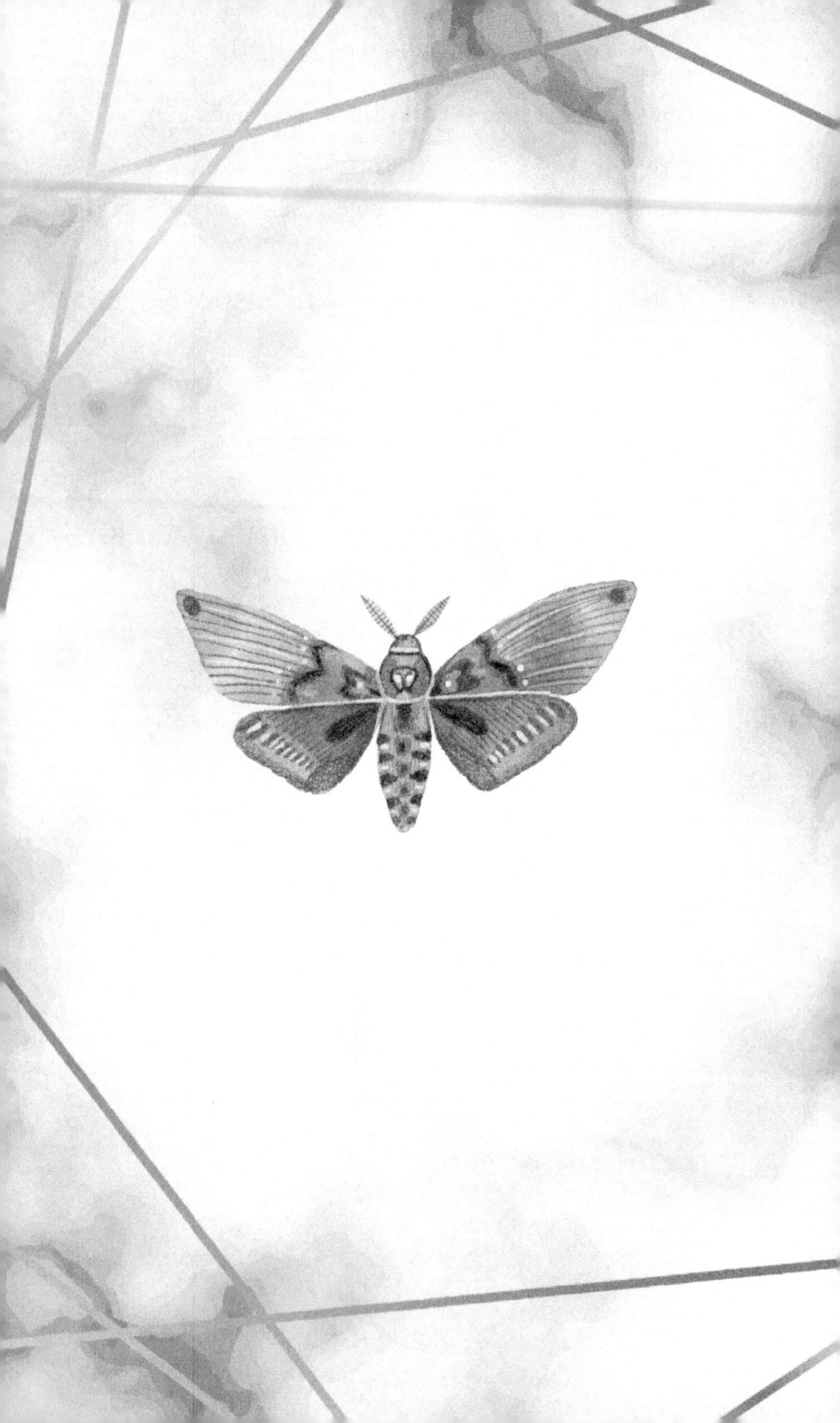

Twenty-Eight

I blinked, scared of the warrior's sudden intensity, but tried to stand my ground. Yanking my arm out of Alder's grasp, I turned back to the open street, wondering why I was able to walk freely now after being locked away for the past week.

"Why were we thrown into the dungeon?" I risked the question as we turned the corner onto another brightly lit street. The white buildings of Ferindale glistened in the sun. Everything from the cobbled pebbles on the road to the exotic hanging flowers in the shop windows glowed in jewel-toned colors as if fae magic infused it all.

"Because you were strangers from a forbidden land. We had to make sure you weren't a threat."

I looked up at him towering over me and laughed. "Sure. Like Bennett or I pose a threat to *you*."

"Not me, personally." He puffed out his chest.

"Then what? Did you really think two kids from Connecticut just randomly showed up as part of a hostile takeover?" I scoffed at the ridiculousness of it all.

"Perhaps. Or that you came to steal from us like most outsiders do."

Stopping dead in my tracks, I looked through the window of the nearest building, taking in the cutest bakery I'd ever seen. A full-figured woman with iridescent wings flitted back and forth between shelves of steaming bread, arranging the baskets and her adorable ceramic wares.

"Who would want to steal from the Light Kingdom?"

"Everyone." Alder nudged me to move on. "Outsiders who somehow show up randomly, or basically anyone from the Dark Kingdom if they make it this far."

His ominous words hung in the air as I took in more quaint shops and friendly fairies flitting about. "What is Dartmoor like? That's the capital city of the Dark fae, right?" I disguised my question based on his earlier statement back in the field.

"Yes., and it's nothing like this. Like its name suggests, you'll find only darkness there, in the streets and in the hearts of the people who live there too."

I thought of Gideon and couldn't believe it. Though I had my initial doubts about him, there was no way the Dark King who was friends with my mother for years—the man who'd been helping us this entire time—was the leader of some seedy, heartless place.

"Are your kingdoms at war?" His words hinted that they were, but I saw no evidence of it.

"No. After the Dark King vanished many years ago, his people spent most of their time warring between themselves. We just stop the thieves who cross into our borders, looking for an easy score."

The brightness that filled the streets should have lightened my mood, but as we neared the castle's main entrance, a knot formed in my stomach. "What are we doing here?"

"The King wants to meet you." Alder smiled, like it was somehow an honor I should be excited about.

"Why?" I pressed, hoping he'd reveal something about the man Gideon fled to escape.

"It's not often someone from your world stumbles into ours. I think he's curious to find out how you managed it."

I took a deep breath, preparing myself to stick to the facts and nothing else. I refused to let anyone know I'd been in contact with Gideon, or that we were looking for the lost fae book back in the other world.

We passed between two massive white pillars and were immediately ensconced in the inner court of the Light fae. Dancing fairies flitted about while small silver ponies galloped between a smattering of younger fae children. Laughter bubbled from every corner of the castle, giving the illusion of unadulterated joy. But that was what worried me… what if all this was merely an illusion for my benefit? To fool the outsider into thinking she was safe.

"This way." Alder's brusque tone caught me off guard, reminding me of our prison guard and the fact that Bennett was still stuck in our cell.

"Why wasn't Bennett allowed to come with me?" I asked as we moved up a set of sparkling marble stairs and strode toward an imposing wood-carved door. Images of fairies, trees, and flowers came to life in the wood, thanks to the detail and care the artist instilled throughout his work. "This is beautiful," I admitted, interrupting my own thoughts.

"Thank you." He smiled proudly, his hand resting atop his sword.

"Wait. Are you saying *you* carved this door?"

A somber nod. "This one and others. I've been the King's chosen woodsman for many years."

"Wow! A man of many talents, I see."

Alder smirked. "Yes, well, woodworking has been a passion of mine since I was a boy, but since my size lends itself to the King's Guard instead, that's where I've spent most of my recent years."

I looked up, ready to offer another compliment, but the words stalled on the tip of my tongue. His eyes seemed shadowed as a hint of sadness passed over his face. He quickly righted himself and held out his arm. "Shall we?" He gestured me forward through the beautiful door.

Marble floors, glittering white walls, and crystal chandeliers flecked with gold decorated the interior of the Light King's castle.

"Is there anything specific I should know before meeting the King?" I didn't want to end up back in a prison cell or worse, just by curtsying wrong or something stupid like that.

"Not that I know of. Just be polite and answer any questions he has."

Pushing through another set of intricately carved doors, Alder stopped a few steps inside of what I assumed was the King's throne room.

More sparkling columns rose from floor to ceiling, holding up a roof painted with a fresco that could rival the Sistine Chapel. Mountains, rolling hills, and glittering lakes all came into view far above my head. I squinted when something moved within the image and watched in awe as a herd of strange creatures I didn't recognize stampeded across the scene.

"Wow."

"I'm glad you approve." A deep voice rang out from the corner of the room.

I stepped back, bumping into Alder's chest as the Light King walked towards us, his white cape wafting out behind him in a spectacular display. "My name is Thadius. It's nice to meet you. It's been so long since we've had a visitor grace our land." He didn't stop to shake my hand, and barely looked at me when he strolled by, climbing the marble steps to take his place upon his gleaming throne.

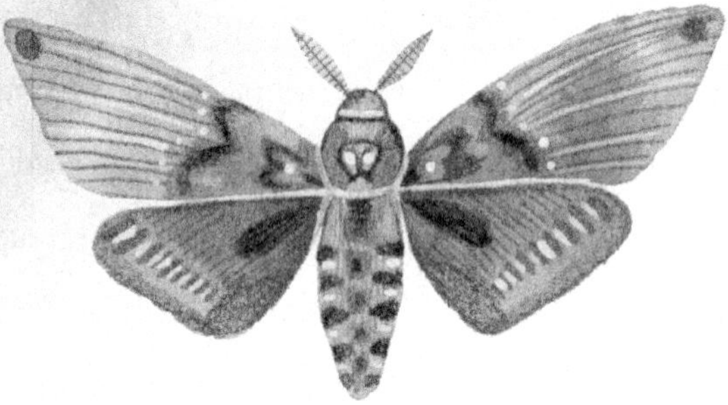

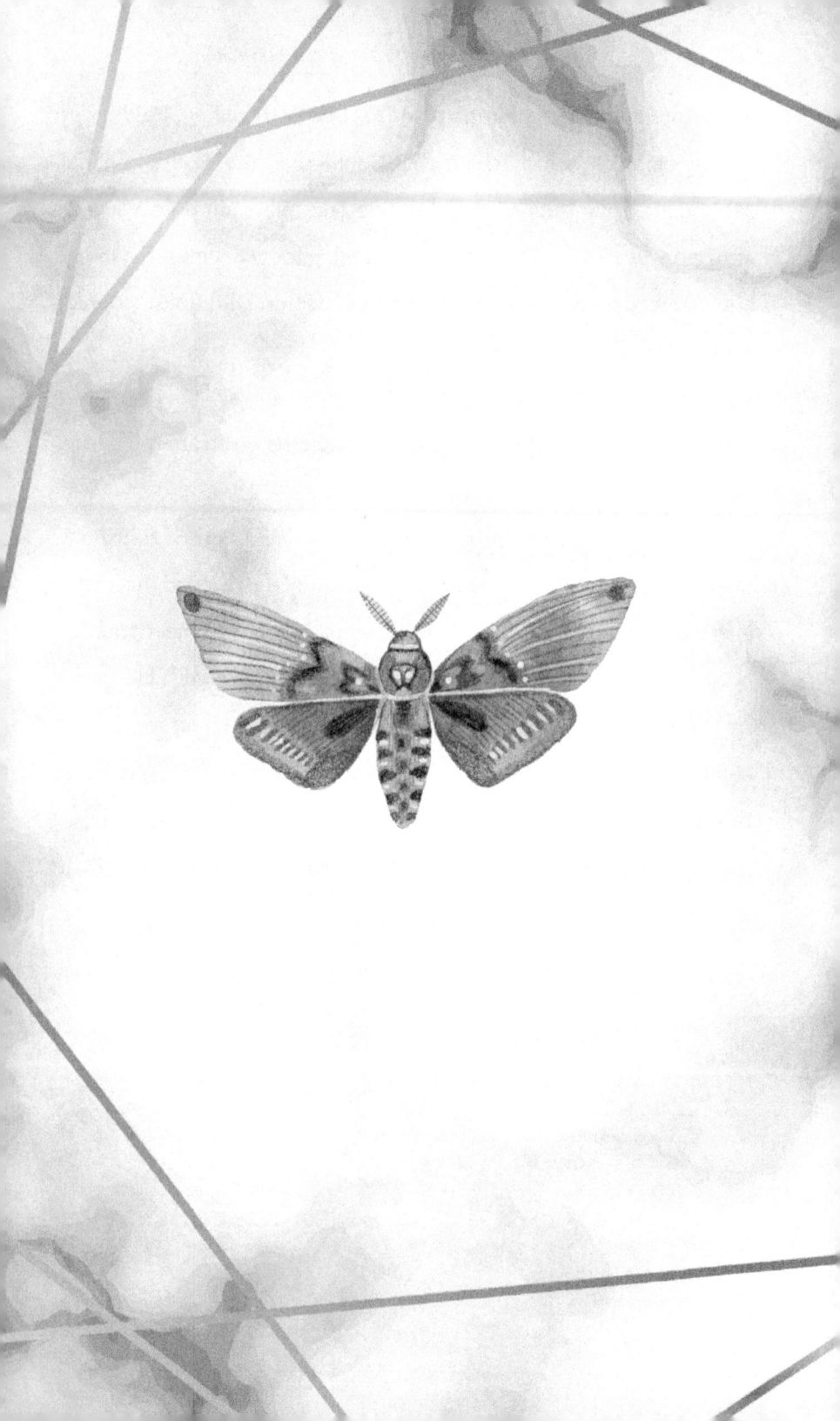

Twenty-Nine

"It's nice to meet you, too," I lied, bowing awkwardly.

A scrape across the floor made me jump as Alder slid an elaborate gold chair into place beside me.

"Please, take a seat," the Light King instructed.

Easing onto the ornate cushion, I crossed my ankles demurely and folded my hands in my lap.

"What's your name?" Thadius asked.

"Lily."

"Hmm…" He thought for a moment. "I like it."

"Thank you?" I wasn't sure how to respond.

"I noticed you arrived with a young man in tow."

I frowned, confused by his meaning, but also creeped out that he knew about Bennett. "In tow? No. He just happened to get pulled through behind me."

"So, your arrival here was by accident?" the King surmised.

"Yes," I replied flatly. No way was I going to elaborate about the newly formed portal in the middle of the woods.

"Interesting."

I squirmed in my chair as King Thadius studied me more intensely than I liked. After several seconds of silence, I could no longer hold my tongue. "When will we be allowed to return home?"

The King shook his head, muttering to himself, and I squeezed my hands tighter together until my fingers started to hurt. With one question, I knew I'd made a mistake.

Pushing off his throne with both hands, he stumbled down the steps like a man under the influence. Scurrying forward, he circled my chair, sniffing me like an animal about to pounce on its prey.

"I'm sorry if my question offended you, Your Majesty. I'm just frightened and would like to go home."

Alder stepped closer to my chair, staring at me with fear in his eyes. "Your Highness. Would you allow me to escort her back to her cell while you and the crone decide her fate?"

My heart leapt into my throat at his words. For the first time since entering the King's throne room, I noticed a darkened corner hidden at the back of the room where something writhed in the shadows. In the next moment, it felt like a fist was tightening around my throat.

Coughing, I reached up and rubbed my neck.

"Your Highness? Do we have your permission to depart?" Alder pressed, thankfully breaking the tension again.

The King continued to mutter under his breath as he waved us off and slunk into the corner, disappearing from view.

"Let's go." Alder hooked a hand under my arm and quickly lifted me from the chair.

Our exit was much hastier than our arrival, and I, for one, couldn't be more grateful. "Thank you for getting me out of there when you did." I paused before asking, "What's wrong with him?"

Alder's shrewd eyes carefully scanned every alley and corner as we made our way back to the keep where Bennett was still being held. This time, he didn't bother to answer my question or mutter a single word.

"What? You're not talking to me anymore? Did I mess up *that* bad?"

Alder yanked open the wooden door to the dark corridor that would lead me back to my friend. But before he passed me off to the decrepit old guard, he leaned down and whispered three words that chilled my blood. "Be careful, Princess."

Before I could turn and ask him what he meant, the door slammed shut and he was gone.

"This way." The familiar flame lit the corridor ahead, and I was once again shoved toward my cell.

Bennett scrambled to his feet the minute the old fairy led me inside. "Are you okay?" He rushed forward, kicking the bowl at his feet in his haste.

I bent down and gathered up the dishes, handing them to the elderly guard before he locked us up again. "I'm fine." Walking to the wall, I slid down to the ground, propping my back against the cold stone. "I met the King."

"What?" Bennett exclaimed as he joined me in the dirt.

"Yeah. And it was… *something*."

"Something how? Good, bad? What was he like?"

"Both, I suppose." I listened to make sure the guard had fully walked away. "The town and castle are beautiful, but the King himself… There's something wrong with him. One minute he was fine, asking questions like a normal person, then the next, he seemed almost crazed, pacing and sniffing around me like a wild animal. It was weird."

"Wow, that does seem strange. Did he mention anything about the book?"

I looked around, hoping my eyes would adjust to the dark again soon. "No, but I think the crone was there."

"Oh my God. And you managed to get out unscathed?"

"Thanks to Alder."

"What? You're joking."

"No. It almost seemed like he was trying to protect me from the King's wrath."

Bennett sighed and fell quiet.

"I asked when we could go home," I admitted.

"I assume from our current accommodations he didn't give you a favorable response."

"You assume correctly. In fact, I think my question somehow drove him mad."

"Strange." Bennett scooted further away, stretching out his legs as he prepared to go to sleep. "Good night, Lily. Maybe tomorrow you'll have better luck."

I opened my mouth to ask what he meant, but suddenly didn't feel like talking anymore. Curling up into a ball, I closed my eyes, hoping I didn't dream about shadows, crones, or kings.

I had no way of knowing what time it was, but from the footfalls scraping toward our cell, I at least knew it was time to eat.

"Wake up," I nudged Bennett. "Food's here."

"Sorry, Princess. No gruel this morning. Looks like you're both getting an upgrade." Alder snapped his fingers and flame burst to life in the center of his palm.

I gasped, staring at the elemental magic as he opened the cell with his other hand.

"You can control fire?"

"Seems like an obvious answer, but yes." He waved me out, waiting on Bennett who had yet to move.

"Come on, sweetheart. You get to join the party, too," Alder chided.

"Party?" I asked, wondering if he meant it literally.

"Yes. Apparently, the King has determined you're no threat to the kingdom and has decided to celebrate your visit by throwing a ball."

"And if we don't feel like attending?" Bennett snapped, crossing his arms.

Alder laughed. "Then I guess you stay right here." The warrior tensed, waiting to see if Bennett would make a move.

I turned to my friend with pleading eyes. "Bennett, please. I want you with me."

No one spoke until Bennett was clear of the cell, then, of course, Alder had something to say.

"Aww… you guys are just too sweet for words."

I took Bennett's hand and started toward the door. "Shut up, Alder. You're just jealous," I teased, hoping he'd leave us alone.

"You got that right, Princess." Light as a feather, his words drifted on the wind, reaching my ears just as we stepped outside.

Thirty

"Wait. Don't I get my own room?" I turned back to Alder as he closed the door on the most palatial bedroom I'd ever seen. Bennett was already in the bathroom, taking full advantage of the immense shower to clean away days of caked-on filth and grime. I couldn't believe this was actually happening.

I wasn't sure what I expected after leaving the Light Kingdom's dismal dungeon, but being marched into five-star accommodations certainly wasn't it. I tried not to gape as Alder ushered me and Bennett through winding hallways that were oddly devoid of inhabitants. That was why I was surprised when the warrior fae ushered us into one room. Surely there were hundreds of empty bedrooms to choose from.

"Nope. Sorry. Easier to guard you when you're both in one place."

I pointed a finger at his barrel chest. "Ah! So we *are* still prisoners!"

"Until the King deems otherwise, yes, I'm afraid so. Though the term 'prisoner' seems so negative. Why don't we go with 'constantly escorted guests'?" Alder stepped outside the room, grinning at me from the hallway.

"Why don't we go with, get the hell out?" I slammed the door in his face.

"Your turn." I spun around at Bennett's voice, coming face-to-face with his bare chest. His lower half was wrapped in a towel, but the ribbed muscles of his stomach were on full display.

"Jesus!" I covered my eyes. "Put some clothes on."

"Relax, I'm working on it." He walked to the armoire Alder had pointed out when we first entered the room. "Oh my God… look at this dress."

I lowered my hand and gasped. The slip of material he held between his fingers wasn't enough to cover a cat. "No way… there's absolutely *no way* I'm wearing that."

"Yes, you are, unless you want to offend the King," Alder's words drifted from the other side of the door.

"Damn it," I whispered, snatching the white beaded dress out of Bennett's hands.

Glowing water flowed down my back, warm and fragrant like a sunbaked rose. If I wasn't being held captive, this would be the best vacation a girl could ever wish for.

Drying off, I sniffed the elegant bottles of creams and perfumes that littered the marble countertop. Selecting the scent I liked best, I dabbed it on my wrists and behind my ears like I'd seen Mom do my entire life.

Wiping fog from the mirror, I pushed my wet hair out of the way and stared at my own reflection. Tears welled in my eyes, and I didn't bother trying to hold them at bay.

No more than two weeks ago, I was at home with my sisters, taking Ms. Buckman's candle order in my favorite place in the world. And now here I was, sharing a room with a guy and getting ready to attend a fairy ball in the most scandalous dress I'd ever seen.

I missed my family. At this point, I'd even take Aster's constant nudging and contemplate attending Yale rather than being here, dealing with all of this. I was grateful to be out of that dingy cell, but something here seemed off. And attending a party where I would be paraded around in front of a bunch of strange fairies wouldn't change my mind. I needed to get home and find that damn book, and if getting through this fiasco was the first step toward my freedom, I would do just that.

Wiping my eyes, I lifted my chin and looked around for the items I'd need to do my hair.

The modern amenities here should have been a surprise, but after learning that fairies lived for centuries and had been visiting our world even before the portals were in place, I guess it made sense they were as advanced as us, if not more.

I dried and curled my flame-red hair and left it loose to trail down my front and back, hoping the curtain of loose waves would provide additional coverage where needed.

Eyeing the dress hanging on the back of the door, I reluctantly grabbed it and slid into the feather-light material.

Sheer panels comprised most of the gown, with small sections of white fabric and beading strategically placed to cover certain areas, while leaving others exposed. Once fully dressed, I looked in the mirror again, barely recognizing myself as I donned the final touches: a glittering array of jewels that had been left for me next to the sink.

My skin glowed like the fairies' and my green eyes shone as brightly as the portal that would hopefully lead me back to my world. Cracking the door, I walked into the bedroom, nervous and feeling more vulnerable than I ever had before.

Bennett gasped. "Wow! Lily, you look gorgeous."

I kept my eyes on the floor, not ready to look at Bennett just yet.

"Here. Alder brought you these."

A pair of glittering silver heels slid into view. The shoes were the final piece to my ensemble, but I still didn't feel ready. I had no idea what to expect, but if the pit in my stomach was any indication of how the night would go, I might choose to go back to my cell instead.

"Shall we?"

I looked up and met Bennett's kind eyes. His radiant smile almost blinded me from how resplendent he looked in a black tux with his arm held out for me to take. "Wow! You look great, too."

He snickered. "You sound surprised."

"No, it's just—"

The door opened and time froze.

Alder stepped inside, wearing what I assumed were his warrior dress-leathers. His wild hair had been tamed and his antlers had been polished until they gleamed. With his sword firmly at his side, he was the epitome of a proud fae warrior. The image took my breath away.

"Shall we?" He repeated Bennett's words, offering me his arm instead.

I looked between the two men and the knot in my stomach tightened.

Bennett dropped his arm and his head, and my heart sank. I didn't want him feeling second best, and after everything we'd been through, I wouldn't abandon him. Stepping up beside him, I threaded my arm around his while smirking at Alder. "Lead the way."

Bennett looked up, shocked by my decision, but happy all the same.

"Fine. But if I may make a suggestion?" Alder dropped his arm. "Stay close to me tonight, Princess."

"Why? What's going to happen?" I asked, not bothering to argue about his annoying nickname for me this time.

Alder's smile stretched until it almost felt menacing. "At a fairy revelry… you never know."

The pit in my stomach tightened again and didn't let up as we traversed the gleaming hallways that led to the castle's ballroom.

Compared to the normal everyday shine, tonight the palace sparkled with the intensity of the stars. Stepping into the ballroom, I didn't bother stifling my audible gasp of appreciation. Wide banners of luminous silver hung from the ceiling high above our heads, while a band of fairy musicians dressed in all white played softly at the front of the room.

Tables lined the far wall, and seated in the middle of the largest one was the Light King. Pushing to stand, he waved his hand and the music stopped. "Tonight, we welcome guests from the forbidden land. May their visit be merry and bright."

All eyes turned toward Bennett and me, and despite the King's flowery words, I didn't think merriment or fun was truly in the cards.

"Let's take our seats," Alder whispered, then led us to the King's table.

Seated a few chairs down to his left, I was grateful for the buffer of bodies between the King and me. Alder slid into the chair next to mine, leaving Bennett to take the one on the end.

With another imperious wave of the King's hand, the band picked up their instruments and played a lively tune. Fairies of all sizes flitted around the room, joining each other on the floor and in the air as they danced to the music.

I leaned close to Alder. "I've heard you shouldn't dance with fairies or eat their food. Are we safe here?"

A huff of laughter escaped his lips. "Lily, you've been eating and drinking our food since you arrived. Why would you think tonight would be any different?"

I shrugged. "I don't know." I looked down at my gown and glowing skin. "I feel like everything is different now."

Alder reached under the table and took my hand. "Princess, you'll always be safe as long as you're with me."

A loud bang made me jump as Bennett slammed his wine glass down on the table and roughly pushed out of his chair. Yanking my hand out of Alder's guiltily, I scooted away and ran after my friend.

"Bennett, wait!"

He spun and caught me in his arms, twirling us onto the dance floor in one smooth movement. "You like him." His voice was low and even, but his arms quivered with rage.

"No! I mean, yes… He's been helpful and kind to us both."

"Kind? To me?" Bennett scoffed and shook his head. "I don't think so."

I squinted, worry lines creasing my brow. "What do you mean? Did he hurt you when I was gone or something?"

"No, but his incessant teasing is pissing me off." He spun me around in time with the other dancers on the floor.

I looked up to meet his eyes. "You just have to ignore him. He's only doing it to get a rise out of you."

"Yeah, well, it's working."

With our next turn, I glanced back at the table and found Alder's seat empty. Scanning down the line, I found him talking to the King.

Both men stared back at me, their eyes unnerving and unwavering.

"Let's go get something to eat." I took Bennett by the hand and led him to the far wall where an assortment of food was laid out in a beautiful spread.

Fruit, bread, cheeses, and meats, along with other steaming dishes I didn't recognize, all filled the long tables. Picking up a plate, I loaded it with food I probably wouldn't even touch, but anything to distract me from the King's unflinching appraisal was a welcome distraction.

"Do you mind if we sit here?" I asked Bennett, noticing a high table with stools near the door.

"Sure." Bennett set down his plate and started picking at his food. "Have you given any thought on how we're going to get out of here?"

I surveyed the room, looking for Alder, and shook my head. "Not really."

Bennett tracked my eyes. "And why is that?"

I met his gaze and huffed. "Because there's no way we can make it back across that field to the portal without getting caught. Besides, who knows if the damn thing is even still there?"

"True. But maybe you can summon another one out of thin air."

I gasped. "What are you talking about? I didn't summon that portal in the tree. It just… appeared."

"Fine. Don't get all worked up. I believe you." Bennett popped a grape into his mouth.

I sighed. "I've been thinking about it, and I think it probably formed like an off-shoot geyser when the energy of the main portal was blocked by the coven's spell again."

"Like a lava exhaust point," he surmised.

"Yes. That's what I was thinking."

"Yeah, you're probably right."

"Or… she's the missing fairy princess with Light magic running through her veins," a scratchy voice sounded from over my shoulder.

I turned to find a decrepit old woman standing right beside me. Unlike the rest of the partygoers, she was dressed in rags, with a sickly pallor to her skin.

She reached for a curl of my hair with her gnarled fingers. "It's been a long time, child," she croaked.

I realized then—this was the crone.

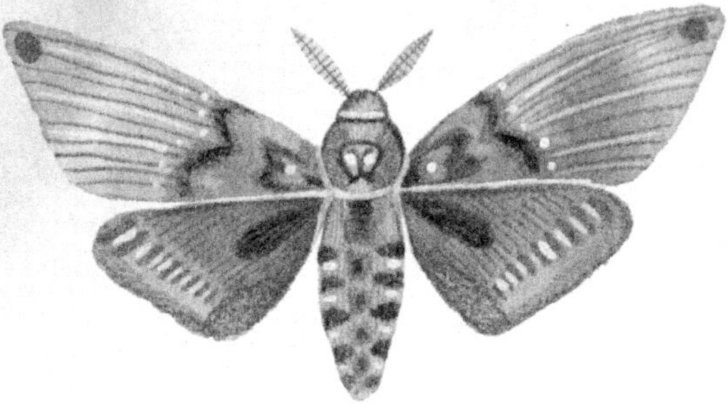

Thirty-One

Scrambling to the other side of the table, I grabbed Bennett's arm and hid behind him as the hunchbacked old woman crept even closer.

"Don't fret, child. I'm not going to harm you *here*." The crone's voice seeped into my veins like an icky virus, spreading fear all the way to my heart. Her ragged gray robes matched her stringy hair, both out of place in the sparkling ballroom.

I searched for Alder frantically but didn't see his hulking form anywhere.

"No one else can see me, child," the crone whispered menacingly. "Only the two of you. But even *he* can't save you from my grasp!" She lunged forward, reaching for me with spindly fingers that reminded me of the tree limbs back at the garden center, her dry skin flaking off like loose bark.

"What do you want with her?" Bennett yelled, struggling to free me from her bony fingers.

The crone's eyes were wild. "To finish what I started, of course!" she cackled. "To complete the binding and seal her in the other world as the changeling she was meant to be."

The room spun and I felt myself fall as another vision began to form—

A beautiful woman with blonde hair struggled as she gave birth to a crying babe. Thadius was there, stroking the face of the woman—his beloved wife and Queen.

"Take care of her, my love. For she is now the rightful leader of our realm." With a final breath, the woman perished, leaving the babe in the King's grieving arms.

Wails of loss and contempt flew from the King's mouth, transforming him from a loving husband into a vengeful father and King.

Waking on the floor of the ballroom, Bennett knelt next to me with the crone hovering over us both.

"You see, child, you *are* the missing Princess and the rightful leader of the Light fae, for only a female is meant to reign. Until you were stolen away."

My chest rose and fell in rapid breaths, words failing me. Thankfully, Bennett spoke up.

"If she was your rightful Queen, why were you trying to cast her out of your world as a changeling?"

The crone flicked a finger at Bennett's head. "Because, boy, with no female to rule, the King could claim the throne."

I gasped and my head swam. I was on the verge of passing out again.

"Wait. If she's the princess, does that mean Thadius is her real father?"

When the crone nodded, I lurched to the side, becoming sick.

"It will never be yours..." The words played in my head; now I

knew them to be my father's. I searched for him in the crowd, knowing he would never willingly give me the throne.

Just then, glass shattered above our heads and a horde of warriors fell from the sky. Dropping into the center of the ball, they quickly fanned out around the room, taking up defensive positions and drawing the swords at their sides. Another boom rattled the room, and Gideon walked through the double doors dressed in all black.

"Ah, Brother. Seems you forgot to invite me to your ball." He splayed his regal cape out behind him, looking every inch the wrathful Dark King he was.

Thadius appeared across the room, his white cape flaring wildly as he ducked behind a row of his own guards.

Gideon's eyes quickly scanned the scene until they landed directly on me. He rushed to my side. "Lily, are you alright? Have they hurt you?"

I shook my head, letting Bennett help me stand.

Gideon's eyes were mournful. "I assume you've learned who you are in this realm, and who you are to me?"

I nodded, still unable to form words, but realized that if Thadius was my father, Gideon was my uncle. "Yes, but I don't understand," I muttered.

"I'll explain everything once we're safe." Gideon motioned to his Dark warriors that it was time to leave. They converged around us as a protective cadre of bristling swords. Tall, in black leather, and with their swords held aloft, they reminded me of Alder.

"Wait!" I searched the room, looking for him, but he seemed to have disappeared.

"There's no time. Let's go." The instant Gideon gave the command, we were ushered out of the ballroom and into the hall, where six familiar figures stood at the end.

"Mom! Aster! Sybil!" I ran toward my family and the leader of the Acrucian coven, wondering how in the world they could possibly be here. Squeezed tight by all my sisters, I finally felt safe. But I should have known better.

"You'll never escape me again, *Brother!*" Thadius's voice raged from inside the room as an ominous, roiling darkness I recognized crept down the hall with greedy fingers.

"The crone!" I gasped. "She's here, but invisible to the eye."

"Not for long." Sybil reached into the pouch at her side, pulling out a handful of white powder that she immediately blew into the air. "Lily, use your revelation magic, *now!*"

I closed my eyes and concentrated on the only magic I'd ever known, connecting me to my witch's soul. "Reveal that which cannot be seen. Expose the lies and in between. Hidden in darkness no more will you be, I cast you into the light, so mote it be."

My magic exploded through the hall, revealing the truth of what the Light realm had become.

Crumbling walls caked with vines, tarnished light fixtures, and broken glass all emerged at once as the fairies from the Light realm came streaming out into the hall.

Their wings were no longer glittering or bright, but instead, tattered and dull with holes slowly eating them away.

"We must go. Now!" Gideon commanded.

One of his guards stepped forward and tossed a metal ball onto the floor between us and the invading crowd. A new portal opened, and Gideon's warriors pushed us all inside.

"Holy shit!" Bennett gasped as we emerged in a different location.

Inky darkness surrounded us so I couldn't see where we were, but as the crone's wailing cry faded into nothingness, the portal snapped closed behind us, cutting her off completely.

"Now that everyone is here and safe, please follow me." Gideon's voice penetrated the deep shadows just as a sliver of light appeared in a vertical slit before us.

I realized he'd opened a door, and I stepped out behind him into another castle's throne room.

"Welcome to the Dark side. We have cookies." Gideon smiled, obviously trying to lighten the mood.

"Seriously, where are we?" I stumbled forward as the rest of our group pushed in behind me.

"My home. My *true* home," Gideon announced with a smile. "You've arrived at my castle in the capital city of Dartmoor."

I gazed around the room, stunned by its grim sophistication. I'd expected far worse based on Alder's description, but the style here was organic and moody. Swaths of rich green covered the walls and most of the exposed surfaces with gold, black, and wooden accents used to highlight the rest of the room. Live plants trailed from the glass ceiling and dangled from multiple shelves, giving the whole place a kind of upscale greenhouse vibe.

"It's beautiful here," I admitted.

Gideon laughed. "Why do you sound so surprised?"

Before I could answer, I was swept up into another sisterly hug, crushed between Aster and Fern as the others wrapped their arms around us. Pulling away, I found my mom and walked into her waiting embrace. "How are you all here?" I murmured against her shoulder.

She nodded to Gideon, who called out to his guards. "Take up defensive positions. I doubt it will be long before my brother tries to reclaim his prize."

"Prize?" I scoffed. "From what I understand now, he tried to throw me away the second I was born!" I looked back at my mom—the woman who raised me—with tears swelling in my eyes. "Why didn't you tell me about any of this?"

"Lily, please. Let everyone get settled and then Gideon will explain."

Her words sounded hollow but I nodded anyway, feeling completely numb and imbalanced, like my world was teetering on its axis and ready to fall into the abyss.

Thirty-Two

Seated around a large, intricately carved table, we all picked at the food in front of us, waiting for Gideon's explanation as promised.

Once the final guard shut the door to the dining hall, Gideon began. "Lily, you're correct. You are Thadius's daughter and the heiress to the Light Kingdom's throne. Inherited from your birth mother, Genevieve, only females are meant to rule the Light Kingdom, while males rule here in the Dark. It's how the balance has always been maintained. Light, Dark. Male, female. Ying, yang. However you want to describe it, it's always been our way… until the day you were born.

"Grief stricken by the loss of your mother, whom he truly loved, Thadius grew power-hungry and decided to seize the throne for himself. He figured if he could cast you to the forbidden world as a changeling, no one would be aware of your existence and unable to challenge him in his claim."

"That's when you saved me," I inserted, remembering my vision. "Before the crone could complete the task."

He nodded. "Yes. When I realized how lost he was, I took you and her spell book and fled for my life… and to protect yours."

"Wait," Bennett interrupted. "I thought the way changelings worked was that a fairy child was left in our world while a human child was exchanged and brought here. If the King had succeeded, wouldn't a human version of Lily have been raised as the princess in the Light realm this whole time?"

"Traditionally, yes, that's how it works, but my brother had no intention of bringing a human back here at all."

I dropped my head. "He only wanted to get rid of me." Aster, who was seated beside me, reached for my hand beneath the table. I pushed her away. "And all of you knew this the whole time? Who I was and where I was from?" I cast accusatory looks around the table, burdened by crippling hurt at the hands of those who were supposed to love me the most.

Mom shook her head. "Not all of them. Just me, Aster, and Sybil."

Slashed by the pain of betrayal, I looked away. "Right, but you couldn't tell me because of the bargain you made with *him*."

Silence fell until Gideon forged on. "Lily, I couldn't allow anyone to know of my existence in your world, so I suppressed my magic in an attempt to hide from my brother and his crone in order to keep you safe."

"And what…?" I looked back at my *mom*—the only mother I ever knew. "You couldn't even tell me about the book?"

"Gideon left it for me and Aster to protect, so we transformed it into a children's book. But shortly after, it disappeared from our shop and we never saw it again."

Tears pressed at the corners of my eyes. "Then explain how I've been able to be around the portal all this time without triggering it like Bennett's magic did."

Sybil finally spoke up. "Lily, we had to suppress your true magic, just like the book, so the crone couldn't track you in our world. But the more time you spent with Bennett, the quicker it began to return."

Bennett eyes snapped to mine. "It was *you*."

I jerked back at his accusation, not sure what he meant.

"*You're* the one who transported us, not me. It only worked when we were touching."

I shook my head. "No… I was just boosting your fae magic, that's all."

"I'm afraid not, Lily," Gideon confirmed. "Bennett was the one who was boosting *your* hidden fae magic all along."

Tears fell in earnest, wetting my cheeks as I pushed away from the table. "How could you all do this to me?"

Gideon rose from his seat, determined to stay by my side. "It was for your own good, Lily. And for that of your sisters to come."

"What are you talking about?"

Gideon looked at my mom, who nodded her permission for him to continue.

"Once I left you with Camellia and Aster, it was imperative we kept your magic suppressed and the wards on the shop maintained… So, we struck another deal."

"What deal?" My voice trembled with anger.

"Just like the power of a magical square of fifteen, your mother agreed to give birth to three more daughters in specifically chosen years. By doing so, the magical span between your births would help maintain the wards."

I gawked around the room at my sisters, trying to figure out what he meant.

From the story Mom told us growing up, she gave birth to us with a specific number of years between each child because when Aster was born, she had been all alone with no help, and refused to be so again. The story went like this: four years after Aster was born, the twins came along, then there was another five years between them and Daisy. I was born six years after that, all in all, putting a fifteen-year gap between Aster and me, which was why she was there on the day I was born.

They were all lies.

Despite my youngest role in the family, I *wasn't* the child here. I was a fairy princess who aged differently than her human sisters and had been deceived her entire life.

"I need to be alone." I reached for the door but was stopped when Gideon grabbed my hand.

"Lily, I'm sorry, but I can't let you go. We have to stay together and make a plan."

"A plan for what?" I screamed. "For me to overthrow my father and take my place as Queen in a land I know nothing about?" I stomped toward the wall of windows on the far side of the room, looking out over the city below.

Night had descended, or perhaps this was how it always looked here in the realm of the Dark fae. Sparkling lights twinkled inside the buildings, illuminating the outline of bodies moving within. Homes, businesses, even a large amphitheater could be seen in the distance. I suddenly wanted to be shown around like I had been by Alder back in the Light Kingdom.

I felt Gideon behind me, though he didn't speak a word.

"Is it always dark like this here?" I asked.

"Basically, yes. Though it does lighten to a twilight hue in the daytime hours, providing enough light for us to move around unimpeded."

I let my words drop because I didn't want to fight, but none of this lessened the sting of all I'd learned. "Your castle is beautiful, Gideon. The fae realm and the two kingdoms are beyond my imagination, but…" I looked up to meet his eyes, "what exactly is your plan?"

With a wide smile plastered on his face, he guided me back to the table. "I thought you'd never ask."

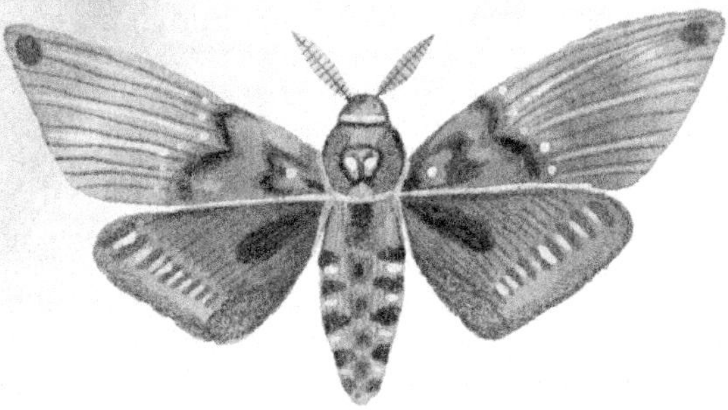

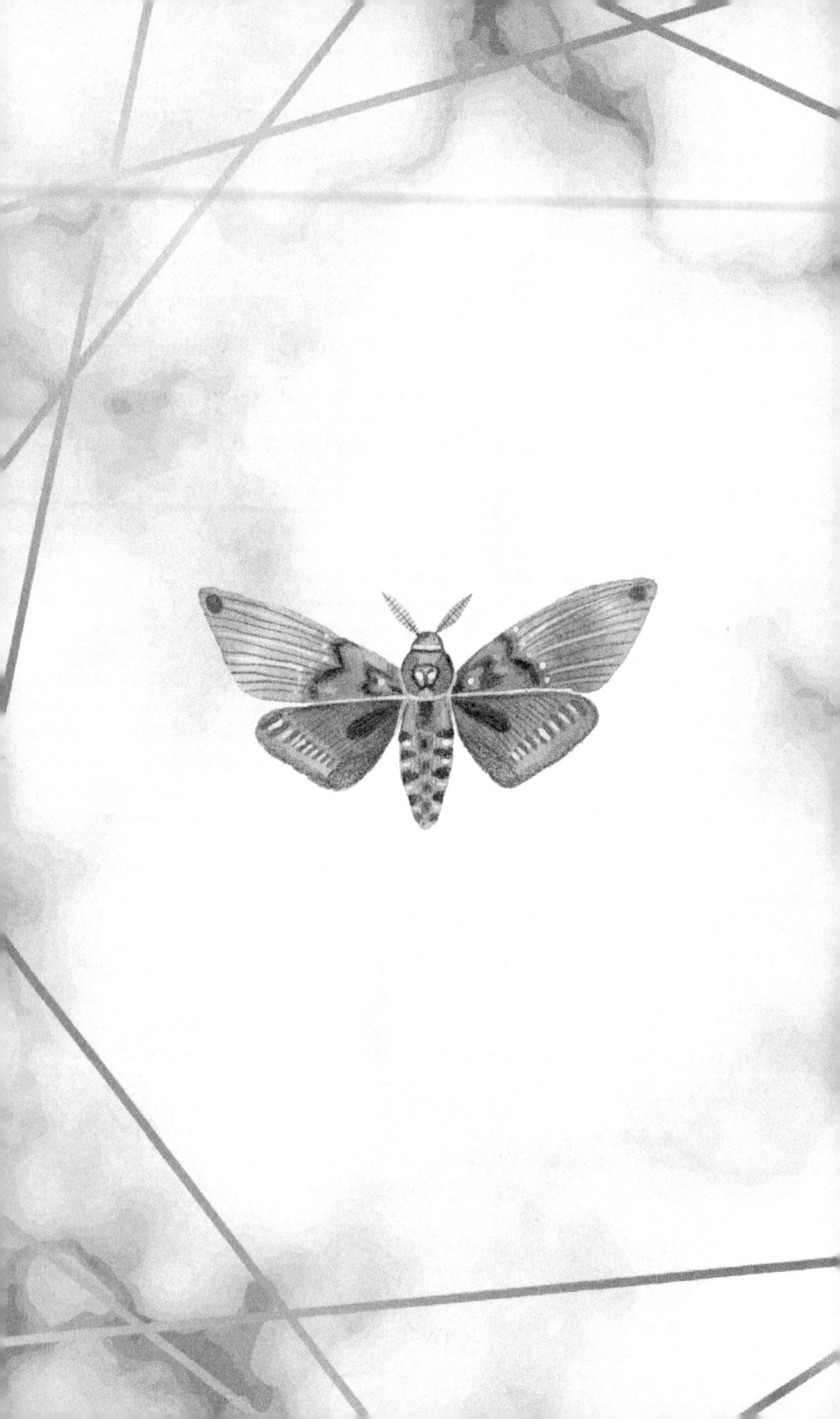

Thirty-Three

Lying open on the carved wood table, the witch's handbook to magic and mayhem revealed its true form, as Sybil and my family of witches used their combined magic to contain the evil inside.

Sybil had explained that after realizing Bennett and I were missing from the Acrucian forest, she tracked our signature to the yew tree. With her help, Gideon released enough of his magic to trigger the portal again.

Placing her witches on guard in the new location, she and Gideon flew back to the States, where they quickly brought my mom and sisters up to speed.

Aster described their whirlwind trip to the Yale campus, where she and my sisters used their combined magic to reveal the location of the book. Ironically, they found it in the campus library disguised as a cookbook, with the most disgusting recipes you could ever imagine listed within.

No wonder it stayed hidden for so long.

After returning home with the book and using its original spell to repair our shop's magic, they all followed Gideon through the portal in our basement with the witch's handbook in tow.

I watched Sybil and my mom work in unison as warriors ducked in and out of the room, receiving orders from their Dark King as he continued to lay out his plan.

"If we can destroy the book now, there should be no reason for you to return to the Light realm. Once you're gone again, my brother will stop looking for us both." Gideon held my gaze, the truth swimming in his eyes.

"You're not coming back with us, are you?" I asked, emotion thick in my voice.

"No. I've been gone from my people for far too long. Once I know you're safe, it's time I reclaim my throne."

My lip quivered, realizing all I was going to miss. "Can I ask you something?"

"Of course."

"What will happen to Bennett? I mean, he's from here originally, right? Sent to my world as a changeling?"

My world, I thought. Now, I wasn't even sure which one that was.

Gideon glanced across the room to where Bennett was talking to Sybil. "I suppose it's up to him" he offered kindly. "Though I have no way of tracking down who his true family is, he's more than welcome to stay here with us."

Bennett caught my eye and smiled, giving a little wave as he continued to help Sybil gather ingredients for another spell.

My mom surmised that since we were in the fairy realm now, their spell to siphon off the book's magic would work fully, instead of merely suppressing it again. Once void of its fae energy, we could destroy it like any other book.

At least that was the hope.

Bennett tapped me on the shoulder, pulling me from my morose thoughts. "Would you like to go for a walk?"

I looked up at Gideon, thinking he'd disapprove.

He nodded encouragingly. "I'll arrange for my most trusted guards to accompany you, if you'd like to look around."

I beamed. "Thank you. That would be great. But first…" I looked down, realizing I was still wearing the ridiculous gown my father had provided. "Is there somewhere I could change?"

"Of course." Gideon snapped his fingers and the doors to the dining hall opened, revealing a thin, middle-aged fae woman with chestnut hair. "Gretta is one of my most trusted helpers. She will show you both to your *separate* rooms."

I laughed, feeling like Gideon was acting more like a father-figure than an uncle.

"Thanks."

Waving to Mom, I followed Bennett and Gretta into the hall and through the stunning castle, gawking at the paintings and statues carefully placed throughout. Gretta caught me staring at one piece in particular. The painting depicted a beautiful doe surrounded by dark flowers in a moonlit forest.

"The Dark King has good taste," I commented.

Gretta nodded. "Yes, he does."

We continued up two flights of stairs, the black onyx floor sparkling in the moonlight with each step I took.

"Here are your quarters, Miss Lily." She opened the door to another palatial room dressed in dark tones and moody accents.

"And Mr. Bennett, here you are." She pointed to the door directly across the hall.

"Thank you, Gretta. We won't be long." I noticed two guards walking towards our doors, realizing they'd been tailing us all along. I turned my attention to Bennett, who still looked dashing in his tux. "I'll only be a minute."

"Same. Meet you back here."

I returned his smile and disappeared into my room.

Rummaging through a free-standing dresser, I found a pair of black pants and a thick black sweater to match. Tossing them onto the bed., I started to pull the paper-thin dress up over my head when a voice stopped me cold.

"I don't know… I can't decide if I'm going to like you better in black, or if I prefer you in the white instead," Alder's voice teased from the shadows just behind the bed.

Pushing open a hidden door, he strode breezily into the room with a flame alight in his hand, like it was no big deal.

I gasped and tugged the dress back down. "What the hell are you doing here? They'll kill you if you're caught."

He flopped down onto the bed. "I had to make sure you were alright."

I gaped at how casually he lounged in my new room. "Where were you when the crone ambushed me? I thought you said you'd keep me safe," I accused.

"No, I *said*…" he drawled, "that you'd always be safe as long as you were with me… which you weren't." His tanned skin glistened in the glow of his flame, the bright warmth of his honeyed eyes threatening to melt me where I stood.

I scoffed. "That's just semantics."

"No, it's the literal truth. You've been under my protection since the day you were born... *Princess*."

I cocked my hip, sick of his arrogant attitude and hidden meanings. "What the hell is *that* supposed to mean?"

"It means... you and I have been bound together, destined to rule side by side from the moment we were born. The heiress to the Light crown, and the heir to Dark throne."

My eyes bulged and I suddenly felt sick to my stomach.

"That's right," Alder continued. "You're the Light Princess, and I'm the Dark Prince, fused together and protected by our royal magic for all eternity as long as we're together." He shrugged. "I knew it the moment I found you in that field, shaking like a leaf."

My head swam. "I don't understand."

Alder hopped off the bed, striding to the tray of food Gretta must have prepared in advance of my arrival. "What's there to understand? Thadius and Genevieve were your parents, and Gideon and Fawn were mine."

Fawn. I recalled the painting of the beautiful doe in the hallway and looked up at his antlers. "Your mom was a deer shifter."

He nodded, suddenly serious. "After my father disappeared with no explanation, my *uncle* decided to kidnap me as a boy and put me to work as his woodsman, eventually indenturing me within his Guard." His eyes roamed the room. "He also had my mother killed, so there would be no one to claim my father's throne."

Jesus. I was the spawn of a monster.

My mind rolled over all the information, sticking on one important note. "Oh, Goddess. Doesn't that make us cousins?" I cringed.

"No. Relax. Besides, that kind of thing isn't a big deal here anyway."

"Well, it's *certainly* a big deal to me! Explain!" I shifted uncomfortably in my mostly see-through dress.

The Dark Prince turned his attention back to me, his expression thoughtful. "Your mother was the Dark Queen's sister, Gideon's first wife. It wasn't until after she passed that he met my mother and had me. And despite how they address each other, Thadius and Gideon are not true brothers. They were only in-laws, related by marriage through their wives, until Gideon's first wife died."

I shook my head. "So we're not blood relatives?" I confirmed.

"No, but we are both of royal blood and in line to our respective thrones, which is enough to enact the blood protection."

Oh, thank Goddess. I'd never felt more relieved in my life. Then I was struck by a sudden thought.

"Wait. If Gideon is your father, then why did you sneak in here to see me instead of coming to join us in the dining hall? If you're the prince, then this is your home, too."

Alder downed a glass of wine, slamming down the golden chalice. "Well, it's not like I want to see the father who abandoned me and left my mother to die." He rolled his thick shoulders and popped his neck. "Like I said, I only came here to make sure you were okay."

Oh no. He blamed Gideon for everything that happened, and rightfully so, I supposed. At least from his perspective. But he needed to know the truth. I walked toward him and reached up to place a hand on his cheek. "Alder, your father disappeared because he was trying to save *me*. From what I understand, when my biological mother died, my father went mad and was about to cast me into the other realm as a changeling so he could claim the throne for himself. Which, obviously, he did, but I wasn't supposed to survive. The crone was in the process of taking my magic from me when your father stole me away. Once we emerged into my world, the portals were sealed and he couldn't get back without alerting them to where I was." I held his gaze unwaveringly. "Don't you see, Alder? He stayed away to protect me." I dropped my hand. "If you want to blame someone, blame *me*. It's all my fault."

Alder flew from the chair, the crash of it ringing throughout the room. "No, none of this is your fault, Lily. Don't ever think that."

We stood face to face, breath to breath.

"Fine, then blame my bastard of a father," I snapped.

"Oh, don't worry. I already do." His eyes fell to my lips, his chest heaving.

"Am I interrupting?"

I turned and found Bennett fuming at the door.

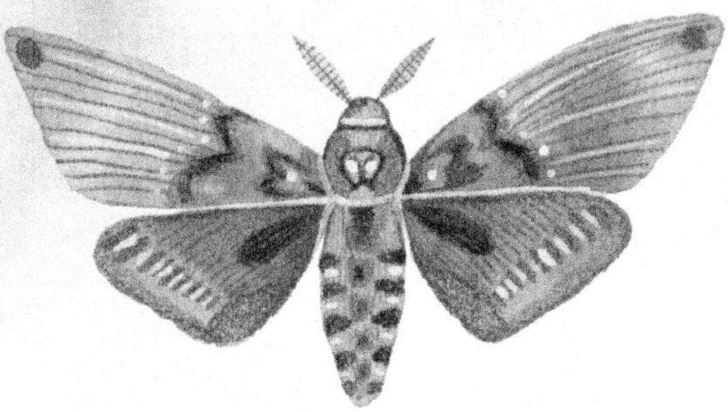

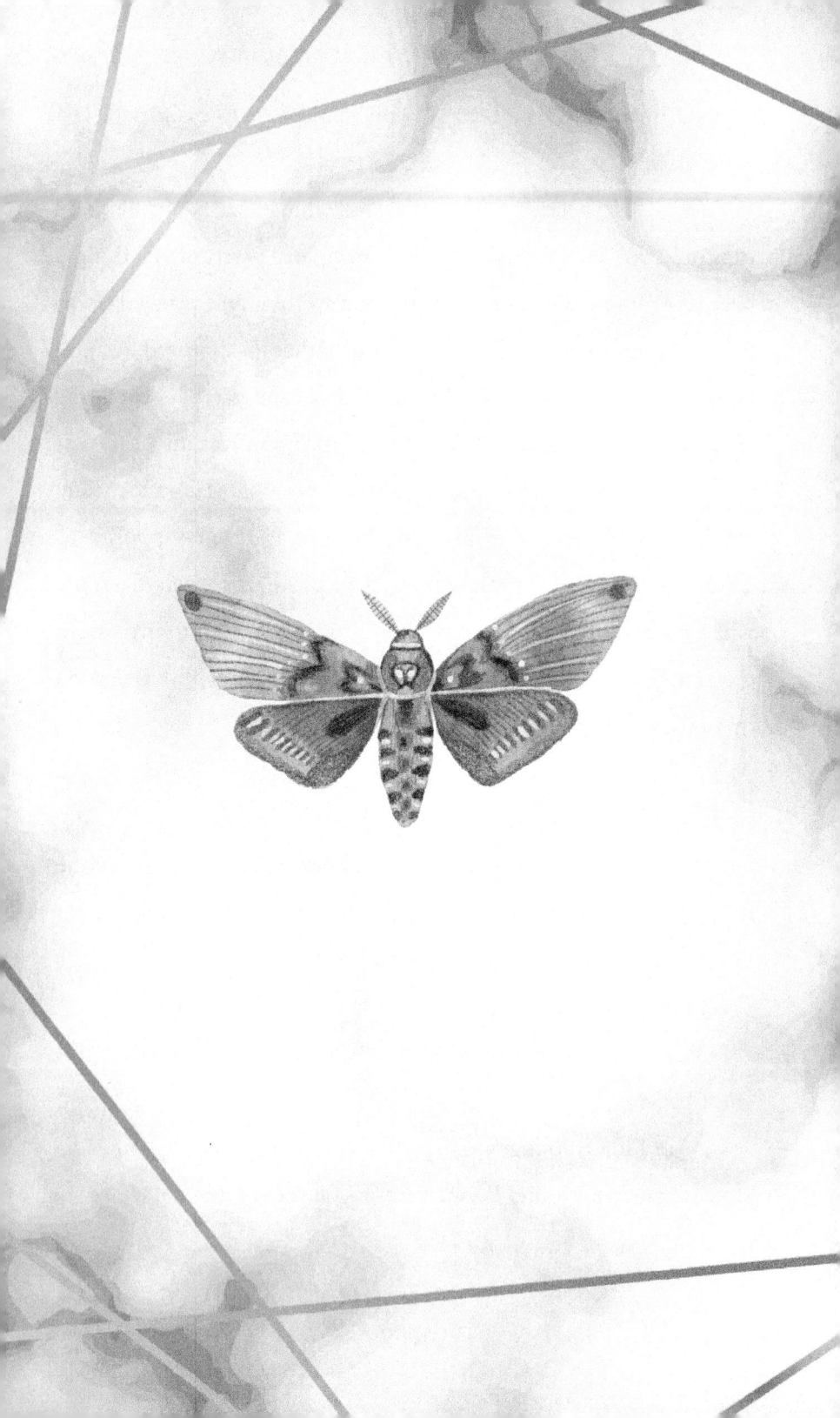

Thirty-Four

"Bennett, wait!" I chased him down the dark, glittering hallway, trying not to slip in these goddess-forsaken shoes.

"Why, Lily?" He spun around. "Why should I wait? You've already made your choice."

"My choice?" I balked. "I didn't realize I had so many options, or that I had a decision that needed to be made."

He flung his hands in the air. "Oh, come on. Like you can't tell how I feel about you?"

"I... I..." Stuttering, I struggled for something to say. Standing in my uncle's castle—the Dark King, dressed in a gown provided by my psycho father—the Light King... I was literally torn between two worlds and at a loss for words.

Alder chose this precise moment to saunter out of my room. "I'm... gonna go." He hitched a thumb toward the stairs. "I think you're right. I need to go find my father."

Bennett's nostrils flared. "Who is his father?"

"Gideon," I breathed.

"Of course he is." Bennett slammed his fist into the wall, the hard crunch of his knuckles making me flinch as blood dripped to the floor.

"Jesus. And how does this help anything?" I reached for his hand, cradling it in mine.

He shook his head, tears blurring his eyes from the pain.

"Bennett, please. Let me look at it." He uncurled his fingers, his broken knuckles bleeding into my palm. Leaning down, I placed my lips against his skin and whispered a healing spell.

Blue magic flared between our hands and fire rose in his gaze. Crushing his lips to mine, he wound his fingers in my hair.

It was my first real kiss, and as far as kisses went, I thought it was a good one.

By the time Bennett and I walked back into the dining hall, the shock of Alder's arrival had cooled to a tolerable level from what I could tell.

When his eyes met mine from across the room, I fiddled with the sleeve of my black sweater, yanking at a loose thread.

"Lily?" Gideon called out. "I hear you've already met my son." He waved me over.

Bennett huffed under his breath, but left me to go check on Sybil. I walked to the table and sat down next to Gideon. "Yes, I have. And I'm glad he found his way home."

Gideon threw an arm around Alder's shoulders and pulled him in for a fatherly hug. "Me too. I honestly can't tell you how happy it makes me to see the two of you hitting it off already. The new Dark King and the Light Queen together will unite the kingdoms as one."

"I'm sorry, what?" The last time we'd spoken, he'd confirmed my family and I would be going home as soon as the book was destroyed.

His eyes were alight with glee. "Yes! Just think about it. With our two realms united, there will never again be the threat of war."

"War?" I gasped. "I thought you said once the book was destroyed, Thadius would no longer come looking for you."

"Yes, that is true, but there has always been a tenuous relationship between the Light and Dark fae."

"You don't say." I glared at Alder, who only smiled back. I swung my gaze back to my uncle. "Gideon, I don't plan on staying here, so whatever ideas you have, they can't include me."

He shook his head earnestly. "No, Lily, you don't understand. Now that Alder has returned, there is a true heir to each of the thrones, which means you cannot leave."

Can't leave? My chest tightened and my insides began to quiver. "What do you mean? That it would be a bad idea if I went home and forsook my throne, or that since our royal blood connection has been activated, I *literally* can't leave this realm now?"

Gideon cocked his head, his dark eyes reading my face.

"The second one," Alder answered for him. "With the blood pact in place, we both have no choice but to rule."

Oh my Goddess. I jumped up from the table, stomping over to where my mom and sisters were seated on the steps at the front of the room. "Did you know about this? That I have to stay here?"

All my sisters looked up at me with tears in their eyes. "We didn't know." Mom scooped me into a hug, holding me tight. I wrapped my arms around her back, going through the motions as my brain struggled to catch up. Aster, Fern, Iris, and Daisy stood beside us, sniffling and sobbing as they all joined in.

"No!" I pulled out of their embrace, shaking my head as I ran back to Gideon. "I won't do this. You cannot make me leave my family!"

With a deep breath and sincerity pooling in his eyes, Gideon reached for me. "Lily, if there was another way, I'd let you go." He looked back at Alder. "Being apart from your family is one of the hardest things a person can endure."

I looked up at the glass ceiling and the sky beyond and tried to lose myself in the stars. My head spun, and darkness pushed in from every direction, suffocating me until I could no longer breathe. My legs buckled, but before my head hit the floor, I heard Bennett say, "Don't worry, Lily, I've got you. I'm not going anywhere."

Light hands caressed my forehead, jerking back when I opened my eyes.

"Oh, thank goodness. We were all so worried." Gretta turned and dipped something into a bowl, laying a cool, wet cloth back across my head.

I moved to sit up, realizing I was back in my assigned room.

"No, Miss Lily, lay still. You must stay here and rest."

I flung back the covers defiantly and crawled to the opposite side of the bed. "I'm sick of everyone telling me what I can and cannot do!" My head reeled the moment the poisonous words left my mouth. Gretta covered her mouth, taken aback.

I immediately felt like an ass.

"She's just trying to help, you know." Alder's voice carried in low from the corner.

Bending at the waist, I dropped my head and placed both hands on the mattress. "I know. I'm terribly sorry for snapping at you, Gretta."

The kind fairy stood and dipped her head. "I'll take my leave. You're in good hands." She bowed to us both before exiting the room.

Crawling back under the covers, I pulled them up to my chin. "So, this is really happening, isn't it?"

"Afraid so." Alder rose from the chair and stood at the end of the bed. "I'm sorry if this connection isn't what you wanted."

I met his eyes, gauging his smirk.

"Do you mean the royal blood connection we now share or something else?"

He lifted a shoulder. "Whichever one bothers you more."

"They both bother me."

"So you admit it… we *do* have a connection." He flopped down, making the mattress bounce beneath me.

"No! I mean yes…" I huffed out a frustrated breath. "I'm just saying this entire royal blood thing is a little too much to take. Then, throw in the fact that your dad thinks we should practically get married today to unite the kingdoms, and I'm freaking out!" I yanked the covers over my head. "I haven't even had a real boyfriend yet."

The bed started to shake and I risked a look to see what he was doing. "Are you seriously laughing at me right now?" I sat up and threw a pillow at his head.

Alder's face was creased in a wide smile as he fought to control his laughter. "What? I'm sorry, but after seeing you in that dress and watching you with Bennett, I just assumed—"

"Well, don't. Don't assume anything about me!" I yelled, completely embarrassed. "Now get out!"

Alder fell back onto the bed, twisting and laughing until his antlers were stuck in the sheets.

"I said, get out!" I pointed at the door.

He stood, taking the blankets with him. Untangling them from his head, he dropped them on the floor, leaving me completely exposed.

I wrapped my arms around my middle, thankful Gretta or my mom had dressed me in the nightgown I was currently wearing.

Alder's body didn't move, but his eyes greedily roamed my exposed skin.

Keeping the thin black gown in place the best I could, I leaned over the side of the bed and snagged whatever sheet or blanket I could reach and pulled it back on top of me. "Can you please leave now?" I barely whispered.

"Whatever you wish, Princess." His blazing eyes held mine as he sauntered out of the room.

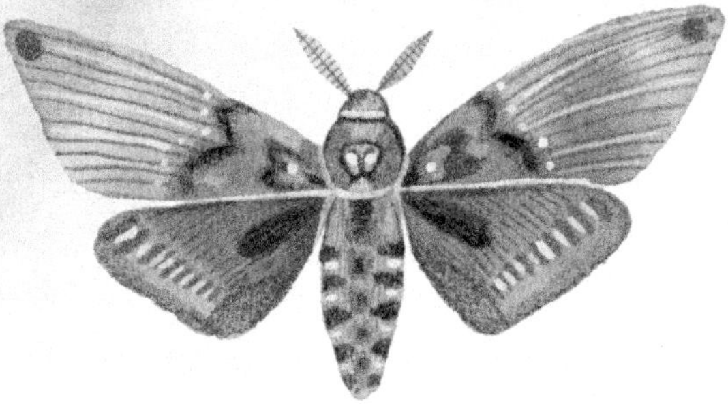

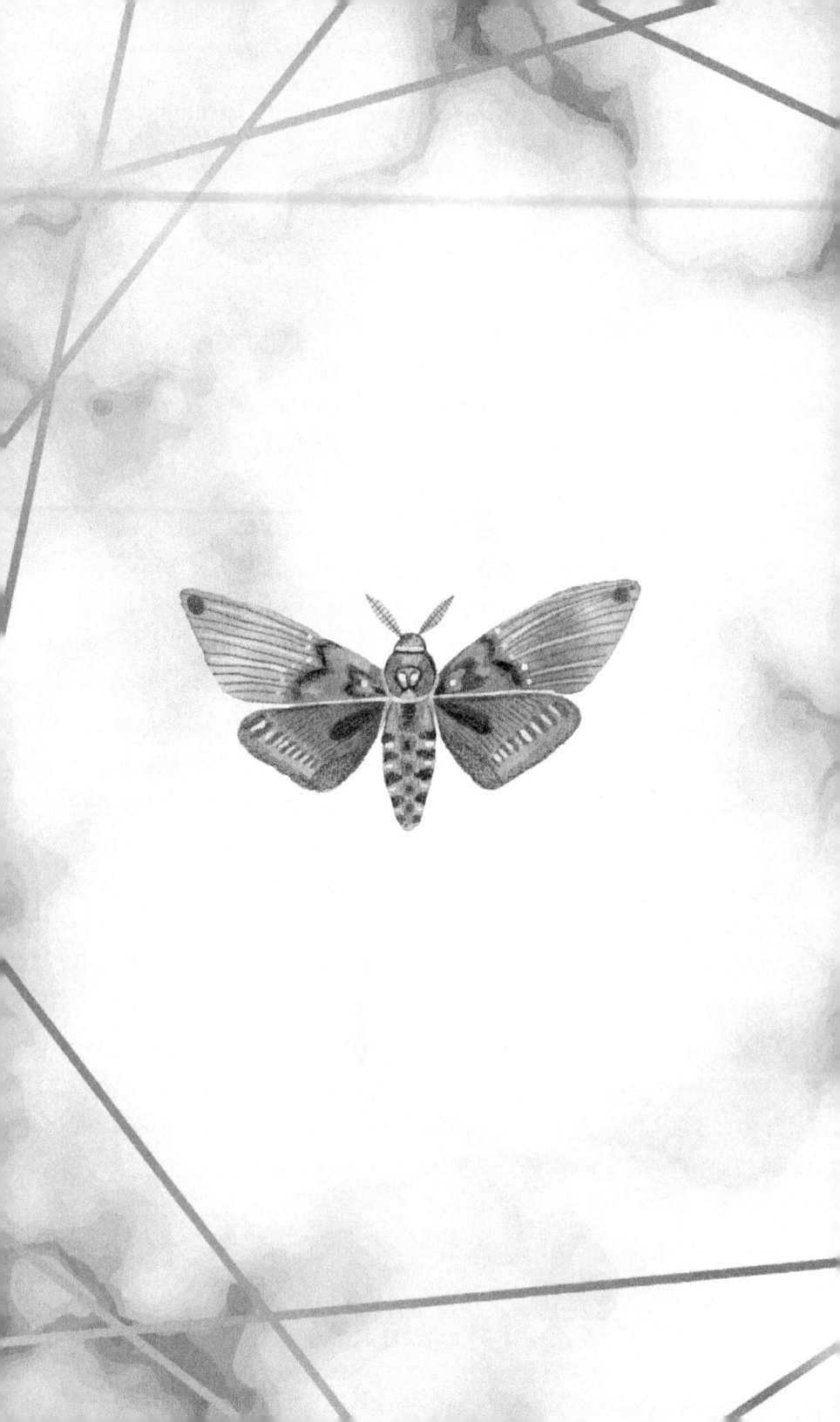

Thirty-Five

Visions of flowers, deer, and frolicking fairies plagued my dreams, tangling me in a pile of disheveled blankets as twisted as when Alder left.

Dressing for the day, I donned the same black pants and sweater I'd worn before, hoping we could actually get something done. I knew Mom and my sisters had been working on the spell to destroy the book with Sybil's help, and I figured they had to be pretty close to figuring it out by now.

A knock sounded at my door.

"Come in." I pulled my boots on just as Bennett walked inside.

"Good morning," I offered, watching his eyes roam the room until they landed on the bed and the tangled mess of blankets and sheets.

He raised a brow. "Sleep well?"

I shrugged. "Not really. Bad dreams."

He lifted his chin and smiled, probably imagining something else. "They're getting ready to serve breakfast. I didn't think you'd want to miss it." He popped a grape from the tray on my bedside table into his mouth. "Personally, I'm kind of sick of all this fruit."

I laughed, sharing the sentiment. Closing the door behind me, we walked down the hallway in silence until we reached the stairs.

"Can I ask you something?" Bennett asked.

"You just did," I teased.

"Ha, ha. I mean, can we talk about what you plan to do?"

I sighed. "I'm not sure there's anything to talk about. In case you didn't hear, it doesn't appear as if I have a choice in the matter. I can no longer leave this place."

"So, are you really going to take the throne?"

I gawked at him wide-eyed. "Not sure how to do that, seeing as my psycho father is still holding onto the Light Kingdom with a white-knuckled grip."

Bennett stiffened at the mention of my father, and I didn't blame him. I froze up every time I thought about what he'd done.

I shrugged. "I guess I'll just stay here until Gideon figures out how we can stop him for good."

We entered the dining hall and my mouth started to salivate. Breakfast meats, croissants, and pastries littered the table, accompanied by more fruit and multiple carafes full of different kinds of juice.

"This looks and smells delicious." I scanned the room for Gretta, knowing she was probably behind the elaborate spread.

"Please, come sit with me." Gideon motioned to the chair on his left, which was placed directly between him and his son. Mom, Sybil, and my sisters occupied the other seats.

"Morning," Alder offered as I slid into the chair, an onery smirk pulling at his lips.

"Good morning," I replied flatly while keeping my eyes plastered directly on the pastries in front of me.

"Camellia and I believe we'll be ready to destroy the book soon," Sybil piped in. "Maybe in another day or so."

Gideon nodded, scooping more of his breakfast onto his fork. "And what about the two of you? Are you both resolved to the roles you now play?" He looked at Alder and then me, but all I could do was stare straight ahead, meeting Bennett's eyes from across the table.

"I'll take that as a no. But it's not something either of you can ignore." Gideon took a swig of juice, its bright pink color reminding me of strawberry milk. "Meet me in my study at ten this morning. There's much we need to discuss."

I caught Alder's nod in my periphery and Bennett's frown from straight ahead. Mom and Sybil continued to converse in hushed tones, while my sisters laughed and marveled at the beauties and wonders of the fairy realm. "If you'll excuse me, I'm no longer hungry." I stood from the table and rushed from the room, wishing I was as invisible as I felt.

"Lily, wait!" Alder caught up with me halfway down the hall, his hand gently taking my arm. "Please, I know you're upset, but can we go for a walk?"

The pressure that had been building inside burst from my lips. "How do you know I'm upset? You don't know me at all!"

"Well, the fact that you just stomped out of the room without eating anything, even though I know you're practically starving, kind of gave it away." His hand moved down my arm until his fingers entwined with mine. "Come on, Lily. Let me show you my world."

I took a deep breath and followed Alder out of the castle, leaving everyone else behind. A pale pink tinge of morning light blanketed the Dark Kingdom, bringing a subdued peacefulness I never imagined here. Fantastical flowers, trees, and gardens of all shapes and sizes encircled the Dark castle, lending their lush softness to an otherwise hardened place.

Gray buildings blended in with the shadows, their surfaces twinkling with some type of embedded mica.

"I grew up running along all these streets." Alder's voice held a wistful quality as we wove our way between an outdoor market that was being set up by an elderly pair.

The fairies here had darker wings, but they were just as beautiful and sparkled with an iridescent glow. "Did you have any friends?" I asked cautiously, not sure how he'd react to such a personal question.

"I did… from what I remember. Mom used to bring me down to the public school so we could play together." He hung his head. "I was six when she was killed and I was taken, so I don't remember much beyond that."

My blood boiled as I looked around at all the friendly faces starting their day. Hardworking couples selling their wares, young men offering their services to help in any way they could, girls cooking or tending to a variety of animals that didn't even exist in my world. My father had ruined so many lives with his grief and greed, and my heart ached for each and every one. Gideon lost his wife and son. Alder, his mother and father. But me…

What had *I* really lost? A kingdom I didn't want and a life I never knew to miss?

I shook my head, feeling petty and sorry for myself. "I'm so sorry for all my father's done." I wiped a tear from my cheek, understanding why Gideon was so desperate for peace. "Thank you for showing me around today."

Alder took my hand again. "You're welcome, Lily. But we're not done yet. I have a surprise for you."

Nearing the end of the street, a path led away from town and into the forest beyond.

"Where are we going?" I asked nervously.

His eyes gleamed in the early morning light. "There's something I want to show you that only a few people know exist."

I met his gaze, and the childlike wonder I found sent my heart racing. "Okay, let's go."

Hiking the path for another mile or so, I took in all the wonders of the woods. Glowing flowers with pulsing stems, insects and toads the likes I'd never seen. And all the while, Alder looking more at home in the forest with each step he took. *The King of Woods.*

We dipped under a canopy of blue-leafed trees, their foliage as vibrant as the wings of a Morphinea.

Alder turned to me, his eyes sparkling. "Welcome to Devonshire." He lifted a low-hanging branch out of the way, revealing the most pristine lake I'd ever seen. Along its shores stood dozens of pure-white unicorns, their horns sparkling with an intense silver light.

"Oh my Goddess, unicorns actually exist?" I shuffled forward as softly as I could, hoping not to spook the ethereal creatures with my presence.

"Yes. But here, they're called Moonbiens."

I laughed at the playfulness of it all and felt lighter than I had in days. "Thank you for bringing me here."

"You're welcome." He walked us closer to the lake's edge, sitting down along its shore. "My mother used to bring me here. It was the only place I ever saw her shift and run free."

I looked up, shocked. "Was she not allowed to do so in the castle?"

"Oh, no. It was nothing like that. My father loved her completely and never denied her true nature. Devonshire is just where she felt most at peace with that side of herself, I think."

I looked out over the lake, its still waters a soothing balm to my soul. "I can certainly understand that." I turned and met Alder's piercing gaze, and another personal question popped into my head. "Are you able to shift?"

He huffed out a laugh. "No. Both of your parents would need to be shifters to be able to do that."

"Oh. Okay, sorry. There's so much I don't understand about your world."

He reached for my hand again. "It's our world now."

Thirty-Six

Seated in the Dark King's study by ten and on time, I dodged Alder's continual smile by looking at anything and everything that caught my eye around the room. The deep green color that Gideon seemed to favor throughout his castle colored the walls here as well, and with the large oak desk set squarely in the middle, it was a masculine but cozy space with a fire blazing in the oversized hearth.

"I understand the recent chain of events has been overwhelming for you, Lily," Gideon began, "but it's my hope you'll come to find your *true* realm to be a place of happiness and peace—once you unite our kingdoms, of course."

I barked out a sarcastic laugh. "Of course."

"Alder. My son," Gideon continued. "I cannot tell you how happy it makes me that we've finally been reunited. Being separated from you and your mother was the most painful thing I've ever experienced." He shook his head sadly. "I'm sorry I wasn't here to stop what happened to either of you."

I lowered my head and clenched my hands in my lap to keep from crying. It was my fault Gideon wasn't here for his family when they needed him most. My fault Alder was ripped away from the once joyful life he knew. "I'm sorry." The words fell from my lips in a whisper, but the sound of them weighed heavily upon my heart.

"No. Don't do that." Alder was at my side in two strides, kneeling next to my chair. "Look at me." With a feather light touch, he turned my chin to face him. "None of this is your fault. You were a baby when your father decided to ruin all our lives with his crazed idea. And while I blamed my father for a long time, I realize it wasn't his fault either. He did the right thing in saving you."

I wiped my eyes as Gideon strode around his desk, placing his hands on both our shoulders. "Our kingdoms will be in good hands with the two of you, I have no doubt. Now, why don't we return to the dining hall so Lily can finish her breakfast? Your mother, sisters, and Sybil are still there, finalizing the spell to destroy the book."

My stomach clenched, realizing the one name he didn't mention… Bennett. "I need to return to my room first, but I'll meet you both there in just a bit."

Alder stood and offered me his hand, helping me from my chair. I met his warm gaze and tried to let the idea of the two of us together sink in, even as I headed off to find my friend.

Hurrying down the hall toward our rooms, I planned to ask Bennett to stay here in this realm with me while I navigated through everything coming my way. It might be hard on us both, but I'd rather have him here, close to me, than gone completely and returned home.

But isn't that selfish? I chastised myself, unsure what the right thing to do was. I'd already spoken to my family and knew they'd be returning home to our shop as soon as this was over. We'd talked and cried until all our tears ran dry, but in the end, I knew it was the right thing for them to do. And whether Alder and I were truly together, I did hope to unite the realms so my family could be free to return whenever they wanted through the portal at our shop. *Maybe that's what I should offer to Bennett as well.*

Easing up to Bennett's door, I gave it a light knock.

"Coming." His voice was steady, but it echoed from the room, reminding me he was all alone. He opened the door and looked at me quizzically.

"Hi! Can I come in?" I smiled, hoping what I had to say would brighten his day.

"Actually, do you mind if we go for a walk?" There was a bite to his response that I didn't miss.

"Sure."

He closed the door to his assigned bedroom and started down the hall without another word.

I took a deep breath. "So, you asked me before what I was going to do. And while the situation remains the same… that I really don't have a choice, I wanted you to know that I think there could be some benefits from me taking the throne… eventually," I rushed to add. "And, if you're okay with it, I'd really like you to stay here with me and help me navigate it all."

His head popped up, meeting my gaze with a wide grin. "I…" he stammered.

Just then, a crash sounded from the dining hall. We raced the rest of the way to the door. As Bennett and I rounded the corner, we watched in horror as a battalion of Light soldiers crashed through the glass ceiling, dropping into the heart of Gideon's operation just like his Dark warriors had done at the Thadias's ball.

"Get down!" Alder called from the other side of the room.

Bennett tried to pull me down the hall, but I was seized by blind fear. "No! I have to help my family! I can't leave them alone!"

Metal swords clanged and shouts erupted as the Dark realm warriors stormed down the hall, running to protect their King, but with a burst of magic, the door slammed shut before they could reach him.

Banging my fists against the carved wood, I screamed for the only family I'd ever known. "Mom, I love you! I love you all! Please don't die!"

Magic welled inside me, fighting to burst free, but it wasn't my witch magic I needed now. Only my fae magic could save us all.

"Lily, you must embrace who you are!" Bennett shouted above the chaos.

Fueled by an innate rightness, I screamed to the heavens and accepted my fate. "My name is Lily, daughter of Genevieve, and I am your rightful Queen!"

Lightning streaked the sky beyond the shattered glass ceiling, backlighting the clouds with sharp bursts of purple and blue. Energy flowed from the heavens and down into my outstretched arms as the rest of my suppressed magic burst free from its bindings. Blasting the doors open, the Dark warriors and I rushed into the dining hall to assess the scene.

Gideon and my father stood in the middle of the room, facing off as Alder dispatched the last of the invading guards with a swipe of his sword. Blood splatters covered his face, a true Dark warrior for all to see.

"Mom!" I raced to my mother and sisters where they huddled on the steps, protected behind Gideon's outstretched arms.

The Dark King's face was grim as he faced down his opponent. "It's over, Brother. Your plotting is at an end."

"You were never my brother!" Thadius shouted, spittle flying from his lips.

Gideon's eyes turned sad. "You were always family to me."

Thadius rushed forward with a crazed look in his eye, bringing his sword level with Gideon's chest.

"No!" I threw out another blast of magic, but it was too late.

Swords clanged as Gideon and Thadius fought like enemies instead of brothers, screaming of grief and betrayal as magic flooded the room. Blinded by the warring power of the Dark and Light Kings, we all covered our eyes until a suffocating silence fell across the room.

With final gasps of sorrow and pain, the two Kings fell to the floor, run through the heart by each other's blades.

"Oh, Goddess, no!" My mom ran to Gideon's side and cradled his head in her lap. "Sybil, help me!" she pleaded.

The high priestess of the Acrucian Coven dropped to her knees and placed her hands on Gideon's chest, but I could tell by the forlorn look in her eyes that there was nothing she could do. "He's gone, Camellia."

My mom sobbed, her tears dropping into the Dark King's hair. With a start, I realized who had fathered my other sisters.

I searched for Alder and found him in the corner sitting on the floor. Walking to him with wooden steps, I lowered myself onto the dark onyx tile, letting its absence of light absorb the sorrow from my soul. "I'm so sorry, Alder."

He sniffed and wiped the blood from his cheeks. "It's not your fault."

Tears ran down my face as the pain in his voice reached my ears. "Maybe not, but you just got him back."

His warm eyes met mine. A somber moment passed, then— "I never expected to see him again, so in a way, I should thank you for giving us the little time we got back."

A wretched cry burst from my chest and I threw myself into Alder's waiting arms. "I'm so sorry." He cradled my head and back, holding me close as we both shook with grief.

"Lily?" Mom's soft voice pulled at my heart. "Honey, we still need to get rid of the book in order to stop the crone from seeking you out."

I looked up, ready to destroy it here and now. Shoving to my feet, I started across the room, but Mom's gentle voice once again pulled me back to reality. "Lily. It must be done right, in the forest where it was first created."

I froze and stared at my sisters, who continued to protect the book. Its cracked bindings and worn leather face showed its true nature, including the blood and bone the crone used to bind all the changelings' magic she'd created over the years.

"Then we head to the forest tonight," I proclaimed, refusing to live in fear a minute longer.

Flames flared in the glowing forest of the Light fae. Now that I'd claimed my birthright, I could pass between the realms unimpeded. My sisters stood in a circle around the fire, waiting for my signal. Mom and Sybil had completed the spell earlier today, before our world fell apart. And after burying Gideon, there was just one thing left to do.

I glanced at the portal in the center of the tree, smiling as Alder stood with his arms crossed before it.

"Lily, are you ready?" Bennett asked, placing his hand on the small of my back.

I turned to him, meeting his kind eyes and thinking back to all we'd endured together. He'd been there for me since stumbling across the threshold of our shop, all while discovering he wasn't who he seemed. I reached for his hands, pulling him away from the crowd. "I can't believe we started all this as a way to save you, but in the end, it was *you* who saved *me*."

He stiffened at my words, pulling away. "No, Lily. You saved yourself. And I want you to remember that no matter what happens next, I'm so glad to have met you and that you got to see the real me."

I frowned, concerned by his statement. "What do you mean? Have you decided to leave?" I looked back at my mom and sisters, knowing they'd have to return home to reopen our shop soon, but heartbroken if I had to lose Bennett, too. "No. You can't leave me! You have to stay." My voice shook and tears welled in my eyes.

Bennett walked back to the circle, picking the ancient book off the ground. "I'll always be with you, Lily. Please remember that." He tossed something into the fire and the flames shot into the sky.

The portal flared with a flash, and my mom, sisters, and Sybil screamed.

I ran forward with outstretched hands, trying to grab them before they were sucked inside. "No!" I wasn't ready to lose them yet.

Alder jumped away from the tree as the portal exploded, chasing Bennett into the forest as he escaped with the crone's precious book clutched in his duplicitous hands.

I raised my arms, welcoming the distant words now reverberating inside my head. Standing in the ancient forest of my ancestors, their voices echoed from the place beyond, revealing

Bennett's truth to me.

He was the son of a Light fae witch, tasked with retrieving the crone's book from our world to buy favor for their outcast clan.

He'd known all along who he was and where he was from.

My heart clenched in my chest. I had so many questions, but it was too late.

I watched as Bennett fled into the woods with the book in hand, shattered by all the broken promises he'd made. It was my fault we just lost the one thing that could keep us safe. The one thing his clan had always coveted. The witch's handbook to magic and mayhem was now theirs and there was nothing I could do to stop it.

I wandered through the gloomy forest alone and bereft, casting my desires into the starlit sky.

"Lily, where are you?" Alder's voice pierced the night, dropping me to my knees—the guilt and sorrow too much to bear.

"I'm here." I tried to shout, but the words barely floated past my lips.

Maybe I didn't want to be found. Maybe I should just lie down and let the forest take me.

Flattening myself atop the dense blanket of cold leaves, I stared through the circle of trees to the cosmos beyond. I had never been scared to die, but wondered now if it would hurt. I wondered now if I would join my ancestors in the place beyond, or if I'd be cast somewhere else due to my failures.

I closed my eyes and wondered now if dying from a broken heart would make it easier or worse.

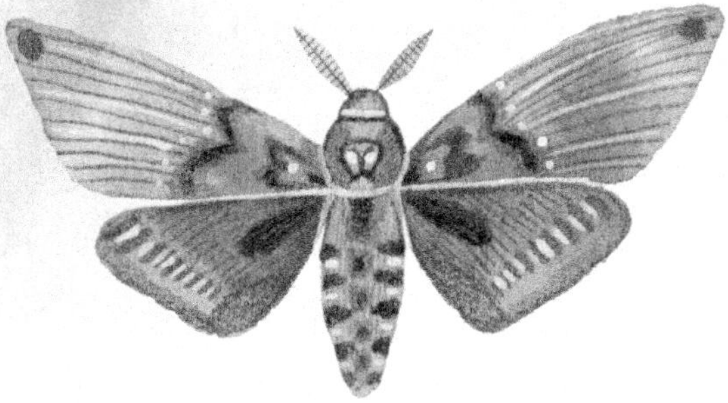

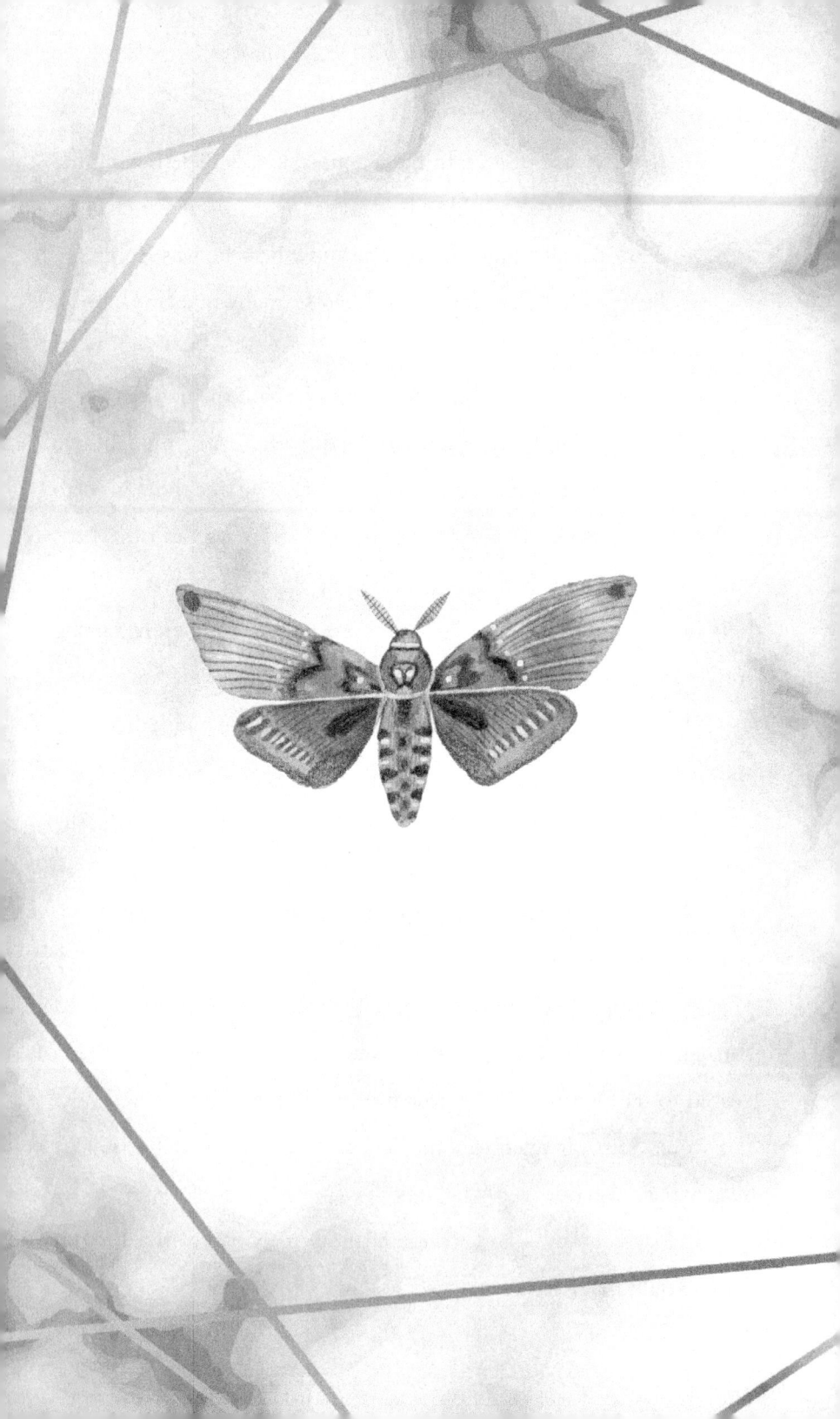

Continue reading for Lily and Alder's

next adventure...

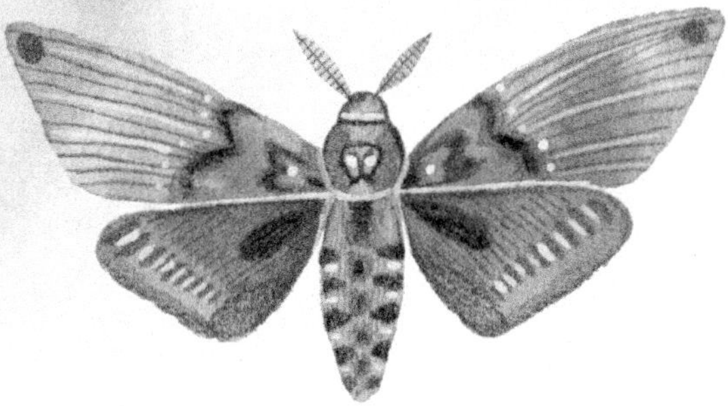

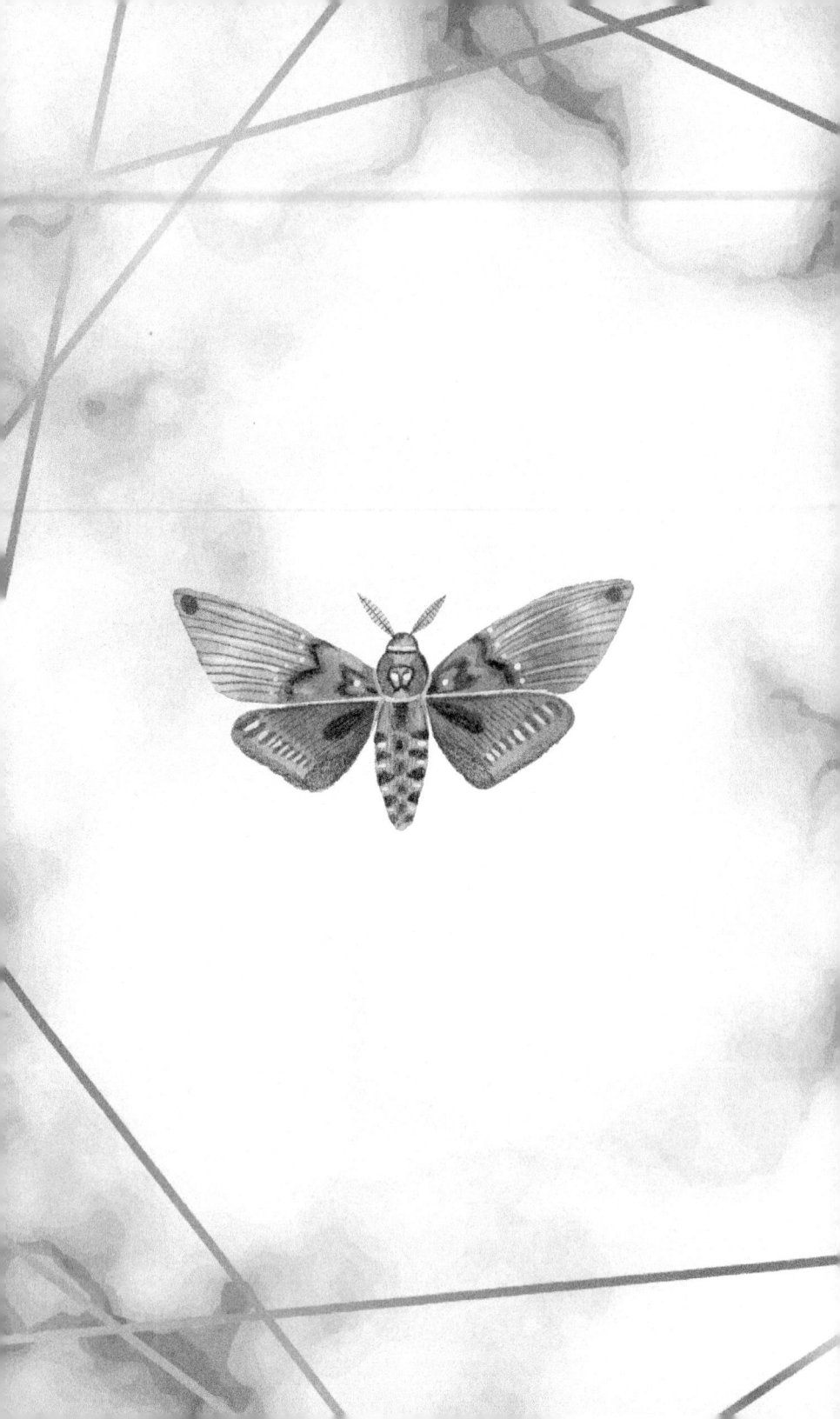

THE FAIRY HANDBOOK TO SPELLS AND SALVATION

(Book 2 in the Stolen Spells Series)

by

Tish Thawer

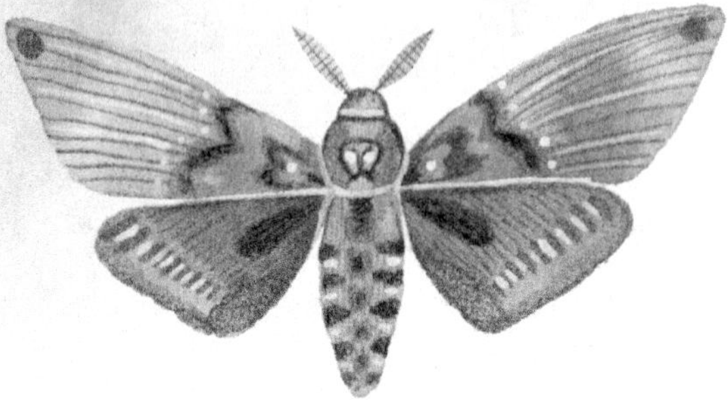

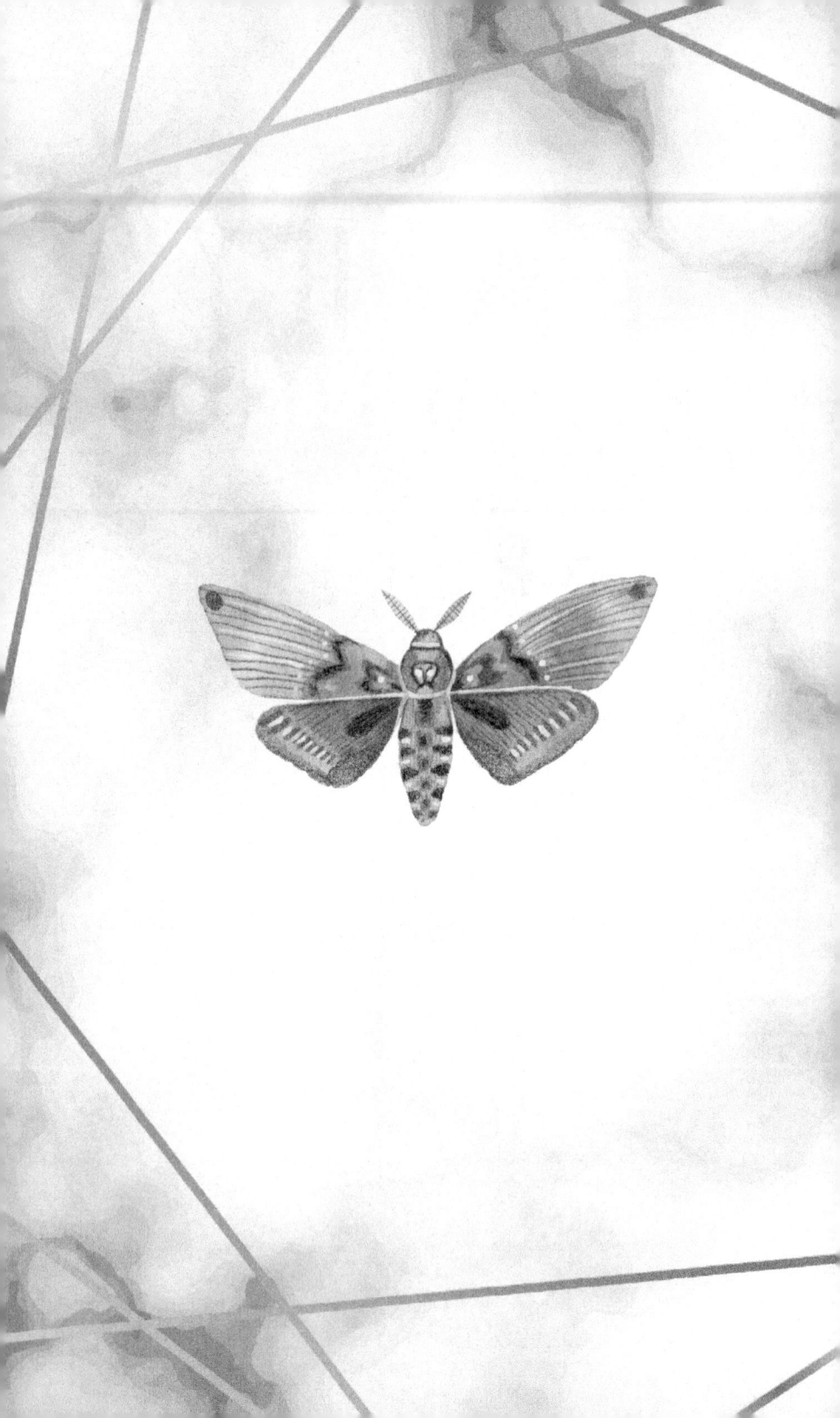

One

"All hail, Lily of Ferindale! Your true and rightful Queen!" I forced a smile onto my face, going through the motions like we both agreed to do.

"It's almost over; just wave." Alder's hand on my waist was the only thing holding me in place.

I waved to the boisterous crowd of fairies below, grateful for their cheers. Three months ago, our fathers killed one another in the castle of the Dark realm—and afterward, Bennett escaped with the crone's magical book. Things could have taken a very different turn, but thankfully, both our peoples were happy to accept me and Alder as their new King and Queen.

Now, officially crowned, we could begin merging our two realms into one… a harmonious Light and Dark Kingdom, just as Gideon envisioned.

"Let's get you inside." Alder guided me off the balcony and back into my glittering stateroom.

It took countless days to learn the layout of the Light castle, once we verified the crone was gone. She'd disappeared just like Bennett, and we hadn't been able to track either of them down.

I flopped down onto the white leather couch, pushing the ridiculous amount of tulle that comprised my skirt out of the way.

"Have you received word from any of the search parties?" I asked hopefully.

Alder bent down and eased the blister-inducing shoes from my feet. "Not yet, but I expect them to return in the next few days."

I furrowed my brows, irritated. "And what are we supposed to do until then?" I quickly learned I wasn't cut out for all the meetings and events that came with being Queen.

Alder's hand slid up my leg, caressing my calf with gentle strokes. "I could think of a few things to pass the time."

I laughed, true joy bursting from my lips.

I couldn't thank the goddess enough for bringing Alder into my life. After he captured me, took me to prison, then saved me from my psychotic father and explained who he really was, we'd been together ever since—him the leader of the Dark fae, and me the rightful Queen of the Light. But those labels didn't matter anymore, or they wouldn't soon enough.

It was Gideon, the father of Alder and my half-sisters, who wanted us to unite the realms.

To honor his sacrifice, that was exactly what we planned to do.

Acknowledgments

To my husband: My cheerleader. My hero. My soul mate... I love you never feels like enough.

To my children: Always follow your heart, no matter how rough the road is along the way. You are beautiful and brilliant, and capable of wonderous things! I love you with all my heart.

To Molly Phipps: Thank you for designing the perfect cover to wrap my story in! I'm so excited to be working with you on this duology, and hopefully many more projects in the future.

To my editor, Stacy Sanford: Thank you for your amazing professionalism and your perfect suggestions. This book wouldn't be as good without you.

To Cortney, Kristie, Belinda, Stacey, and Sharon: Thank you for reading *TWHMM* before publication and providing your feedback and editorial reviews. I'm so grateful to have such amazing friends in this industry. You are all the best!

And finally, to my readers, old and new: Thank you for following me down the primrose path and into another adventure. I can't wait to embark on our next one together!

About the Author

#1 Bestseller in Historical Fiction
Top 100 Bestselling in Paid Kindle Store
Best Cover Award Winner
Readers' Choice Award Winner
Best Sci-fi Fantasy Novel Winner (x2)

Author Tish Thawer writes young adult fantasy and paranormal fiction for all ages. From her first paranormal cartoon, *Isis*, to the *Twilight* phenomenon, myth, magic, and superpowers have always held a special place in her heart. Best known for her *Witches of BlackBrook* series, Tish's detailed world-building and magic-laced stories have been compared to Nora Roberts, Sam Cheever, and Charlaine Harris. Tish's books have been featured in *British Glamour* and *Elle* magazines. Tish has worked as a computer consultant, photographer, and graphic designer and has bylines as a columnist for Gliterary Girl media, *RT* magazine, and *Literary Lunes* magazine. She currently resides in Missouri with her husband and three wonderful children, and operates Amber Leaf Designs, an online custom swag retail store, and Amber Leaf Farms, a lavender and flower farm that opened in 2022.

You can find out more about Tish and all her titles by visiting: www.tishthawer.com

<u>Connect with Tish Thawer Online:</u>
Instagram: @tishthawer
Facebook: www.facebook.com/AuthorTishThawer
Twitter: @tishthawer
Pinterest: www.pinterest.com/tishthawer/

If you'd like an email when each new book releases, please sign up for my mailing list. Emails only go out about once per month and your information is closely guarded.
http://www.tishthawer.com/subscribe.html

Also, to get an email for new releases, book updates, and special sales, follow me on BookBub and Goodreads at the links below:
www.bookbub.com/authors/tish-thawer
https://www.goodreads.com/tishthawer

Again, thank you for reading. If you'd like to stay connected and hang out for more magical adventures, you can join my private reader group here:
https://www.facebook.com/groups/TishThawersBookCoven

Blessed be,
~ Tish

Also by Tish Thawer

Stolen Spells
The Witch Handbook to Magic and Mayhem - Book 1
The Fairy Handbook to Spells and Salvation - Book 2

The Witches of BlackBrook
The Witches of BlackBrook - Book 1
The Daughters of Maine - Book 2
The Sisters of Salem – Book 3
Lost in Time – (A Legends of Havenwood Falls novella, and a Witches of BlackBrook side-story)

The Women of Purgatory
Raven's Breath - Book 1
Dark Abigail - Book 2
Holli's Hellfire – Book 3
The Women of Purgatory: The Complete Series bundle

The TS901 Chronicles
TS901: Anomaly – Book 1
TS901: Dominion – Book 2
TS901: Evolution – Book 3
The TS901 Chronicles – Complete Set

Havenwood Falls Shared World
Lost in Time – (A Legends of Havenwood Falls novella, and a Witches of BlackBrook side-story)
Sun & Moon Academy – Book 1: Fall Semester
Sun & Moon Academy – Book 2: Spring Semester
Havenwood Falls Sunset Anthology

The Rose Trilogy
Scent of a White Rose - Book 1
Roses & Thorns - Book 1.5
Blood of a Red Rose - Book 2
Death of a Black Rose - Book 3
The Rose Trilogy – 10th Anniversary Edition

The Ovialell Series
Aradia Awakens - Book 1
Dark Seeds - Novella (Book 1.5)
Prophecy's Child - Companion
The Rise of Rae - Companion
Shay and the Box of Nye - Companion
Behind the Veil - Omnibus

Stand-Alones
Weaver
Guiding Gaia
Handler
Moon Kissed
Dance With Me
Magical Journal & Planner (non-fiction)
Found & Foraged (non-fiction)

Anthologies
The Monster Ball: Year 3
Fairy Tale Confessions
Losing It: A Collection of V-Cards
Christmas Lites II

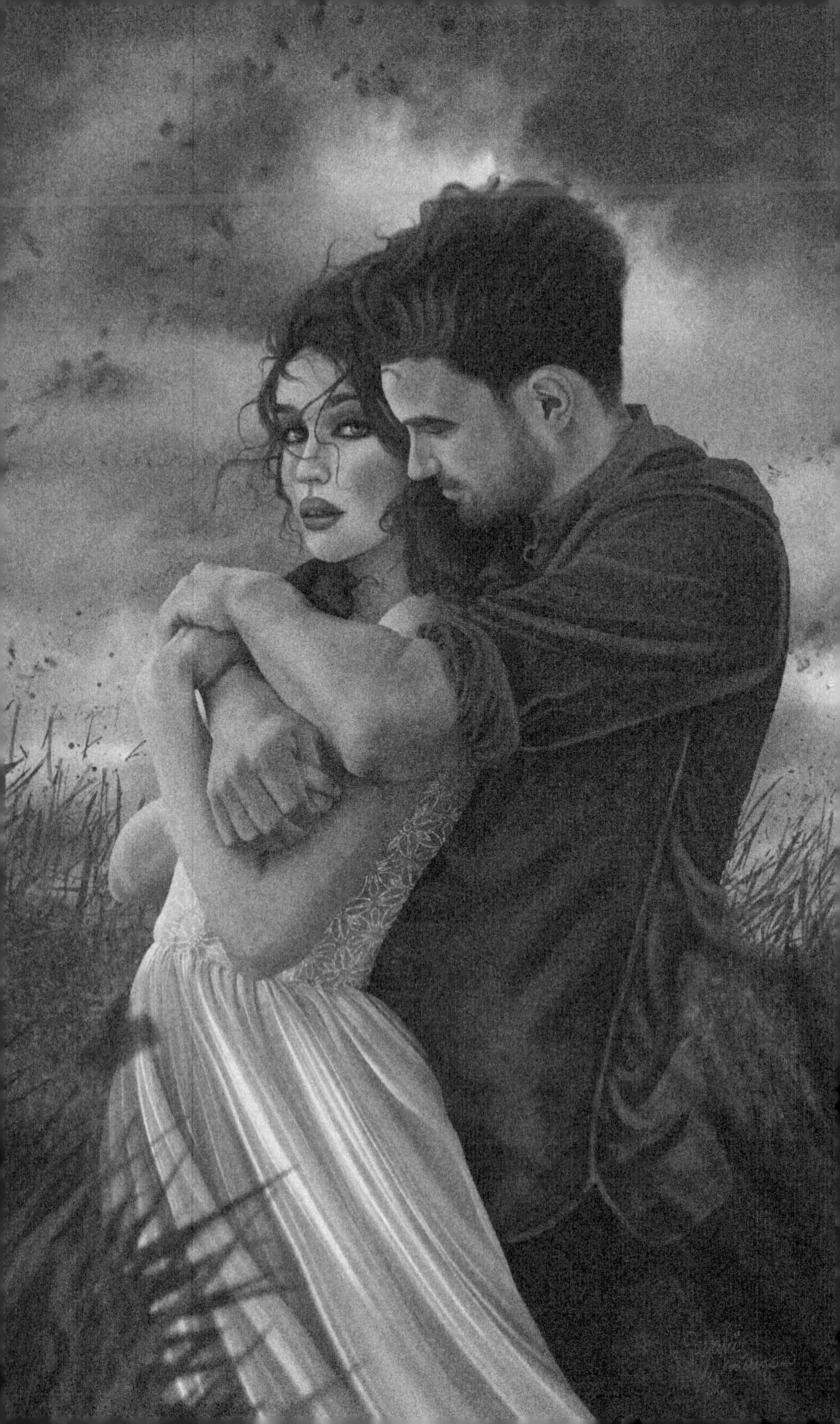

For another adventure
please enjoy this excerpt from *Weaver*

He walked out of my dream, identifying himself only as the Weaver. In a black cloak, with eyes like stars, there was a shimmer to the way he moved. He was beautiful.
Ethereal… and I was going to make him mine.

***

Alone for most of her life, Milly is determined to make the man of her dreams a reality. Using her hereditary magic, she sets out on a lifelong quest, entering a world of shadows and secrets. But little does she know, to possess his heart, she'll have to give away her own… for the only way to love a Dream Weaver is to become his Queen of Nightmares.

***

The choice between love and magic is a dangerous thing.

Prologue

Roarke – Colorado, 1847

I tilted my head to the sky, lifting a hand to block out the blinding light. A torrent of shooting stars streaked across the black expanse, filling it with cosmic rays, practically turning night to day.

"My son, it's you. You've been chosen." My father clapped me on the shoulder.

I looked to my brother, his head hanging in disappointment. The stars were so bright and unnatural. I couldn't deny my father's claim.

"Tonight, as soon as you fall asleep, you'll travel to the gate and receive your powers." He continued.

"What happens after that?" I asked, my voice cracking and unsure.

"Then you'll claim your destiny as the next Weaver."

I shook my head. I spent my entire life waiting for this moment, but now that it was here, I wasn't sure I was ready—wasn't sure I'd *ever* be ready.

I stared at my father as my brother returned to our cabin, my mother's cries spilling out the open door. We both knew what this meant. My father's time as the Weaver was over, and my family would be forced to leave. For only one Weaver could remain hidden here at a time.

"Is there no way you can stay?" My voice hitched.

He met my eyes with tears in his own. "You know we can't. You're a grown man now, and as soon as you receive your powers, your soul will begin searching for your queen." He reached out and pulled me into a hug. "I'm not going to lie, son. It can be a long and lonely endeavor. But promise me you'll never give up hope."

I tightened my hold, not ready to let go.

"I promise."

Milly - Rhode Island, 2016

A blazing sun scorched my skin, baking me in its heat along with the wilted tomatoes dried on the vine. "Mama, what should I do with these?" I yanked the dead plants from the dirt, grasping one in each gloved hand.

"Toss them into the compost. Their demise will soon help provide life for another." She turned to me, smiling and with love in her eyes. "You're doing so well, Milly. The earth has truly responded to your magic this year."

I held my head high, proud to receive my mother's praise as I looked out across the blooming beds of our gardens.

At thirteen, our hereditary magic now flowed through my veins. And thanks to my mother's guidance, I knew this was my calling too. Our souls were connected to this land, and my magic grew stronger with each and every season.

"*Milly...*" Mother whispered, her voice sounding wrong.

I turned in time to watch her fall.

"Mama!" I raced to her side and grabbed her hand. "Mama, what's wrong?"

"My darling girl. I've taught you everything you need to know. And now it's time for you to be brave. Promise me you'll be brave."

Tears streamed down my cheeks, and I knew this was it. Mama was finally leaving me. After falling sick over the past few years, she made it her mission to teach me all she could about our magic and how to make a living off our land, but I prayed this day would never come.

"Milly, promise me you'll continue your education, and more than anything, promise me you'll follow your heart."

Mama's eyes closed, and something inside me broke. The plants and flowers surrounding us wilted alongside my pain.

"I promise."

One

Present day…

Darkness surrounded me as I opened my eyes, its emptiness clinging to me like a second skin. A shiver rattled my bones as my feet hit the cold planks of my cottage's hardwood floor. Smoothing my nightgown straight, I walked to my altar, ready for my next attempt.

It had been two days since my last dream, and all I could remember was that I didn't want it to end. I tried to force myself back to sleep—back to *him*. Dark, sparkling eyes from beneath his hood were all I could remember before being ripped awake without warning. Now I was desperate to get back. There was something about him I needed to learn. Something magical calling to my witch's soul.

My last batch of skullcap, rosemary, and mugwort sat cold in my mortar. This time, an added pinch of passionflower should stop my mental chatter. I needed to focus if I was going to make this work.

Three times before, I'd seen him shimmering in the distance, watching me from afar. The most recent dream I recalled was like a fairy tale. With glistening castles and lush forests surrounding me, it was full of mythical creatures who let me frolic alongside them without a care in the world. I spotted him standing behind a stone outbuilding, staring and monitoring my every move.

The dream before that took place in a desert where I lived a fabulous life as the close friend of an important sheik. There he'd been huddled behind a spice cart in the market, but I could still feel his eyes upon me.

Regardless of my dream's location, my watcher was always there. Unfortunately, my last dream had been yanked away, leaving me with a complete void. Something had changed, and I was determined to find out what.

The cold feel of my pestle in hand was a welcome shock to my system. A signal to my body we were about to begin. Grinding herbs was a ritual I cherished.

"Take care now, Milly. Too harsh a stroke and you'll bruise the lavender."

I smiled at the memory.

For six years now, I'd tended the gardens of our humble cottage alone, honing my craft in the Arcadia Forest outside of West Greenwich, Rhode Island. Mother always said it came naturally to me.

Squinting against the dim morning light, I reached above my head and pinched off a sprig of dried passionflower, adding it to my mortar. Now nineteen, book-smart, and full of Mama's wisdom, I rolled my wrist as she taught me, grinding the herbs in a soft motion until the sharp fragrance filled the air.

It was ready.

After setting the kettle on the burner, I bound three pinches of the herbal concoction into a small square of cheesecloth and dropped it in. Once steeped, the elixir should work right away. Within minutes, I'd be back asleep.

Busying myself while the water boiled, I combed my dark-auburn hair straight, then braided it into two plaits and wrapped them into a bun again. Closing my eyes, I could almost see him. *Almost.*

He moved like a wisp of fog through my dreams, seeping in and out of my mind and settling between the cracks of my heart. The dark hood of his cloak was always in place, concealing his features from my view, and only once had I seen his eyes. Like a galaxy of stars contained in a marble, they shimmered from beneath his hood. I held his silver gaze, my magic rising. Then all was lost. The connection slammed shut, jerking me awake as if somehow he kicked me out of my own dream.

But tonight I had a plan.

Instead of experiencing my dream while he waited on the sidelines, I was going to seek him out. Find out if he was real or just a figment of my imagination. I'd had many book boyfriends over the years, but this was different—as if the man of my dreams could somehow be real. And if he was, I wanted to talk to him, ask him questions, and find out exactly who he was. I wanted to know why he continued to appear in my dreams. And, more importantly, how he managed to leave a lasting mark upon my soul. But most of all, I wanted to know what he was about to say the last time we were together, before I'd been ripped away.

I smiled as the kettle whistled. Tonight, it would be me who was stalking him.

Steam swirled around my face as I sipped from the cup. The sharp taste of skullcap, mugwort, and rosemary was still present, softened only by the addition of the passionflower petals. This was the first time I'd used this combination, but I was confident it was going to work. The only concern was how well. Getting lost in a dreamscape could be a dangerous thing.

Raising the carved-wood cup to my lips, I drank and then set my intention.

Lucid dreaming come to me. Find the one that I do seek. Grant me control in this way. Bring me to him on this day.

I relaxed my head into the feather pillow, readying myself for our next encounter.

A bloodred sun blazed behind my closed eyes, my outstretched arms and fingers floating on the surface of the cool water below. A bright blue sky and green leaves welcomed me, mocking the colors of my mismatched eyes. I rose from the rectangular pool filled with the bluest water I'd ever seen and was met with dolomite pillars lining both sides of the space. My eyes followed their structured lines to a square building standing directly ahead. Fountains and flowers trailed down its sides, so beautiful they could rival the Hanging Gardens of Babylon. I looked left and right, trying to spot my watcher, but I didn't see him... *yet*.

Emerging from the pool, I walked up the marble staircase and was met by two young men. Tanned and with gold bracelets encircling their upper arms, they were dressed in nothing more than white loincloths. The first approached, reaching out to drape a white dressing gown over my gold swimsuit, the thin material floating behind me in the warm summer breeze. The other bowed at the waist, keeping his head low as he raised a platter of grapes on outstretched arms. I plucked the fruit from the tray, then followed the cypress-lined walkway up the stairs and through the courtyard, heading straight for the building. Tonight, it seemed, I was in ancient Greece.

Gauze curtains floated around me as I pushed my way through the entrance and into a massive bedroom. My ancient history lessons rushed back to me as I took in the Grecian architecture. More pillars lined the space, and carved bands of Greek reliefs encircled the ceilings. Gold braziers hung from the walls, their charcoal flames providing the only light throughout the room. Finally, I noticed an oversize four-poster bed sitting atop a raised dais against the far wall. Its sides were curtained in more of the gauzy material, and lying atop it was a white chiton and a golden crown. I was clearly meant to put them on.

Changing quickly, I slipped the gown over my head, the gold shoulder clasp and laurel headpiece making me feel as if I were somehow important here.

"That's because you *are* important."

There he is.

His deep voice floated from the shadows, sending a chill up my spine. I wondered if he had watched me change.

"It's not polite to spy on a lady."

"It's hard not to when you're all I can see."

Flushed, I placed a hand on my chest and turned to face him.

The room was empty.

"Who are you, and why are you stalking my dreams?" I asked, taking a deep breath.

"Stalking is such a harsh word." His voice again drifted to my ears.

"What else would you call it?" I tilted my head, trying to pinpoint his location.

"Maybe... *enchanting* your dreams."

Before I could utter another word, the ceiling exploded into a thousand stars. Tiny silver lights twinkled against a black expanse, enveloping me as if I were inside the private cosmos of the gods.

"So... are you enchanted?" His voice sounded from directly behind me, his warm, featherlight breath brushing across my skin.

"Yes," I replied. There was no reason to lie.

"Good. Then I'll see you again tomorrow night."

I spun around, desperate to lay eyes on him, but the room was empty once more. "At least tell me who you are," I called out.

From the shadows drifted, "It's time to wake up, Milly."

I woke abruptly, the familiar scent of my cottage permeating the air. Sitting up, I rubbed my chest then startled, wrapping my arms around me as another chill raced up my spine.

Someone was here.

Squinting into the darkness, I caught a shimmer in the shadow across the room and shrank back beneath my wall of blankets, unable to move.

"Don't worry. I've only come to answer your question." His voice was the same but somehow sharper. Clearer. "They call me the Weaver."

The Weaver? I must still be dreaming.

Emboldened more than usual, I slid from my bed and crossed the room. He remained deep within the shadows, his form slowly coming into view.

Broad-shouldered and at least a foot taller, he towered over me. But I wasn't intimidated. I felt safe. Safe enough to lean up on my tiptoes and place my lips against his.

My elixir worked. I was in control here.

After a shocked breath, his lips began to move against mine. Strong arms encircled my waist, pulling me close. Pressed against his body, I no longer felt like myself. Like somehow I wasn't my own person but instead a welcomed part of him. Or maybe it was the other way around. Perhaps he was becoming a part of me.

Pulling back, he inhaled sharply. "Wait. We can't do this. It's not allowed."

"Says who?" my dream self boldly asked.

The shadow around us shimmered, his now-dark eyes flaring silver. Then suddenly he was gone, leaving me alone to question everything I knew—which clearly wasn't much.

The cold press of my lips against my mirror jerked me back to reality. The wood planks beneath my feet were frigid, the fire in the hearth reduced to barely an ember. I waited for something else miraculous to happen, another shift in my dream that would bring him back. Instead, I startled when my familiar rubbed himself between my ankles, winding in and out of my legs as cats normally do.

"Jenks, what are you doing in my dream?" I picked him up and nuzzled his black fur. "You're meant to stand guard over me, not join me."

I focused on the room again, the space coming into sharp relief as my eyes continued to adjust in the dark. Mr. Jenkins had never entered my dreams before, and as he writhed in my arms, I realized he hadn't still. This was not a dream. I was wide awake... and a complete fool.

Two

The Weaver—two words bound to plague me for the rest of the day.

I considered drinking another cup of elixir but instinctively knew it would no longer work. He seemed to be in total control when it came to my dreams. Instead, I decided to set about my daily tasks. With the sun rising, a soft fog lingered between the trees, the dew on the ground still glistening and wet. The chirp of crickets provided an early morning soundtrack I happily busied myself to, working inside as I waited for the day to warm. Dusting my shelves and reorganizing my oils and herbs filled a good portion of my morning, though regardless of the mundane tasks, I couldn't stop thinking about him.

Had he really been here? In my home? Or was it all in my head—my perfect dream man brought to life? If not, I needed answers, like how had he broken through my wards? All I could do was hope he was true to his word… that we *would* see each other again tonight.

I looked to my altar and considered crafting another spell. A new one. One powerful enough to give me more control. Mr. Jenkins meowed from beneath the kitchen table, and I knew he was right: None of my attempts would work against the Weaver. I needed to shift my focus to learning instead.

With the house dusted and cleaned, I dressed for the day in my favorite cornflower-blue dress, pulling my black lace-up boots into place beneath its well-worn hem. The ensemble was witchy enough to deter the people in our modern town from trying to engage with me, which was exactly how I preferred it. Though I'd lived here my entire life, I was still considered an outsider. A lesson I learned a long time ago.

Living quietly alone on the outskirts of Arcadia Forest, Mom and I had crafted a solitary life of magic and gardening that fulfilled any desire of connection either of us ever had. My dad died when I was three from a war injury even Mama's magic couldn't heal. But together, she and I learned to survive and grow until she passed away when I was thirteen.

Left to fend for myself, I drew on everything she taught me and continued my home education with regular visits to the local library in West Greenwich. One day—when I was feeling brave—I attempted to make friends but was starkly reminded of just how different I was. Not only did I have one blue and one green eye, but a young girl living alone in the woods caused people to talk… *harshly*. But thanks to my magic, no one entered our grounds uninvited.

My only friend in town remained the librarian, Keelyn. She had witnessed my awkward demise at the hands of the townies that day and ever since had been the only person I chose to talk to on a regular basis.

"Good morning, Milly. How's the bean crop coming along?" Keelyn smiled, the delicate lines at the corners of her eyes pulling tight as she waited for my response.

I snagged one of the carts from beside the front door. "It's good. Thank you. I'm getting ready to harvest some fresh peppers later today. I'll save you a bag if you'd like to stop by."

Vegetables, flowers, crystals, and creams were how I made a living. The small farmers market held in the area produced a weekly income that comfortably got me by.

"That sounds wonderful! I get off at four. Will that work?"

I thought about the timing. A few hours here for research, then home to harvest and sort... "Yes. That should be fine. I'll put on some tea."

Keelyn's eyes brightened as she gave me a wink then waved me on as another patron neared her desk. She'd been the librarian here since she was a teenager, and now in her early forties, she was well-respected within the community. I was happy to call her my friend.

Ducking into the far back corner of the old redbrick schoolhouse, I settled into my usual spot. The round table offered an unobstructed view of the second-story windows on either side of the belfry but concealed me enough from the ongoings on the main floor that I wouldn't be disturbed.

I placed my notebook and pen down beside my water bottle and wheeled the cart into the nearby stacks. Most of the books I read were located here, hidden in the shadows of the New Age section. Metaphysics, astrology, and anything regarding a "kitchen witch" had graced my reading list since a very young age. Thankfully, Keelyn never judged me for what some might find *odd* selections. Today's research, however, would be even more focused.

Running my fingers along the spines, I quickly found the dream section and pulled a few new titles from the shelves. I'd studied lucid dreaming and dream symbology, as well as how to unlock the power of your dreams, but unfortunately, none of those books mentioned a Weaver. Honestly, I wasn't sure if I was on the right track at all, but somehow this felt like the correct place to start.

With my selections spread out on the table, I hovered my hands above them and closed my eyes. The magical signature of each book was different, and with my intention set, I focused on finding the one giving off the strongest vibe.

Ripples of energy met my palms, and when my skin warmed, I opened my eyes.

The book was the oldest among them, with worn edges and a tattered spine. I wasn't surprised. All true magic was documented so long ago that hardly any original texts still existed. However, with books like these—beautiful reproductions from a witch's point of view—we could still get close to true information, even in the modern world today.

This one in particular was written by Genevieve DuWant, a pseudonym for sure, but I found the title oddly subdued for the subject matter within. *Magic of the Mind* didn't exactly scream "dreamscapes" or "Weaver."

I flipped open the cover, reading the introduction:

> **The mind is a wonderful thing as long as you don't lose control of it.**

Hmm... What could any of what I'd experienced have to do with losing my mind? I was suddenly unsure if this book was going to be of any help at all, but I read on.

> Dreaming is a way for your mind to let go, taking you through a subconscious minefield planted by your memories and fears, your hopes and dreams. But never once were we told it could also be where you lose yourself or that it could be controlled by another.

Now we were getting somewhere.

> While I cannot prove what I say is true, I can document my experiences and share them here as a warning—a warning that mind magic does exist and can be woven in and out of your dreams by the one given ultimate control.

She hadn't mentioned the Weaver by title or name, only using the word *woven* instead. And while the *one given ultimate control* could be talking about the Weaver, it could also be a metaphor for gaining control over one's self. I skimmed through the rest of the book, but in the end, I decided if what she had written couldn't be proven, it wasn't going to do me any good. I placed the tome back on the shelf and moved on to the other books in my pile.

Three hours later, I still had no additional information on my Weaver.

My Weaver. A warmth flushed through me.

Was it odd that it really did feel that way? That some strange man within my dreams felt like he belonged to me? Or odder yet... that I somehow belonged to him?

Returning home, I buried my hands in the garden dirt, harvesting the peppers, beets, and beans I'd need to shell over the next few days. My mind drifted over the information—or lack thereof—I had read in the library today. Not a single book produced anything useful, but the words *mind magic* kept needling my brain. Could the Weaver be a real person using this type of magic to manipulate my dreams? If so, I had to find out why. Or more specifically... why me?

"Milly, are you back there?" Keelyn's voice pulled me from my thoughts.

"Hi, yes. Just beyond the fence."

Keelyn pushed through the wooden gate, joining me in the garden and bringing with her a welcome reprieve. I needed to focus on something else for a while before I went utterly mad. *The mind is a wonderful thing as long as you don't lose control of it.* I chuckled as the words from the old book drifted through my head again.

"What's so funny?" Keelyn pulled her long silver-blond hair into a ponytail, then bent down to relieve me of the burlap bag I was dumping the beans into.

"Just something I read today that stuck with me." I tossed another handful of the legumes into the sack.

"Well, I have to say it's good to see you laugh." Jiggling the bag to settle the contents, she cinched the top between her hands. "Can I help you inside with these?"

"Yes, thank you. I'll put on the tea." I led her inside, thinking about what she said. I supposed she was right—it had been a long time since I felt this joyful. Not that I was unhappy in my life, but as the wheel of the year turned and the seasons repeated, the days could edge toward doldrum. The Weaver's appearance had brought on something unexpected. Something new and wonderful to look forward to. Something to laugh at and bring a smile to my face.

"Did you not enjoy your books today? I noticed you didn't check out any of them." Keelyn dropped the bag of beans on the floor, steadying them against the kitchen cabinet with her leg.

"Oh… I was just doing a little research, but nothing panned out." I shrugged.

"Really? Is there a certain book you'd like me to order instead?"

Her offer was kind, but I had no idea if one even existed, so I kept my answer vague. "Sure, if you come across any dream-type books that mention the word *weaver*, that would be great."

Keelyn tilted her head. She had always accepted how different I was with my solitary ways and soft-spoken oddness, but I never shared my magic with her. With anyone, actually. And as much as I enjoyed her company, I still didn't feel comfortable doing so now.

"Here's your batch of peppers." I shoved a grocery bag of freshly picked sweet peppers into her hand, my oddness striking again.

"Thanks!" She laughed. "These will go great in my next salad. Speaking of—would you like to join me for dinner tonight? I'm hosting a book club at my house and think you'd have a really good time."

Gnawing the inside of my cheek, I tried to be brave, but people just weren't my thing. Besides, I needed to prepare if I was going to search out the Weaver again tonight. "Thank you, but I'll have to pass. Harvest season affords me no breaks. I'll be off to bed early again."

Keelyn dipped her head, a knowing smile pulling at her rose-colored lips. "Well, if you ever change your mind, or when you finally do get a break, you're always welcome. We'll be meeting every week on Thursday nights."

I smiled, my cheeks flushing as she graciously accepted yet another of my excuses. "Thank you for stopping by. I'll be sure to save you some fresh currants next time, if you're still interested."

"Absolutely. I love using them in my yogurt cakes." Keelyn winked and gave me a little wave goodbye. "See you soon, Milly, and I'll let you know if I come across a book you described."

I waved to Keelyn just as the kettle began to whistle. Realizing I'd ruined an afternoon of what could have been lighthearted camaraderie with my friend, I poured myself a cup of the lavender-mint tea and filled the bowl on the table full of beans. Shelling the pods was a relaxing, monotonous task I'd done over and over, year after year, and I had the calluses to prove it. Rough around the edges, I was all work and no play, and while I truly did prefer being alone, sitting here in this empty house, I was regretting my friend's rushed departure. I couldn't deny I was considering Keelyn's offer to join her book club, and there was certainly no doubt I couldn't wait to see *him* again. It was all so unlike me, and I wondered how the Weaver had broken through that facet of my life.

Once processed, I stored the shelled beans in the freezer, planning to use them in my ham hock soup when the weather turned cold. Grabbing my wicker basket, I traipsed back into the garden to gather the ingredients I'd need for my spell tonight. My goal wasn't for more control but instead to open my heart and mind and to see things more clearly. Perhaps if I could pierce the veil of the dreamscape, I could see what was truly going on.

Snipping nine heads off my peppermint and lemongrass plants, I returned to the kitchen and dropped them into the mortar. Adding a chunk of ginger, I began to grind.

Reveal the truth. Allow me to see. Magic being hidden from me. Open my heart, and my mind. Show me the truth, nine by nine.

I muddled the herbs into a fine powder, setting the kettle again to steep on the stove. After adding a pinch into my cup, I dripped in a dollop of honey and poured hot water over it all. Sweet steam rose into the air, spinning at the base, then continuing upward into a smoky, straight line. The spell was energetically clear.

Normally I'd work in the garden past nightfall, but tonight I was ready to start my next adventure by 7:00 p.m.—a good, magical number.

"Now you stay close tonight, okay?" I scratched Jenks behind the ears and tucked myself beneath the blankets as he walked atop them, settling near my feet. I quickly drifted off, the dream enveloping me like a blooming cloud—a watercolor painting rendered right before my eyes.

Rolling green hills and a bluish-gray sky surrounded me. I thought I might be stateside until I saw a unique stone castle perched atop the nearest hill. The air was balmy and carried with it the thick, cloying fragrance of my favorite flowers.

I turned and gasped.

An ocean of blush-pink roses spread up over a hill as far as the eye could see, some so plump they looked like peonies. I buried my nose in the nearest cluster, inhaling the familiar scent. "How did you know these were my favorite?" I asked, feeling the Weaver's presence behind me before even seeing him.

"I know a lot about you." His deep voice drifted to my ears.

That statement put me on edge, but as a clear sense of contentment settled over me, I knew my spell had worked. I was seeing the truth beneath his words and was confident I had nothing to fear.

Spinning slowly, I kept my eyes down but tried to catch a glimpse of him in my periphery. A flash caught my eye, and I looked up to find a gorgeous Victorian greenhouse standing nearby. Traipsing along the manicured path, I let my fingers graze the soft petals, making sure to avoid the hidden thorns. Entering the glass greenhouse, I inhaled deeply, enjoying more roses, foxglove, periwinkle, and poppies, all in full bloom and filling the space. The skirt of my sundress swished lightly against the leaves as I nonchalantly moved between the manicured rows. Hummingbirds flitted among a rose of Sharon while the largest monarch butterfly I'd ever seen slowly opened and closed its wings from its spot in a wild honeysuckle bush.

"I have so many questions." I began. "Exactly how do you know a lot about me? And what type of magic are you using to control my dreams?" I hoped my directness didn't scare him off, but I needed to understand.

Silence settled throughout the space, taking with it even the slightest rustle of leaves. Behind me, a wall of energy pressed against my back. Slowly, nervously, I turned around and came face to face with the Weaver.

He stood in front of an enormous rip in space, his eyes matching the stars behind him. A swirling galaxy of silver with the faintest hint of blue and purple shimmered against a black expanse. He lifted a muscled arm from beneath his cloak, extending his hand to me. "I have all the answers you seek. You only need to surrender and join me."

Surrender?

I wasn't sure I liked the sound of that.